[Cargo]

[Based on the original screenplay by James Dylan]
J.C. Maçek III

Print ISBN 978-1-912175-88-8

For Novara

1 The Box

Anthony Peterson was in pain.

His head throbbed, and the dream interpreted that pain as a severe injury.

He found himself on his knees out in a field, sure that he was injured. He was calling out to his wife and reaching for her in his pain. But Susan remained just out of reach. The wind blew her white dress around her in slow motion, and the pollen of the field flowed around her in a cocoon. He reached again, and she was even further away, causing his pain to flare even higher.

Every painful place on his body was lit by sickly starlight, and strangely, that starlight hurt. It was as if the light was piercing him. Crucifying him.

One beam actually cut right through the center of his forehead like a deathblow.

Bring it on, if it would end the pain.

He was in agony. He was terrified.

Finally, Anthony Peterson could no longer handle all of this discomfort, this pain, this helplessness. Thus, he reached out to Susan, his bride, his strength. She would care for him. She had to. She was his trophy wife. She had better. He had invested.

But as he cried out for her, Susan was suddenly different. To his horror, his young, beautiful wife had degenerated into an old crone, and she seemed not to recognize him.

Peterson fell back as he watched her walk away down a blood-stained dream street. The field was gone. The pain was not. He held his head and repeated her name as he collapsed onto the bloody path.

Then vibrations rolled through his head like thunder, irritating his headache more.

Tremors. Something was shaking the ground. Were there machines coming? Didn't they know he was hurt? Wherever he was, he was hurting! How could they not know or care? What was this?

The vibrations paused then came again.

Over and over to his increasing pain, he felt the vibrations pause and restart. Just when he felt it was time to relax again, they returned.

Make it stop! he thought. *Stop it. I'm hurt!* But the agonizing vibrations did not stop.

For the first time in as long as he could remember, Anthony Peterson felt fear. Pain was one thing, but fear? Fear was not like him.

He held his head, curled into a fetal position, and shivered on the cold hard floor of the desolate field with the bloody trail widening through its center.

Each buzzing vibration felt like a reminder of something ominous coming. Every buzz increased his fear to the point that his heart was pounding in his chest, exacerbating the throbbing in his head.

Then, the blue flashes came. Blue flashes like unearthly lightening reached out for him. As the noise rose and the blue flashes overtook his consciousness, he knew that the thing he feared had finally come for him.

*

And then, Anthony Peterson awoke in the darkness with a series of heavy, terrified gasps.

It was a dream. Only a dream. All a dream.

Susan would be next to him, still young, still beautiful, still his trophy. Should he wake her up and tell her or–?

Anthony Peterson froze as he reached for her. He suddenly realized something quite disturbing.

He was not in their bed.

Had he rolled onto the floor? He must have. It was *hard* where he was lying.

That must have been one hell of a dream to eject him straight from his bed. He felt ridiculous.

What time was it? He looked around and saw nothing. Where was his clock? Had the electricity gone out?

Goddam, he spent all this money to live in the swankiest part of town and the electric company couldn't even do their fucking jobs, right?

His heartbeat finally slowed, but his head continued to throb in a defiant reminder of his bad dream. How in the name of fuck had he ended up on the floor? Was that how he had hurt his head?

Slowly, he sat up, still holding his head with one hand, and felt around in the darkness.

He narrowed his eyes in confusion. This was metal. He was on some kind of metal floor.

Where was he?

Equally disturbing was the realization that he was not wearing his night clothes but instead was still wearing his suit and tie from the office.

What was this, a prank?

Nobody did this to Anthony Peterson! Nobody ever! Didn't they know that? Well, if they didn't, they soon would. They would know who they had been fool enough to fuck with.

He felt groggy. His body ached nearly as much as his head.

And then, there was the fear. The fear now came to him in the waking world as if reaching straight out from his nightmare to wrap around his throat.

He would never admit this to anyone but himself, but he was indeed frightened. Whoever the fuck had done this to him would pay dearly for it.

Pranks like this? Not funny.

He looked around wildly, trying to see anything that might give him a clue to where he was. Slowly, he made his way to his feet and put his arms out, gasping and breathing hard, walking forward and feeling for…anything.

He was a blind man in the darkness. Alone.

He tried to remember what had happened before…this. Was he hung over? A night on the town? Maybe this was a friend's garage he was sleeping it off in or–

His hand touched something, and he started. It was cold. A wall? His other hand touched it, and he recoiled slightly in shock.

Where am I?

He placed both hands flat on the wall and pushed.

Metal. Like the floor. He began tracing his way around, feeling along the wall, guiding himself.

He was baffled. No explanation he could come up with made sense. None of the people he knew would consider a prank like this. He didn't remember running around with any of his young girls recently. No party invitations, no happy hours, no drugs. And his kids weren't talking to him, so a night out with them was improbable. It was baffling. Shocking. Where in the name of God was he?

And with that, his dream came into reality. He felt the vibrations again. Heavily.

The machinery from his dreams was here.

It was loud, grating, painful, yet…familiar. It was coming from all around him. What was it, and how could he stop it?

He turned around and leaned against the wall and saw that the blue flashes from his dream had also come reaching into reality.

It was…a blue glow, slight, but bright in the darkness. It flashed every time the vibrations shook the room and reactivated his headache.

He made his way closer, moving his arms blindly in front of himself to avoid any collision. When he was close enough, he realized exactly what was making both the vibrations and the flashes.

It was a cell phone.

He shook his head to clear it as he leaned in and walked closer.

A cell phone…taped to the wall. It was taped in a way that left it flat against the metal with the screen facing forward so as to be seen. He could see the readout on the phone indicating an incoming call along with the time…1:16 AM.

The metal walls amplified the ring notice vibrations and carried it through whatever this place was like a metallic megaphone.

Who could be calling? Who knew he was here and…where was here?

His grogginess cleared somewhat, and he found the presence of mind to reach forward and rip the phone from the wall.

He wadded up and tossed the tape with a few hand flaps, hit the answer key and quickly said, "Hello?" in an expectant voice, sounding more scared than he intended.

There was no immediate response.

The silence was as heavy as the darkness. He imagined some serious and brooding stranger on the line waiting to for the right second to talk. He wrinkled his brow in frustration.

"Hello?" he said again.

After a moment, a deep, serious and fast voice boomed back at him. "Anthony Peterson?"

He almost jumped, but directed his energy into his voice demanding, "Who is this?" with anger.

"Is this Anthony Peterson?" the voice asked again, not intimidated.

"Who the fuck is this?" Peterson asked again in his most authoritative, businesslike voice. He wanted them to know he was no one to fuck with.

"Is this Anthony Peterson?" the voice asked again with the same tone and inflection. He was patient and had his own way of showing who was in charge, whoever the hell he was.

"Yes, this is Anthony Peterson!" he barked back.

Without a pause, the voice said "This is *Mrs*. Anthony Peterson."

Peterson's mind reeled in confusion. What did that mean?

Quickly, he was answered by his wife's own voice. She was clearly terrified and close to tears. "Anthony! You've got to help me! They've got me tied to a chair and blindfolded! I don't know where I am. They won't tell me anything. I have no idea who they are!" she shouted, and he heard her being violently pulled back from the phone.

"Susan? Susan!" Peterson shouted back in shock as Susan's cries faded into the distance.

But the kidnapper had the phone again with the same, steady, emotionless voice. "You give us what we want, or we take turns gang fucking her while live-streaming the whole thing to the web." The caller paused for a second to let his words settle in, then added, "And *then,* we kill her. It'll be the world's first *live* snuff film."

Peterson was shocked. Right button, first try. If there was anyone in the world he loved besides himself and his money, it was Susan.

"No! Don't hurt her! Please don't hurt her." He had intended it to be a shout into the phone, but it came out more like a pained and terrified moan.

"A pretty thing like that will get lots of views, don't you think?"

"Please, just don't. Don't do this."

"Then give us what we want," the kidnapper said plainly.

It was all very direct. Peterson was not given options. It was either this…or *this*. Obedience…or bloodshed.

They had Susan and, well, obviously, they had him… somewhere.

If they already planned to do that to Susan, what might they do to him?

"Where am I?" Peterson groaned.

He didn't expect an answer but he got one.

Immediately, overhead lights flooded the space with white brilliance. Peterson was blinded again and almost dropped the phone to shield his eyes which were clouding over with visual purple.

The kidnapper remained silent. Patient. Plotting. Waiting.

Deliriously Peterson shook his head and forced his eyes open and adjust to the visual onslaught. As the maroon cloud of rhodopsin faded from his eyesight, he finally got a good look at his surroundings, such that they were.

Everything around him was plain. Slate grey. No…more like…what did they call this?

Gunmetal gray.

He shivered as he traced every corner.

To his shock, he found himself in what looked like the inside of a cargo container, the kind they ship things in, overseas or cross-country. His company used them all the time down at the docks, though he had never been close to one, let alone been inside.

It was about forty feet long, he estimated. Maybe eight feet tall and as many feet wide. His very own forty-foot coffin.

Suddenly, everything was more real for Anthony Peterson. This was no extension of his nightmare. This was stark, cold reality, and the acknowledgment of that made him dizzy.

His pained head spun as his captor mirthlessly explained his situation. "You've been kidnapped, Mr. Peterson. Trapped. What's the last thing you remember?"

Nothing. he thought. He paused, thinking…what had happened? He spoke the words as soon as they came into his head. "I remember…being on the street and then…being smothered." He closed his eyes and looked up, trying to think of something else. Anything…but nothing came. "Then, I woke up here," he said.

The fast-talking, low voice of the kidnapper took over. "We drugged you, pulled you off the street. The exact kind of thing that happens in human trafficking circles a hundred times a day around the world."

Peterson winced at those words. Human trafficking. His head throbbed again. His fear was quickly being replaced by anger. What gave them the right to do this?

"Then again, traffickers rarely pinpoint bags of bones like you. Their usual targets look a whole lot more like...well, sweet Susan over here."

Peterson heard her whimper at those words, and then, a door slammed in the background, separating him from even her voice.

"Where am I?" he demanded.

The kidnapper's drone continued, speedily, "Maybe you're in Siberia. Maybe the Middle East. Maybe in a pit in Mexico. Maybe you're in a New York back alley. Maybe you're just down the street from your pristine home," the kidnapper said as if he had the speech prepared.

A chilling thought entered Peterson's mind. "Are you... outside this container right now?"

"Maybe we are. Maybe we're a hundred miles away. Maybe we're next door. The thing is...you'll never know."

No stone unturned. They had kidnapping down pat, and they knew exactly how to terrorize a person.

"What do you want?" Peterson asked wearily.

The kidnapper waited a moment, as if for maximum impact, then answered, "Ten million dollars."

Peterson panicked. "What? Ten mill–? I don't have that kind of money!" he insisted into the phone.

The kidnapper didn't hesitate. If there was any emotion in his voice at all, it showed only that he was self-assured. "We both know that you do."

Peterson shook his head in panic and cried out, "Why me? I'm just a businessman."

"*Because* you're a businessman," the kidnapper said as if the answer was the most obvious thing in the world. "A very wealthy businessman at that."

Peterson was incredulous. "Well, wait, wait! Is this... something personal? Do I know you?"

"Shut...up," came the kidnapper's curt response. There was a tone of definitive finality.

Peterson obeyed and waited.

The kidnapper fired off instructions rapidly as if ready to be done with the very sound of Peterson's voice.

"If you contact the police, your wife dies, then you die. If you contact the FBI, your wife dies, then you die. If you contact any authorities, your wife dies, then you die. If you contact anyone that doesn't have to do with collecting the ransom money, your wife dies, then you die. You've got air for twenty-four hours. That should be more than enough time to get the money together."

Peterson winced at every sentence, but the timeline his jailer quoted forced him to interrupt.

"Twenty-four *hours*?" he responded with shock. He composed himself fast and responded with authority, "No! No! No! That's not enough time! You've got to give me more time."

The kidnapper continued as if there was no interruption, paying no mind to Peterson's words. "Once you have the money, we'll send you the account to wire it to. You do as we say, we let you go, and we let your wife go. If you deviate from the plan one iota, you're both dead. We'll rape and murder your wife and live-stream the whole thing."

Peterson winced again at the very thought. He clenched and unclenched his free fist in fury as every emotion he had ran across his face.

The kidnapper continued his litany. "As for you, though? You, we will leave to die alone…slowly…of suffocation." The captor paused again for carefully planned dramatic effect, letting his words hang in the air as ominous reminders of the threat. "Chances are, your useless, withered corpse will never be found."

Terrified, Peterson resorted to begging again. "Please! I implore you! Don't do this!"

The kidnapper paused just long enough to give Peterson hope, then said, "Twenty-four hours, Mr. Peterson. No…Twenty-three hours and thirty-three minutes now. You took longer to wake up than we calculated."

"Please!"

"You've got some calls to make," the kidnapper said and hung up abruptly.

Anthony Peterson stood where he was in yesterday's suit… an older but still fit businessman, now a prisoner of…God only knew who.

He let his arm go limp. It had only been minutes since he had awakened.

He was stunned, still groggy and in great pain.

He was alone.

He was trapped.

2 Desperation

1:41 AM

Anthony Peterson was not the kind of man who took orders. He had rarely answered to anyone in years, and when he had, he had never been the kind of man who enjoyed doing so.

After composing himself as much as he could, he slid the phone into his pocket and walked right up to the doors and pushed. They would not open.

Maybe they would slide open?

Nothing.

They must have been locked tightly from the outside. They didn't give even a millimeter. Was he welded in?

Christ!

Peterson felt the fury rising in him. Who the hell were they to do this to him? To his wife? He banged on the door as a substitute for his captor's face, kicked that chosen spot a few times, then banged again. The noise rang out loudly.

Someone had to hear.

He banged again and again, then went to every wall and banged harder and harder, shouting, "Help!" and "Let me out of here!" over and over.

Anthony Peterson refused to let up. "I need help! Get me out of this place!" Someone would come. Someone would hear.

He screamed and banged on the walls until his voice was raw, and his throat burned and his hands were bruised.

"Damn it. Just...let me out," he croaked weakly and fell against the wall.

He slid down the wall to the floor to rest, exhausted, covered in sweat and hyperventilating.

He really was trapped. He knew that now. He had to accept it. That and the fact that either no one could hear him, or those who did hear him were in on this kidnapping.

No one was coming to help him, so he had to find the courage to help himself.

He sighed and summoned every bit of courage he had. This was not an easy proposition considering the situation. Anthony Peterson was never helpless. Never in his life. Never until now. Thus, Anthony Peterson had no way to deal with being helpless.

Shakily, Peterson got to his feet and retrieved the phone from his pocket.

This was not his own phone. Anthony Peterson would never have a phone so cheap. This had been purchased and provided by the kidnappers. He went through the phone. Every app, every folder, every button, everything he could find and came up with nothing. Certainly none of his contacts were in this cheap thing.

He tapped a few icons and thought of who he could call. What numbers did he know by heart? The convenience of cell phones had sounded the death knell for memorized phone numbers for most people. Peterson was not most people. He prided himself on his ability to memorize account numbers, phone numbers, dates, and just about anything else he needed to recall.

The problem now was this dazed state he was in. His mouth was dry. He felt as if he hadn't eaten in a month. Worst of all, his head ached like no hangover he had ever experienced. He was going to have to clear his head if he was going to put these memories together. Maybe the key was to focus on something else. Something like his freedom.

An idea came to him and he searched for a GPS location. If calls could be made, surely the GPS would work through this metal thing.

But no… They were smart. It was disabled.

He inspected the case. He recognized the brand. 'AfterSHOK.' It was a heavy duty, shockproof job that gave maximum protection and even doubled as an external battery. Great product. The commercials for it showed people throwing their phones across the rooms in hilarious parodies of anger and then picking them up and finding them unscathed.

Another comical ad had Frankenstein's monster using a phone with their case while electricity was shooting through him. He turned around and looked at the mad scientist and said, "Dad, do you mind? I'm on the phone! Okay, you were saying?"

The phone itself, on the other hand, was far from state of the art. It was one of those hackable knockoff phones. It was a smart phone, but just barely. It was a cheap phone, the kind they sold in pharmacies. As close to 'disposable' as they got.

The case probably cost three times what the phone did.

The message that sent was clear. They didn't want him to have any extra capabilities with this phone, but they wanted it to remain functioning and powered no matter what. This phone was his lifeline, but on their terms only.

Whoever the hell was behind this had blocked the internet on it as well. All browsers uninstalled, email clients uninstalled. Nothing seemed to work except the clock, the talk feature, and maybe the text app.

But who could he call or text? Who that could help him?

"Tom!" he said out loud. "I've got to call Tom," he added in a determined whisper, then dialed his closest business associate's number from memory, albeit slowly.

Tom Pocase was more than an employee or executive assistant. Tom was a special breed of sycophantic savant. He was smart enough to get everything done that Peterson needed to get done and to remember accounts and passwords like a machine, but also loose enough in his morals to do anything Peterson ordered him to do.

Tom was also probably just dumb enough to stay loyal and not think too much for himself.

Peterson waited for the connection to be made. For a moment, Peterson couldn't breathe. He stood there, frozen, waiting for the call to connect. When he finally heard ringing, he exhaled hard and relaxed.

But impatience got the better of him. "Come on, pick up, pick up, pick *up*!" he muttered, pacing and gesturing with his free hand.

At last, Tom picked up. "Hello?" he said groggily, clearly no happier than Peterson would have been about being woken up in the middle of the night.

Peterson was immediately relieved to hear Tom's voice and exclaimed, "Tom! It's Anthony!"

Tom took a second to digest those three words, then grunted, "Anthony? Jesus, it's two o'clock in the morning."

It was 2:02 actually, but Peterson ignored that. "Just listen! I've been kidnapped."

The sleep left Tom's voice quickly, and he shouted incredulously, "Kidnapped?"

The word hung in the air, and Peterson felt himself unconsciously recoil from it as if the word itself was an adversary. He composed himself to confirm that horrible word, but was cut off as Tom's voice broke the silence and laughed. "What is this? A joke?"

Peterson shook off his fear at the frustration Tom's inane question caused. He began to pace and gestured as if Tom was in front of him. "No! They took Susan too. If I don't give them what they want, they're gonna kill her."

"What? Who is? Who's gonna kill her?"

Peterson wondered with annoyance why the fuck that should matter. "Some people. I don't *know* who."

Tom's voice changed. It was as if he only then accepted that this just might be true. "Where are you?"

Peterson's lower lip quivered. Where could he begin? There was so much to explain. "I'm locked in a metal shipping container somewhere. I don't know where. It...it could be anywhere."

"Well, shit, man, for God's sake, call the police," Tom said, as if Anthony hadn't thought of that and was merely calling for some friendly advice. Tom was reliable, but not the sharpest tack in the corkboard.

Peterson explained as politely as he could. "If I call the police, they're gonna kill her. They could be listening to this conversation right now."

Tom froze. Peterson could hear it. It wasn't a gasp. It was like a sudden fear took his breath. There was no longer any sound coming from anywhere on Tom's side. Tom was spooked even from his safe, warm bed.

"Wha'd...uh, what exactly...what...what..." Tom stuttered, now completely shaken by the possibilities. "What do they want?"

Peterson could scarcely believe the amount he was about to quote. "Ten million dollars," he said, with a cold, incredulous laugh in his voice.

"What?" Tom obviously could not believe what he was hearing, and his voice echoed the shocked incredulity of Peterson's own.

Peterson's mind reeled. He closed his eyes and focused. What he was about to say caused him actual pain. Pain to his very core. This was not the kind of man Anthony Peterson truly was.

"Look, look...just...I need you to sell everything!"

"Everything?" Tom repeated, taken aback.

"Ev-er-y-thing!" Peterson repeated, exasperated to the point of shouting, "All my shares. My whole portfolio. Everything. Then, when you get the money together, get back to me, and they'll give me the account to wire it to."

Tom was silent to the point that Peterson was ready to ask if he was still there. "You're serious about all this, aren't you?" he said at last.

Peterson rolled his eyes in disbelief. What the fuck kind of question was that? Peterson shook his head and ignored the question, waiting for Tom to speak again.

"Anthony...are you sure this is really how you want to roll with this?" Tom asked, with audible concern and even skepticism in his voice.

Peterson sighed and shook his head. He was exhausted and completely out of options.

"I don't know. I don't know...I don't even know what I'm *doing* right now! All I know is that I want Susan back."

"So, you want me to do this? For sure?"

Peterson nodded, as if Tom could see him, then said, "Yeah. Unless I come up with a better idea, I need to have this ready to... to appease them." The words tasted sour as he spoke them.

Tom was silent, thinking. Then, he responded, "I hear you. You gotta do what you gotta do. If I come up with a better idea than this one, I'll share it."

"You do that. But until then—"

"I do exactly what you say, boss!" he said almost comically. Then, his serious voice returned. "I'll get back to you," he said, with a determined tone to his voice.

He hung up, and Peterson let his cell phone hand sag to his side.

3 September Memories

Anthony Peterson, the man who had everything, was feeling decidedly poor at the moment.

And the thing that surprised him the most at that moment was it was not only the money he was thinking of.

Oh, he was furious about losing the money and having to give it to the people he hated most in the world…or, perhaps, one person. Whoever the fuck it was…he hated them…and he was about to make them ten million dollars richer at his own expense.

He was fuming.

But, quite unexpectedly, the thing he felt worst about was the possibility of losing Susan. That surprised him. Of course he loved her. He knew that. However, much of that 'love' came from her value to him as a status symbol. She was a beautiful, young trophy wife, and every man and half the women they came across surely imagined fucking her as soon as she caught their eyes.

But they couldn't have her. She was Mrs. Susan Peterson, which made her Anthony's own. Yet even at his most devoted, Anthony Peterson knew in his heart of hearts that he loved nothing more than his money. Susan was part of the show. Susan was an integral element in the tapestry that made up the successful façade of Anthony Peterson, right up there with his other possessions and all of his many mean green almighty dollars.

Or so Anthony Peterson had always thought.

But now…

At this moment, he was furious at the kidnapper and goddamn cronies he might have, not only for forcing him into this mess and bleeding him dry, but for putting Susan at risk. Susan.

Susan.

If they hurt her…

When he had first met Susan, he was still legally married, but had been separated from the mother of his children for some time. It had been a time of reeling and reanalysis of his life as his first wife Marie slowly succumbed to her illnesses. And Anthony Peterson, never an unselfish man, hadn't the heart to witness it all. And there were other things. Other painful things that he was only able to quench when he met Susan.

Sure, Anthony had had his affairs over the months, the cleaning lady at his office was one notable example, but Susan had caught his eye like few others ever had. Where Marie was old, Susan was young and vibrant. Marie had stopped caring about her appearance and cut her hair into short, sensible curls while Susan let her wild, straight locks flow free. Marie had been content to stay home and spend his money. Susan was a go-getter, an actress always seeking out bigger parts.

His children, Evan and Elena, had been hoping that he would reconcile with their mother. That was never to be in the cards once Susan took his breath away. After their first date, he knew he needed to be free and quickly finalized the divorce.

With Susan on his arm, deals went quicker, faster, easier. Informal country club contacts became major deals with Susan by his side. She impressed everyone, and everyone was impressed that old Anthony could score such a hot little number. He soon knew he was going to have to seal this deal himself and make Susan his bride. And soon he did, much to the joy of his friends and business associates. Much to the chagrin of his children.

Evan and Elena did not show up for their September wedding.

Was it the money Susan loved? Maybe so. Was it her beauty and the prestige she brought him that Anthony loved? Maybe so. All he knew was that things were better with Susan, and he was happy to invest in her. And on his wedding night, he swore to any god who was listening that he would destroy anyone who even tried to take her away from him.

Of course, he always expected this would be some young heartthrob, not a psychotic kidnapper, but his rage was no less. His rage was increased tenfold.

Anthony Peterson would have his revenge one way or the other. There could be no doubt about that. Anthony Peterson always paid back in kind. Many people had found that out over the years.

You didn't *fuck* with Anthony Peterson.

But if they hurt Susan...even a little bit...these bastards would have no idea the hell that would rain down on them. This was Susan. His Susan. Any vengeance in his past would feel like a gentle breeze compared to the damage he was prepared to do. And he knew just how to take revenge and who to partner with for maximum payback.

You did *not* fuck with Anthony Peterson.

The thought of that revenge, which he was quite sure he would have, almost made him smile, in spite of his terror and fury.

And then, the phone rang and startled him back to his wits.

Spooked, he grabbed the phone and answered shakily.

"Mr. Peterson."

It was the kidnapper again in that all-too-calm whisper of his. Peterson already hated that voice. He already imagined making that voice scream.

"Look, I just spoke to my closest associate. He's putting together the money now."

"For the sake of both you and your precious little wife, I sure hope so."

Peterson shook and composed himself. He was caught between gritting his teeth in fury and crying in terror, so he did his best to sound calm and even friendly in the face of this enemy.

"Yeah, look, just tell me something, please. Why are you doing this? I mean, why *me*?"

"Why *not* you?"

It was almost clinical, that voice.

"All right, I understand about the money. I can understand that, but why *me*? Why me personally? There are a lot of rich guys you could have chosen. I'm just an honest businessman. I pay my taxes. I don't understand why you're doing this. I'm a good man."

For the first time, Peterson heard the kidnapper's voice change. Up until then, the bastard could well have been a robot. Now he laughed sardonically as if to say, "That's rich," and when he spoke, the already whispering voice had changed to a hateful hiss.

"A good man? No, no, no, you don't get to where you're at by being good, Mr. Peterson."

"No, it's the truth. Nobody's perfect, but I do *not* deserve this!"

The kidnapper was ready, calling his bluff. "You honestly believe you're a good man?" he asked, with a tinge of sarcasm.

"Yes! Yes, I do!" Peterson yelled back, steadfast in his convictions. "I believe in God, I follow the rules, I give to charity."

"Charity? God? Taxes? Oh, no, no, Anthony Peterson, you're not a *good* man. Your history speaks for itself. Taxes? You've been cheating on taxes more than you have your wives. Charity? Shit, your charitable contributions are just another way to cheat on your goddam taxes. It all filters back to your profits, doesn't it, foundation-boy? And God? What do you think God would say about that sort of thing, Peterson? Let God come and get you out of your little box."

Peterson's eyes widened at the cruelty. "Wait, wait! Even if what you're saying is true, and I ain't sayin' it is, what makes me deserve this in your..." his shaking voice gave way to anger for once, "... sick, twisted little mind? I've never done a goddam thing to deserve anything like this."

"Never?"

"God, no, never! I'm a good–"

"What about September twenty-fifth?" the kidnapper abruptly blurted.

September again? His anniversary?

Peterson's blood ran cold, and sweat beaded on his forehead instantly. Those simple words were a blow to his gut. Images flowed into his head and paraded before his bloodshot mind's eye. He paused, working his jaw wordlessly as he tried to find the words to defend himself.

After a pregnant pause, he weakly managed the words, "What *about* September twenty-fifth?"

"September twenty-fifth. Ten…years…ago."

Peterson's eyes widened, and his brow wrinkled. No, a different September. A different anniversary.

What was this? What were they doing to him? How could they…

"I *don't* know what you're talking about," he said, almost pleading.

The kidnapper pounced on him. "September twenty-fifth, ten years ago, South America. The press, those who reported on it, called it the La Aldea Massacre, but the people behind it were never found. We know the truth."

The kidnapper gave another of his dramatic pauses, then tore into his speech again.

"A business deal of yours went sour. The people you needed to sell to you reneged on the deal. They had a crisis of conscience. You've read about those, haven't you?" The kidnapper laughed coldly at his sarcastic joke. "Yeah, you stood to be out millions, Anthony Peterson, and losing millions didn't sit well with you then any more than…well, any more than it's sitting well with you today." He took a breath to let those last stabbing words sink in, then continued. "So, what did you do? What did Anthony Peterson do when push came to shove and money was on the line? Why, you had them *killed*, of course. All of them. Every last one."

Peterson was shaken. He tried to tailor his voice to its most serious and businesslike, its least emotional so that it would sound the most truthful. He tried.

"No, no, I don't know what you're talking about. It's a lie. It's an absolute lie."

"You hired mercenaries."

"No, now that is an *absolute* fabrication. Who the hell have you been talking to?" He could feel himself losing control of his loudening voice.

The kidnapper spoke louder over Peterson's protestations. "Oh, and not just the men. But the women and the children."

"No, no I wouldn't—"

"Entire families…you had wiped out. Every…last…*one*."

"I didn't! That's a *lie*!" Peterson shouted in his own defense.

"You paid those mercs extra to make examples of the ones who wronged you."

"Lie! Lie!"

"You had them decapitated, and their heads stuck on pikes and planted on the outskirts of the city."

Peterson was enraged now. "What? No! Liar!" he yelled.

But the kidnapper would not be interrupted. "You bathed the streets with their blood!"

Peterson held his breath and just shook his head as the accusations, this one long accusation, continued.

"Ever go back and visit that little town? Of course you haven't. Of course you just put it out of your mind and moved on as if it was just another day to you. Tuesday in Anthony Peterson's busy week. But if you had gone back to La Aldea…you'd see the streets are still stained by all of that blood. Skulls still unexpectedly wash up in the little canals that line the streets. You literally left *that many* dead in the ditches."

"No, you've got the wrong…" Peterson's quivering voice couldn't finish as the graphic imagery bombarded him. He could see it in his mind. Suddenly, he could see everything.

The kidnapper waited for complete silence, then continued, back in a quiet register, as if to let the next words speak for themselves.

"You killed the children last," the kidnapper almost growled. "You made the children watch their parents being murdered as they screamed helplessly. Some of them had the honor of being baptized in their parents' blood and bile before you had them taken care of. Never let it be said that Anthony Peterson doesn't take care of children."

That last mockery twisted Peterson's guts. He could only listen now, wide-eyed and disbelieving the words he was hearing.

"You were sending a message, weren't you? Well, that message came through loud and clear. *'Don't…fuck…*with Anthony Peterson!'"

By this time, Peterson was speechless in his rage. Those words. It was as if they could read his very thoughts. His face twisted into a mask of fury and then relaxed into an angry stare that could have frozen the kidnappers in their tracks, had they the balls to face him directly.

And with every new word, he got angrier.

"You had the money and influence to keep it out of the press, paid off all the right people, judges, cops, politicians. Dummy companies and shell corporations are a very useful thing in what I will ever so generously call 'international relations.' And it was all swept right under the rug…but everybody knew. Those few who did survive? They know too. And they're worse off than the dead. The dead you, personally, are responsible for."

Peterson gasped. He was almost hyperventilating at the verbal assault. All of these accusations. How could they…

"Liar," Peterson finally managed to hiss through his clenched teeth, his lips peeling back like an attacking animal. "Liar!"

"Murderer," the kidnapper said back to him and hung up the line with a slap.

Peterson turned to look at the disconnected phone.

"Murderer."

He shut his eyes and shook with ire and shame.

4 The Rainy Day Cometh

2:37 AM

Anthony Peterson stood in silence, arms crossed, one hand on his chin, deep in thought about the words the kidnapper had spoken to him.

And one word in particular.

"Murderer."

He sighed. Was that what he was? How could they say that? Just look at him. Just look at Anthony Peterson and what do you see?

It was a 'power look' Peterson had cultivated. That was what they called it back in the 80s when he was young, great looking, and carefree, making money hand-over-fist in the glorious Reagan years. Before his wife was even born.

That was what Anthony Peterson was. A money-making, powerful businessman. He didn't take any shit, and he knew exactly when to fight back if he was wronged. So, no. He wasn't a murderer. Was he?

Just look at him.

The 'power look.' He had it. He still had it, actually, but it was useless. Nobody could see him, for one thing, and for another, he had never felt so powerless.

Powerless. Not something Anthony Peterson was used to feeling.

But that feeling was virtually all he had…at least physically. His head was still throbbing like the antichrist of all hangovers. His mouth was dry. They hadn't even had the courtesy to leave him a bottle of water. He felt like he had just come out of the desert. And he was hungry. He had not eaten since the day before…sometime. How the hell did they expect him to function for them when he had no blood sugar to work with?

It was this physical ailment that kept reminding him how real this horror was. This was reality. He would never dream a nightmare this vivid. The pain in his knee, the dryness of his mouth, the rumbling of his stomach, and the constantly booming headache. Without all of this, he might convince himself it was not the reality that it was. But it was.

This was absolute horror. A horror he didn't deserve.

Did he?

Anthony Peterson. Look at him. He was no murderer. This was ridiculous.

The cell phone rang, breaking his pensive introspection (though none of his physical pangs) and demanding his attention. Peterson brought the phone to his ear without checking the number. "Tom. Is everything a go?"

Tom coughed and seemed to battle with the right words. "Uh, yes…" Peterson exhaled and started to smile before Tom completed his sentence "…and no."

Peterson's smile turned to a grimace. "What the fuck does that mean?" Peterson spat.

"We're a-ways short of the ten million."

"How much is 'a-ways'?"

Tom consulted his papers and said "Four…maybe five."

"What? You have got to be fucking kidding me! That's half the money. That's a little more than 'a-ways,' Tom!" Peterson shouted.

Tom was defensive. "Hey, man, you know goddamn well that the last few years haven't been your best. It ain't the eighties anymore, man. Shit, you're still making money, but you're mortgaged to the hilt."

Peterson shook his head in frustration, eyes closed, pained. What Tom said was true. Anthony and Susan Peterson had expensive tastes and so what if they did? What was wrong with borrowing from yourself once in a while? The money was always there…until you needed it.

Tom broke the silence of Peterson's despair. "Look, Anthony, maybe you can make them an offer. That's what you do best, isn't it? The art of the deal? Well, *make* them a deal. Five or six million is still a lot of scratch."

"No, Tom, no, you didn't hear this guy. He won't settle for a nickel less than the ten mil he's demanding."

Tom scoffed in exasperation. "Well, then you've got to let me call the long arm of the law, here. You can't just lie down and go all bitch dog for these sons of whores and you *know* that. You've never bent over for anyone in your life."

Peterson shook his head "This is different, Tom. I told you, if I do that then she dies. They kill Susan. Susan...is...dead!" he said, making his point immensely clear.

Tom considered aloud "Well...would that be...such a bad thing?"

"What...the fuck, man?" Peterson cried out in shock. "Are you fucking kidding me?"

Tom reasoned with him calmly. "Hey, you were the one always saying she was a stone-cold ass bitch. You said the old magic was long gone, and the only reason you kept the marriage going is that it was cheaper to keep her." Then, Tom did his best impression of Peterson's voice to add, "'Divorce is a bitch, Tommy-boy! It's always cheaper to keep her!' You said that shit a lot. Don't you remember?"

Peterson closed his eyes, flustered and ashamed. He had said that. He knew he had said that many times. He regretted it now. "I was...drunk...when I said that, man. Give me a break."

"*In vino veritas*, my friend."

Peterson shook his head. He couldn't believe what he was hearing, especially as desperate as the situation was. Was Tom out of his mind? He wanted to berate Tom back into shape, but alienating Tom would mean certain death for both Susan and himself. "No, no, Tom, I didn't mean it...not ever, I—"

"How do you know this isn't all a con?" Tom asked, speculatively, cutting him off. "And if it is a con, who knows who's in on it? Who knows...maybe...Susan?"

Peterson tensed up at those words. He was ashamed to admit to himself the thought had crossed his mind.

Susan was an actress. What if she had cooked up this whole scheme to get all of his money, then leave him for someone else? He could be in an abandoned warehouse in bum-fuck suburb USA while she was safe at home making plans to leave the country.

But no…he knew better. What the hell was Tom playing at? Tom was a recovering addict and alcoholic, but…he wasn't off the wagon, was he?

"No. She…wouldn't…do that…to me, Tom," Peterson insisted, actually pointing through the empty air with wide eyes.

"Well then, I don't know what to tell you, my friend."

Peterson was stone-faced, unsure what to do or how to feel. What was Tom doing this for? Why was he resisting? Did Tom have something fucking better to do? This was his life! Susan's life!

Peterson started when the phone beeped in his ear.

"Ugh! Hang on, Tom. I got another call." He tapped the screen, sighed in exhaustion and put on his business voice again. "This is Anthony Peterson."

"The money," the now-familiar voice said.

"Yeah, well, I've got most of it."

"Not good enough," came the response without a missed beat.

"Well, I can't just come up with ten million dollars," Peterson argued, flustered. "I mean, that is just crazy!"

The kidnapper remained calm as if playing by a different script. "If you can't come up with the money, take it out of your rainy day fund," he said, matter-of-factly.

Peterson's face twisted in confusion again. "Rainy day fund? What are you talking about?"

"A man like you has got to have a lot of cash on hand. Crooked judges and lawyers don't come cheap."

Peterson shook his head and said, "I have *no* idea what you're talking about."

"Oh, should I not call it that? Well, let me clarify for you. By 'rainy day fund,' I'm talking about an offshore safe deposit box."

The words hung in the air. Peterson was wide-eyed, taken aback, shocked. How could they know about that?

The kidnapper waited a moment and twisted the knife. "Yes, we've been doing our homework on you, Mr. Peterson." He paused again, then added, "And not just that one with your little gold nest egg. We know about the Swiss bank accounts. So secretive. And, lest we forget, the Delaware holdings. Yeah, shell companies again. We know your fingerprints when we see them."

Peterson's adversary seemed to be really enjoying himself now. The voice was still low and largely unaffected, but a sinister, nearly playful, edge could be heard. It was almost like listening to a human predator play with his prey.

Peterson's anger got the better of him. "Who is this 'we' you keep talking about? Are you some kind of fucking terrorist group? Who the hell are you?" he demanded.

The kidnapper laughed again coldly. "*I'm* the one who's going to make you pay, Mr. Peterson. One way or the other."

Peterson pushed back. "I cannot pay you ten million dollars, not in twenty-four hours, it's impossible!"

"Then, you pay in blood. Then, your wife's dead," the kidnapper whispered. "And then, *you're* dead." Peterson recoiled. "Maybe we'll be generous and leave the oxygen on and you can starve to death slowly or maybe you die of thirst. Whichever comes first. And your wife? After we're…" he laughed "…*finished* with her, we'll cut off her head and stick it on a pike. Just like in South America."

Peterson desperately tried to dispel that talking point again. "Hey, now I told you that was a lie, that's an absolute lie. I don't know what the fuck you're talking about. I told you that!"

That grim laughter again. "Sure. Nice pivot. You want me to believe I've got you confused with someone else."

"Yeah, well, maybe you do. Maybe you do!" Peterson said aggressively.

"Right, another egomaniacal sociopath business tycoon with delusions of morality and nobility. You got me there. There are plenty of those in this country, the good ol' You Ess of Aay!" the kidnapper drawled those last words in a sarcastic parody of a southern accent. "But there is only *one* Anthony Peterson."

"No, it's not me. You've got the wrong man! I'm not a sociopath. I'm a good–"

"*No*body thinks they're a bad person," the kidnapper cut him off. "Not even the worst people. Not even a monster. Not even the monster named Anthony Peterson."

"You…you are the monster," Peterson said, the words slithering from his mouth, painfully.

The kidnapper didn't bother responding. "If I were you, I would start thinking about the contents of that safe deposit box you're so carefully protecting. Then the Swiss accounts, then the shell company bucks. Do it."

These assholes weren't getting the message. Impatiently Peterson repeated himself. "I told you, I don't know any goddam thing about any safety deposit box or any fucking rainy day fu–"

"Yeah? Well, all right. I can see you need a little coaxing!"

And with that came another vibrating hum, this one louder than before. He heard it before he felt it.

But this time, it was not the cell phone.

This time, it was everything around him. The entire container was one big electric conductor, and that electricity flowed through his body at that moment.

Peterson froze like a statue. Every muscle in his body tensed as the voltage shot through him. He trembled like a dying man being electrified to the point of near death as the lights faded and came back.

He felt blood vessels burst in his eyes and visual purple involuntarily clouded his vision. Even in his pain, the purple clouds reformed to make blood blossoms and he thought about La Aldea. He wasn't a murderer. But South America…and the blood…and the–

The torturous electrical onslaught continued.

It was agony, and it seemed to take forever to end. But at long last it did end in the reverse of the way it started. The hum ceased while the electricity continued to coarse through his body and finally fade out. His heart restarted, and it beat more fiercely than he had ever felt it before. He fell to the floor in agony, blood streaming from his nostrils.

Had he really been complaining about hunger, thirst, and body pains? How foolish had he been? That was like heaven compared to this hell.

The phone was lying on the metal floor just before his eyes. Shockproof case. Electricity proof. Frankenstein had been right. Now he knew why.

Blood dripped around his face, and he stared straight ahead, hurting, paralyzed. He would have vomited, had he not been so empty.

The kidnapper's voice came from the phone and Peterson could just make out the words "All right. Hopefully you're in a more…harmonious…frame of mind."

Peterson coughed and fought to catch his breath. It took all the strength and effort he had to look at the phone and say "Go… fuck…yourself."

The electrical hum came a second time. The entire container was electrified once again, and Peterson along with it.

The current contracted his muscles and forced him to sit up straight as if on command. His head trembled, and he felt his eyes roll back in his head as his jaw clenched painfully. Blood began seeping from his ears onto his shoulders, and he knew he would soon be dead. This was the way he was going out…shitting his pants on the floor of a goddam cargo container all because of a business deal he barely remembered that went south.

South.

And with that thought, the blood and skulls took over his mind again. He could see them floating up, dead, but the jaws seemed to open with gravity as if to scream at him. After another excruciating moment, the current stopped, the vision vanished, and Peterson fell backward to the floor, hyperventilating.

Peterson reached feebly for the phone, feet away from his grasp. He was ready to tell them that they won. He would do it. That and anything else. Just stop this torture.

But before his fingers could bring the phone to him, he heard the voice again, ominously saying, "Once more...with *feeling*!"

Peterson's eyes widened in horror as the current filled his body again. He convulsed wildly on his back in more pain than he had ever felt in his life. Is this what they were doing to Susan? Oh, God, no! Even if Anthony deserved this torture, surely sweet Susan did not.

It felt like an eternity before the power shut off and the lights rose back to normal.

He went limp, at last, his tortured muscles relaxed and his pain wracked face went expressionless. The agonizing torture had ended for the moment and all was quiet.

He couldn't move for several minutes. He wondered if he might actually be dead, but his brain hadn't yet got the message that his body was shutting down for the season.

His mind wandered crazily back through his life's history. He remembered a fishing trip with his family when his son, Evan, had been just a boy. He recalled Evan catching a catfish and watching it flop around on the metal floor of the small boat they rode in. Of course, Peterson knew, that was exactly how he must have looked minutes before. Just like the fish, he had been flopping around and convulsing in death. He remembered Evan asking his father if the fish was dead, and Anthony had chuckled, "Oh, he's dead all right, son. He just doesn't know it yet."

Was that it? Was Peterson dead, but simply failed to realize it yet?

That must be the case. He wondered, idly and morosely, which ring of hell he would be visiting first. Next, he wondered if Evan would even care.

At last he gasped and breathed and moved. Very slowly he was able to will his body to move into a seated position, then to stand on shaking legs. It took all his strength. But he wasn't dead after all. Not yet.

His legs were shaky, and his knees knocked. He saw blood droplets falling to the floor and making their dime-sized marks on the bottom of his forty-foot coffin. As they flowed together, he thought of the blood-stained streets again.

Could that morose story be true? Is all that how La Aldea had gone?

All he wanted was to lie down and rest. There was not a part of him that was not hurting. He even felt pain in his hair, as if that were possible. He wanted to lose consciousness and try to forget that this was his life, if only for a moment.

But he was still Anthony Peterson, goddammit, and he was not done yet. If he was standing, he was living. If he was living, he was fighting.

He may be covered in his own blood from the waist up and his own shit and piss from the waist down, but they hadn't beaten him yet. Not yet. He was still standing, and he was going to win.

He nodded into the nothingness of his chamber and staggered over to the wall, laying an outstretched hand on it to lean over.

Suddenly, a final jolt of electricity hit his hand. He jumped and cried out in pain. It was like the worst static electricity shock he had ever felt. He jerked the hand away and stared at it in disbelief.

Then, that same sickening, cruel laughter echoed again around the container. It sounded like the villain in some B-movie horror thriller cackling and echoing through a haunted house.

If only that were the case. This was real.

He looked around and then down at the phone.

The kidnapper had not hung up. He had been waiting there the entire time until Peterson showed signs of life. Only then did he laugh at him.

"Well, chicken. Sounds like you're not quite fried yet."

"Asshole," Peterson whispered through his teeth, pulling back his lips again in anger.

The kidnapper hung up in mid-laugh, leaving Peterson leaning against the wall, staring down at the phone with hatred.

"Sa*dist*ic *ass*hole!" he shouted through his clenched teeth.

He leaned his head on the wall, staring at the floor, and allowed himself a short cry.

Slowly, he composed himself and looked back down at the phone. He hated that fucking vile device. But it was his lifeline. Or so he hoped.

He staggered back to it and slowly, carefully, sat down next to it. He looked at it before he touched it and finally picked it up and dialed.

"Tom?" he sighed and shook his head in defeat.

"Anthony, what happened? I lost you there."

"We're going to need to clear out that rainy day fund."

Tom paused for a moment, then asked, "Okay, which one?"

"All of them, man. I need you to arrange for someone to liquidate the safety deposit box and I need the funds from all the rainy day funds."

"Anthony, again, are you sure about this?"

Anthony shook and sighed, nodding. "I'm sure, Tom. In case you didn't notice, it is fucking *pour*ing right now!"

5 The Difference is Why

Anthony Peterson was nowhere near his beloved wife.

But someone else was.

Calderon had spent much of his life following the wrong men and, being that Calderon had few scruples, following the wrong men proved never to be much of a problem. That was as long as the checks cleared.

And Calderon always made damn sure his checks cleared.

Money made the world go round, right? So, what the hell else was there?

Calderon kept to the shadows just outside of the single building on the property.

He lit a cigarette and stayed close to the trunk of the tree he was under.

He had earned this break. He had been listening too long.

The boss…well, this current boss of this one particular job, that is, wanted as little satellite or aircraft visibility of their operations as possible. Even the truck Calderon himself had driven in that morning had to be driven in on a specific schedule. If their intel was right, there was no photography, satellite or otherwise, at that time. If they had done their job correctly up until then, even if they were being photographed, no one would likely be scrutinizing the images.

This place was about as off-the-grid as one could get. It was a hole in the map, if anything. No one knew it was there.

It was Calderon's kind of place. And, again, the job paid well, so what else was there?

He chuckled quietly and puffed again, then surveyed the horizon.

Nothing.

He calmly moved his rifle to hang on his other shoulder and leaned against the tree to relax.

What else was there?

He sighed, forgetting the laugh for the moment and spat his cigarette onto the ground, where he crushed it with his big tan boot.

Well, there was that kick he felt as he brought the box in. That kick from inside the box.

Calderon was not the kind of man who asked questions. The money was good, so he didn't ask. After all, what else was there?

But that kick he had felt as he brought the box in. That made him think. He didn't like it.

He knew abstractly what was going on. This particular job was all about payback. Guy trapped in a metal cargo container. He was going to be tortured and blackmailed and killed. Well, maybe killed. Calderon didn't know. And why should he care? Money made the world go round, right?

What else was there?

Some other hired team had taken care of that part. Wired it up for electricity. Lighting. Oxygen. Other surprises.

Calderon didn't even know where the goddam container even was. Somewhere out there. Hell, maybe under his very feet. He didn't know. He didn't care. It wasn't his business to know or care.

Some other team had picked up the rich asshole the boss of this job was torturing. Maybe the same team who had placed the container wherever it was and rigged it up for electroshock therapy.

Calderon chuckled at that thought.

Calderon's job had been threefold. He and another hired gun were to pick up the wife and bring her right there.

No problem. Easy job. If only they hadn't had him bring her in a wooden box. Too much like a coffin.

But that was the goddam job, so he did it. It paid just right and what else was there?

There was the kick he heard. That stuck with him, strangely.

The second half of the job was to guard the place and pick off anyone who tried to get in if necessary. But, hell, who would find this place? It wouldn't be necessary.

Calderon was bored and when he was bored his mind started to fuck him over, doubting everything about himself.

Thinking about…why.

The third part of the job was maybe the most important. Part of what made Calderon sought after was more than his combat and intelligence capabilities. He was also a skilled communications operative and this particular boss (Calderon didn't know the man's name and never asked) wanted a list of phone numbers monitored and recorded.

Calderon had the equipment, and he brought it with him in a nice, shiny silver case. The system even managed to do a light digitized voice disguise to help keep things secretive. It was easy training the others to use it in shifts. His only rule was that they didn't spill any fucking coffee on the damned thing.

He reached for another cigarette, then thought of the feel of that woman kicking from inside the box. Suddenly, the cigarette didn't appeal to him. Somehow, he was sure it would taste terrible.

What was it that bothered him so goddamn badly?

Calderon wasn't the kind of man who had much of a heart, nor was he terribly sentimental or sympathetic.

Had he gotten soft in his advanced years? He had been everything from a hitman to a soldier of fortune to a trader of secrets for the past twenty-five years.

Calderon was only forty-seven, but he felt so much older sometimes.

Was having seen so much over the years finally wearing on him? Was Calderon that kind of a pussy? He wondered.

Maybe he just wanted to fuck the bitch. He didn't know.

He shook his head.

No, no. Something else. He knew what it was too. He just didn't want to admit it.

But that one thing…that one little…strange thing…that had been wearing on him for months before this job. Wearing on him and telling him he needed to quit all this. Retire to some island full of naked women and eat and drink until he got fat. Fat and happy and laughing. Not ever thinking about his history. Not ever again. And he wouldn't even swat a mosquito or gut a fish. Just leave the blood to someone else and retire.

He had the money. That was all that mattered. What else was there?

He walked back inside, keeping close under the shade so he wouldn't be seen in the unlikely event that anyone happened to be looking. He entered the code and entered the compound.

"All quiet on the western front," he joked to another of their small team, a young female mercenary named Keeler.

He needed to get it all out of his mind. The kick and the memories it stirred up.

It was time to forget everything and just watch some television. Try not to think about what happened months ago and why he was questioning the very living he had made for himself.

Monitor the calls when they came, watch some TV in between.

This was not the job on which to use cell phones. GPS signatures blew apart jobs like this. Even though he was bored at the moment and would love to turn on his phone and watch some old movie, it was not to be. So, he headed for the television, wanting to take his mind off of his doubts.

Morality had no place in the dark underbelly of society where Calderon made his living. You took the right jobs, you asked the questions you had to ask to do those jobs and you didn't ask a damn thing further than that. If your heart is going to give you pangs, you're in the wrong business, aren't you?

But he did have a question that, at least for the past few months, had given him pangs.

And that question was 'why?'

He realized since that one day that still made him so sick, that 'why?' was a vital question that made all the difference. The difference…was why.

He didn't give a shit about Anthony Peterson. He sure as shit didn't sympathize with men like him. Hell, as bad a man as Calderon surely was, he wasn't nearly as bad as Anthony Peterson was. He knew that.

But this wife? That trophy wife? Did she deserve this?

He heard her screaming and crying into the phone before someone taped her lips shut again. And he had just laughed. But when things got quiet again, he started to ask why.

Sure, this was part of the plan. This was part of the torture of Anthony Peterson, but…why? Why this?

And that made a difference, suddenly, in his life. A year ago, it wouldn't have, but as of a few months back…

He shuddered as he walked down the dark hallways.

You can kill a guy because you've been paid to. That's a living. You don't ask questions. Maybe he's being killed because he owes somebody money. Maybe he's being killed because he fucked the wrong man's wife. Maybe he was just as bad as Calderon or even Peterson. Or maybe he was being killed for the wrong reasons. The wrong guy at the wrong time?

The difference is why.

So why was Mrs. Peterson involved in this? Was she as bad as her husband? Had she partaken in the same nefarious deeds Peterson had? Was she some evil bitch who deserved all she got? Or was she an innocent bystander in all of this?

A year ago, Calderon wouldn't have cared. Today, no matter how much he fucking fought it…Calderon cared.

Or, at least, Calderon questioned.

Why? Why not one of Peterson's kids or that partner he used to have or some close co-worker?

If it was just to torture Peterson, that didn't feel right.

He silently cursed himself for giving a shit or even coming close to giving a shit.

Calderon stopped at the windowed door that led to the neatly organized storage room. He looked in on the bound and gagged wife and smiled at her, coldly, trying to show (if only himself) that he was still the badass motherfucker she should be terrified of.

But why?

He shook his head and walked on to the next room where the little TV was. It had rabbit ears and foil on the ends of each antenna. They could only get one station on that little TV, but he accepted it and used the noise of some old game show rerun to clear his brain.

He chuckled at the station's ID. K-OME. Had he gotten into a different line of work, he might find himself there, making sick jokes in their advertisements. "Only one station in the area can make you…K-OME!"

Calderon chuckled.

Then, he fought to put it out of his head.

You don't ask why. Not in this business. Not ever.

And he almost convinced himself to stop thinking about it.

6 The Burning Man

3:35 AM

Anthony Peterson sat against the wall and stared forward. His knees were bent before his chest. He limply held the cell phone in one hand, draped across his knee. The other hand was laid limply on the floor next to him.

He had chosen a certain nondescript point on the wall in front of him and stared, unfocused, at it for far too long.

This was dejection. Nothing else for him to do. Trapped. Controlled. Owned. Indeed, he was even bored.

This was not the kind of situation one expected to be bored in. Life or death, danger, torture. It was not boring.

But this was. He had done all he could, and thus, he waited.

And waited.

And…

He began to idly bang the back of his head against the wall. Calmly at first, lightly. Even casually. His eye remained fixed on the spot on the wall before him, and he found himself interested in the unique feeling of his eyeballs rolling in their sockets while he moved his head and kept them staring at a particular spot.

Bang…bang…bang.

That was how bored he was. He found the sensation of feeling his own eyeballs to be fascinating.

Bang…bang…bang.

Anthony, old boy, I do believe you're cracking up! he thought to himself and continued the banging.

Bang…bang…bang.

But he had done everything else, hadn't he?

Bang…bang…bang.

He had had an affair with an actress once before Susan. She may not have been a big Hollywood starlet, but a recognizable enough face from TV, movies, commercials. He had once told her how fascinating he thought her job must be. She had told him it was actually mostly waiting around. Setting up the camera, hanging around craft services two hours after your call, waiting for the previous shot to be done so you could deliver your three scripted words, and then wait around again.

Bang…bang…bang….

So, I guess…this is the big film, he thought and almost smiled. He didn't smile, though. Smiling might have messed up his rhythm.

Bang…bang…bang…

The place smelled bad. Like one of those canals in…

No, no, no, not that.

The smell was a nauseating combination of sweat, feces, urine, and that old, decaying metal smell that never seemed to be missing from crates like this. It wasn't rust. It was…something else. As if the metal itself had died and was rotting. Sending out its carrion fumes to its captive. From one corpse to another.

After his last call to Tom, while he was still reeling from being fried, he had undressed and used his underwear and undershirt to clean himself as best he could (the bastards hadn't even left him a bottle of water as his parched mouth could attest) and had tossed the soiled underclothes in the corner.

Bang…bang…bang…

It was humiliating.

Bang…bang…bang…

Then, he got dressed again. Even pulled his tie up to the top button. The Power Look. All he needed now were a pair of Ray Bans.

They were stealing his money, they had taken his wife, they had robbed him of his freedom, but whether they knew it or not, he still had his dignity.

Bang…bang…bang…

Suddenly, the cell phone went off again and startled him out of his daze. He almost laughed at his reaction. The one thing he had been waiting for was this phone call, but when it came, it scared the hell out of him.

Maybe he *was* cracking up.

He hit the green icon and stood up to pace some more. It was better than sitting there and banging his head. "Yeah?"

"It's Tom," came the voice. Peterson rolled his eyes again. Why the fuck would Tom bother identifying himself? It was either him or the kidnapping asshole. "Alright, I cleaned the rainy day funds."

"Good."

"No, not good. We're still gonna be a short a couple million."

"Shit." He cursed under his breath. How could this be? There was always money…now…this. "How the fuck did that happen?"

"Don't blame me, Tony-Pete!" Tom said back, using a very forced nickname almost too casually. "Those accounts were always just outliers."

"And the safety–"

"The *safe* deposit box, Anthony. Think about it. We'd have to have someone clear it out, sell the stuff, then deposit and transfer it. Yeah, I got that started, but it sure as hell can't be finished before your time is up."

Suddenly, banging his head didn't seem like such a bad idea. What good was a rainy day fund if…or should he have called it a kidnapped and boxed by terrorists fund?

Tom took advantage of the silence and spoke up again. "Look, uh, Anthony, again, are you sure this is the way you wanna go? I mean, there may be some other options. Do you have *any* idea where you are?"

How thick was this guy's head? "I told you, I'm in metal shipping crate, trapped. Cargo containers aren't generally known for their scenic views, Tom," Peterson barked, impatiently.

Tom was only lightly fazed. "Uh, well, can you hear anything? Outside? That might pinpoint where you are."

Dutifully, Peterson paused then said, "No. Nothing."

"Are you on land or on water? A ship? The air, maybe?"

Peterson was frustrated enough without Tom's nonsense. Did Tom really think he hadn't thought of all of this already.

"I don't fucking know! Land, maybe. I haven't heard or felt anything. No engines, no turbulence."

"How about the weather? Wind? Rain? Anything?"

"Nada," Peterson said firmly, hoping to either move Tom to another subject or at least a part of this one he hadn't thought of already.

"Okay, then odds are you're indoors," the genius deduced. "I assume you've been pounding like a motherfucker to get out of there, so you're probably somewhere secluded. Is it hot or cold?"

"Cold." No question about that one.

"How 'bout the cell phone they gave you? Any phone numbers or any information that might give you any indication?"

Again, as if he hadn't thought of that. "No, I checked, everything's blocked. It's a cheap knockoff, nondescript. Cheaper than the case."

"Expensive case?"

Peterson chuckled without humor. "One of the best. One of those AfterSHOK cases they advertise."

"Right, the one with Frankenstein in the commercial. Well, can you take the phone out? Anything inside? Price tag, maybe?"

Peterson's eyes widened with hope, and he did exactly that. But his hopes were dashed. "Ah... nothing. Nothing at all."

"Dammit." Tom paused in thought. "What about the voice of the kidnapper?"

"Low. Deep. Calm. Cruel."

"No, I mean, accents or anything?"

Peterson shook his head. "The whole time he's talking in this subdued whisper. It's almost impossible to recognize anything in his voice." Peterson thought about it for a moment. "Maybe American, maybe Canadian, I guess. He doesn't sound like a foreigner. He's...an older guy, maybe. He sounds very sure of himself. Confident. Like a man with a gun to your head." Peterson paused, wondering whether to go on. "And he...he knows a lot about me."

Tom didn't get it. "Like what?"

Peterson sighed and pushed out the words, painfully. "South America."

Tom was silent, as if running those words through his mind. Tom knew about La Aldea. Peterson just waited for Tom to put it together. Finally, a pained sigh told Peterson that Tom got it at last. Now Tom understood. Now Tom knew they were fucked and why.

"Oh, fuck," Tom said. He waited, clearly thinking and came back more determined to solve this. For maybe the first time that night, Tom didn't sound distracted. "What's the last thing you remember?"

"Like I told them, being on the street and then being... smothered."

He had been through this a hundred times over the past few hours. He ran through it again in his mind, trying to go backward into the past, working to access the memories of that day.

"Wait...I remember...I *was* at a bar. That's right, I stopped on my way home from work at that joint over on Thirteenth Street."

"That kind of sleazy gastropub?"

"That's the one. I had a few drinks, and I went to the head." He thought some more. "And then, when I came back to my table..." Peterson replayed it all in his mind. "... my drink had a strange taste. Just a little. I didn't think much about it at the time. Could have been a bad shot or something...but now..."

"Can't be a coincidence, chief. You were drugged. That's the only answer. Someone at the bar did it. Did you notice anyone suspicious?"

"Well, it's...the drinks are good, but it's kind of a dive bar. Everyone was suspicious." He laughed in spite of the situation.

Tom was quiet again. He must have been spooked by the story. If it could happen to Anthony Peterson, it could happen to him.

Sadly, Tom didn't come up with anything useful, so he went back to the subject at hand. "So, what do you want me to do about the...the rest of the money?"

Peterson hesitated. All of his money was gone, the rainy day funds were gone too. The gold could not be sold in time. Where else could he go for cash? He really didn't want to have to do it, but he had no choice.

"Sell the houses, all of them."

"I can't," Tom said quickly. He had already thought of that, hadn't he? "You can't transfer property that fast, Anthony. Ever hear of escrow? And, besides, man, you...you're mortgaged in balls deep as it is."

Peterson was annoyed on top of being frightened. Why *Tom*?

"Well, we've got to think of something, you fucking asshole. I need to get out of here! Fast! In less than twenty-fours, I run out of air! And that's not even to mention they've got this whole place hooked up like a goddamn electric chair," he snapped.

Tom was horrified. "What the fuck? Are you serious?"

Peterson practically yelled, "Serious as it gets. They keep torturing me by electrifying the goddamn place. It's a lot like feeling your brains in a red-hot cauldron inside your own head. I might have permanent damage already. I can't take much more of this shit."

"But that would take..." he calculated and then gave up. "Who would have the kind of money to set something like this up? You've just heard the one voice on the phone, right?"

Peterson shrugged. "Yeah."

"Well, maybe it's not a crew. Maybe it's just one guy. Maybe he's some rich fuck with a mastermind complex looking to torture other rich fucks for his own sick fuckin' amusement. Maybe somebody you burned on a business deal?"

45

Peterson bowed his head in complete exhaustion. "I never burned anybody this bad," he said.

It was a serious moment of pain for Peterson, but Tom actually laughed, seeming to genuinely find this cynically amusing.

Peterson's anger roiled again. "What the fuck are you laughing at?"

Tom tapered off the laughter and said, "Nothing, nothing. It's just good to see you still haven't lost your sense of humor during all this."

"You think that's funny?" Peterson demanded.

"No, no, no. Just…you must be joking. You know how badly you've burned people before. You're the king of–"

"Look, I suggest you get on the fucking houses right now! If you can't sell them, borrow against them. For God's sake, you find something we can sell, damn it, or Susan is dead, I'm fucking dead, and that leaves you, Tommy-boy, very, very *unemployed*."

Peterson heard a whimper in the background. "I gotta go," Tom said.

"Damn right you do. You better!" Peterson scowled and hit the hang up button, clearly not amused.

What the fuck was Tom's problem? Laughing at a time like this?

Anthony Peterson knew he didn't deserve this. Nothing like this.

7 Men of Principle

Anthony Peterson paced his cargo cell like a caged lion. Waiting.

Parched, pained, tired, sore, starving, and angry.

Having to appease these monsters was driving him mad. Did they think he owed them something? Christ.

The damnable thing was that now he was rehearsing in his head how he would tell them that they would have to settle for stealing less of his money...and *he* was the one who had to be apologetic.

Damnable.

Frustrated, and finding no other option, he raised the cell phone and hit send.

"Mr. Peterson," the kidnapper immediately answered.

Peterson was tense. He had a nasty taste in his mouth about the whole thing. "Yeah."

"How are you progressing?"

He took a deep breath. "I tapped into the rainy day funds like you said."

"...and?"

He closed his eyes tight as if expecting a blow. "I'm still gonna be short."

The kidnapper showed emotion again, blasting out threats almost breathlessly. "If you're short even one penny or late one second on delivery, I'll kill you and your expensive trophy wife."

"We can make a deal here. The banks aren't even open yet."

"No deals. Ten million or you pay in blood."

Peterson was at his wit's end. He shouted, "This is crazy! You're gonna throw away potentially millions of dollars?"

"I'm a man of principle, you might say," the kidnapper proclaimed with a smile in his voice.

"I might say you're a man who's fucking out of your mind!" Peterson scoffed.

The buzz sound rose again, and Peterson immediately regretted the talkback.

Suddenly, the entire container was a Tesla coil. Peterson's head snapped backward violently, and his eyes rolled back in his head, his body trembling at the voltage.

It was another eternity for Peterson. He felt as if his brain was cooking. It was a physical torture that brought about mental torture. His eyes clouded over with purple again, and he could see skulls floating out of the darkness. It was as if they had floated to the surface of a canal filled with blood. And those floating skulls rose to greet him face-first as if to look upon their proxy murderer, accusingly.

When, at long last, the electricity was turned off, he collapsed, hitting the floor hard.

Gasping for air, he slowly opened his eyes. Gradually, he was able to regain his vision. He focused his eyes to see the phone waiting there for him on the floor.

"Now…I'll bet that was a shock to the system," the kidnapper joked and hung up.

8 Distracted at Work

4:07 AM

Anthony Peterson was counting on one man more than any other, and that man was Tom Pocase.

Tom sat on the floor of the corner of the room and stared forward with angry eyes. This was an unexpected development, and it was surely going to keep him from doing his job quite as well as Anthony Peterson had come to expect.

Tom felt sick. Why did this have to happen tonight?

Didn't the universe know he had shit to do?

Of all nights…tonight?

Why?

Hell, was it even night anymore? He scoffed as he looked at his watch. Morning. Why today? Ugh. Why?

Tom brought his knees to his chest and hugged them. Then, he let one fall to the side and rested one arm on his raised knee.

Here, he wouldn't have to face what he had done. Out of sight, out of mind.

Maybe if he just sat here against the wall and looked at the bed at this angle, he wouldn't need to face reality. He wouldn't need to…

Ugh, but what a fucking mess. Everything was a mess and his life kept getting worse and worse.

He wondered…how could he make this better for himself?

Maybe if Anthony were to take good care of him? After all, Anthony was right. He would soon be very, very unemployed and with this situation he had found himself at the center of.

He also faced the very real possibility that he might face jail time.

How had he gotten himself into this fucking mess?

Anthony.

He had to focus on Anthony to get his money.

Tom needed to get Anthony his money, then Tom would get his. He would make that clear. He had to.

Tom pushed back with his heels and started to slide up the wall. He wasn't quite the athlete he once had been, back in his boxing days, but he was still strong. Damn strong.

He let out a sob as soon as he got to his feet and saw that horrible sight.

Maybe Tom was not that strong.

He stared at the bed and shivered. The phone rang, and he jumped.

It could be Peterson. It could be the other…the other…

He sobbed and walked forward to stare down at the bed. It was not empty.

What had he done?

How had he gotten himself into this mess?

This wasn't him. This…

The phone rang again, and he wiped his eyes. He sat on the bed and reached for the phone and tried to sound calm, but the next ring made him sob again, then dissolve into nervous, ironic laughter.

He tried to compose himself.

Unknown number. It was Peterson. Had to be.

He took a deep breath and pushed the button and immediately heard his name.

He jumped in shock. Sounding normal again was not going to be easy.

9 Party Monster

4:14 AM

Anthony Peterson hated waiting. He had given up sitting and staring at the wall and had given up banging his head against its neighbor, but his frustration was not abating.

He had been calling Tom, and the bastard was not answering.

There was no time for this. Didn't Tom know this was life or death?

Peterson needed this to be finished. Now.

He slowed down his tense pacing and loosened his tie. The air was getting thin. This was the end, wasn't it? Maybe. Maybe just close to it.

The pacing wasn't helping. He needed time. He needed air. He needed Tom to answer the goddam phone.

He hit redial and waited. At last, Tom picked up, and Peterson exhaled, relieved. "Tom!"

"Oh…hey," Tom said meekly. This was not the response Peterson expected.

Tom sounded like he had been crying. In fact, he could hear sniffling right then. What was going on?

Was it the kidnappers? Had they gotten Tom too? Tom's wife? Tom's kids?

"Tom? Tom, what's wrong with you?"

Tom's tears turned to light laughter. It was light, yet somehow crazy laughter that, filtered through his tears, still sounded like crying.

"Tom, have you been crying?"

"No," Tom said defensively and weakly. Then, as if trying to cover up his lie he coughed and deepened his voice again. "No. In

51

fact. Uh… Oh, God. In fact…I was just about to call you back. But, uh…you see? There's been a complication."

Peterson didn't like the sound of that. He forced himself to remain calm. "Compli*cation*?"

That soft, crazy tear-laughter returned for a second, and Tom said, "Yeah. I think you'd better call someone else. We'll talk later. You'd better call somebody else, Anthony!"

Peterson had been putting up with Tom's bullshit for the entire night, and this was not what he needed to hear. He patiently tried to school him, calm him, and get past this shit.

"No, Tom, no. I *can't* call anyone else. You *know* that! You're my closest business associate for a reason; you're the only one with access to any of this, because you're the only one I can trust."

The nervous laughter returned. "You're going to have to call somebody else."

Peterson realized he was going to have to help Tom before Tom could be of any help. And only Tom could help him.

"Tom? What's wrong?" Peterson asked in his most patient, least realistic voice.

Tom was trying to be calm, Peterson could hear that, but he was also afraid to tell Peterson what he needed to know. "Well… see? When you called…I left something out."

"Something? What?"

Peterson's heart drummed in his chest. What had Tom not told him?

The pause Tom subjected him to was interminable. At last he mumbled "I, uh…I wasn't exactly alone. I'm still not."

Peterson knew he wasn't going to like this one bit. "Who is there with you, Tom?"

He sniffled. "A…uh, a…a woman. A girl."

Peterson scoffed. "A girl? You mean a hooker?"

"No!" Tom said quickly. "No, no, no. Just a girl I met online."

It was becoming difficult for Peterson to remain cool. He was impatient. This was his life on the line and Tom was out for some free candy?

"Tom. God knows I'm the last person to lecture anyone on infidelity, we both know that. But for God's sake, man, you know you've got a wife who is *pregnant* and three little kids at home, right?"

"I know," Tom whispered shakily. "Yeah. Yeah, I know. Ah, God, I love her. I do, I just... I made a..." Tom coughed several times before continuing. "But that's...that's not the complication, man. See, this girl, she's...well, it turns out she's quite the party monster."

Peterson closed his eyes tightly and sighed. He had been a notorious partier himself. Somehow, he knew precisely where this was going. "Why didn't you tell me this before?"

"It wasn't...Anthony, it wasn't a problem before. Well, not a big problem. We went out, partied, came back here...did the deed...fell asleep, and then, you called."

"So..."

"So, we both, I...I mean this girl had a few, and I guess she got bored from all the work I was doing...for you, you know?"

"I get the picture."

"So, I guess she got back into the stash on her own."

"Tom?" Peterson calmly spoke. "What did she take?"

"Nothing," he said defensively. "Well, not much."

"Not much?"

"Just a little low-grade acid, you know."

"Acid."

"And some heroin. And...uh, a speedball."

"Heroin *and* a speedball?"

"Well, maybe two? Two or three speedballs."

"Jesus."

"Then, I gave her a little bit of coke to ease her down."

"Is that all?"

"Um..." Tom thought. "Well, that...and some pot...and a little...little bit of mescaline."

"Jesus Christ, Tom, my life and my wife are on the line, and you're busy hitting some girl over the head with an entire fucking pharmacy?"

"…and some vodka," Tom added nervously.

Peterson looked off to the side, frustrated and in almost complete disbelief that this already nightmarish night had to get worse. "Tom?"

"Yeah?"

"Are you high right now?"

"Oh, no!" Tom said. He sounded amused by the question, and it was not quite believable. "You know I don't…I'm straight."

But Tom didn't sound 'straight' to his boss.

"Tom?" Peterson was patronizing, talking to Tom as if he were a small, dull child. "Tom? You've been through two rehabs already. You promised me you had this under control."

"I do," Tom said shakily. "I do… just… don't worry about me, it's her."

"What happened?"

Tom coughed nervously and laid out the scenario. "Well, after you hung up on me, I checked on her, and she was…ugh, she was vomiting in her sleep. I guess she had passed out, you know, after… while I was busy with you. And then, she puked in her sleep."

"Oh, God."

"No, I mean, it's okay. I put her on her side so she doesn't choke. And uh, well, she started coughing up blood too." He sighed, confused and scared. "It's just now…I, I, I can't get her to wake up. I've tried everything. She's, she's uh, she's turning kind of blue, and I, uh…"

"Turning blue? Oh, for fuck's sake, Tom, call a doctor, now!"

Tom laughed-cried a freaky, tearful sound and said, "I cuh…I can't call a fucking doctor, muh-man. I've got two felony DUIs under my belt. Third strike, and I'm a goner. Game over!"

Peterson couldn't believe he had to be sucked into this shit. How irresponsible could one man be?

Tom continued ranting. "And that's not even counting my wife. I call an ambulance, and she finds out about this? Forget the cops, man, she'll murder me. I'll be in worse shape than you are now!"

Peterson would have berated Tom's stupidity, if he could, but what he had said was true. Tom really *was* the only one who could help him. The only one with access to everything and the knowledge of how to move it all. He fought back his highly fucking irritated side and tried to stay calm and give instructions.

"Now, Tom? Tom!"

"Y-yeah?"

"I want you to call a Doctor Ivy. Now, do you remember Doctor Ivy? I'm almost positive I gave you the number. It should be in your phone now. That's Ivy. I-v-y. Check now."

"Okay."

Peterson didn't wait. "He can help you. He's a friend, he's specialist in these situations and he's very…discreet. Just call him up, he makes house calls."

Tom croaked, "Okay, I have it here, but I really think she might be dead by the time he gets here."

Peterson closed his eyes. This just kept getting worse and worse. "Well, then, you've got to get her to him…fast! Hurry! The address should be in your phone too. Where are you now?"

"I'm in a hotel downtown."

"All right, then you should be fine. Wrap her up, pick her up, and get her to your car. Quick."

"You want I should wipe the vomit and blood off her face first?"

Peterson grunted. Tom wasn't thinking straight due to fear and stress. At least Peterson hoped only fear and stress was fucking Tom up. If he really was high…

"Uh, *yeah*, Tom, I think that might be a good *idea*, Tom," he said patronizingly, while actually nodding at the phone.

He heard Tom put the phone down, then rustling noises and a pained "OOF!" as he picked the girl up. The hotel door slammed behind him.

Quietly, Peterson heard, "I'm in the hall…aw, fuck." More rustling followed, then Tom spoke again, sounding strained and nasally. "I'm in the hallway with her now."

"Put me on speaker phone, Tom, don't try to carry the girl and the phone at the same time."

"Aw, yeah. Smart." He laughed. Peterson heard a beep and then a thud that sounded like Tom had dropped the phone onto the girl's chest.

"Now, Tom, we're going to have to get you on a Bluetooth headset or something so that you–"

"SHH, SHH, SHH!" Tom shushed him. "There's some people coming toward me."

"Well, keep moving, then," Peterson whispered sharply.

This was ridiculous. At some point, he had to wonder what was worse, dealing with Tom's buffoonery or being electrocuted by his captors.

"Ha! Hello! Oh, yeah, she's fine!" Tom said, presumably to the other guests. "We just had sort of TOO good a night, if you get my meaning, ah? Yeah. Debauchery. HA HA!"

Peterson rolled his eyes then jerked straight again when he heard a tripping sound, followed by Tom cursing and something heavy falling on the phone. Then, there was silence.

"Tom? Tom? Hello?" Oh, Jesus. Was he on his own now? He looked around the small chamber and his eyes went wild with fear. "Tom? Tom, please!"

Finally, he heard more rustling, and Tom's voice saying, "Sorry."

"What the hell happened, Tom?" Peterson demanded.

"I just dropped her."

Peterson shook his head and closed his eyes, trying to remain calm. "Well, pick her *up*, Tom!"

"Okay."

Had the stakes not been so high, Peterson would have felt like the straight man in a very ridiculous black comedy.

"I'm coming to the car now," Tom said. "Hey, what do you think would be better for her in this state? Put her in the trunk or lay her down in the back seat."

Peterson kept a straight face even in his sarcasm, saying, "Well, you know you *could* be a gentleman and put her in the front seat."

"Front seat. Got it," Tom said breathlessly.

Peterson heard the car door open, and he added, "Fasten her seatbelt, Tom."

"Seatbelt. Got it," he said, breathing heavily.

Peterson listened while the door slammed, Tom pranced around to the other side, got in, and started the car.

"Oh, come on!" Tom said, and Peterson could hear the engine revving, but no sounds signifying it was going anywhere. "Fuck, man!" Tom said and kept pushing the gas.

"Tom?" Peterson asked, impatiently. "Are you in *park*?"

He heard a click, and then, the engine roared.

"Idiot," Peterson muttered under his breath and hoped Tom hadn't heard him.

The car sped backwards with screeching tires and then crashed into something.

Peterson yanked the phone from his ear.

"Tom?"

"Yeah. I'm here. I just…backed into a street light."

This had left the realm of ludicrous a long time ago. He silently hoped he was unconscious somewhere, and this was just some long, dangerous, extremely annoying nightmare.

"Is anyone hurt?"

"No, we're okay," Tom said, almost casually.

"Then drive, Tom, drive!"

The car roared, and Tom said, "Yeah, yeah."

Tom's souped-up Charger sounded like it was rocketing down the street. That was good. Speed would save his ass sooner. The entire container seemed to rumble at the sound of the engines.

"Red light coming up."

Peterson sneered. "How's she looking?"

Tom paused as if checking her, then said, "Not good."

Peterson shouted, "Then run the fucking red light, Tom!"

"Run it?" Tom asked, taken aback.

"You see a lot of cross traffic?"

"None."

"Cops?"

"Nope!"

"Well, no cop, no stop! Run that goddam thing!" Peterson yelled. This was almost fun, in a morbid sort of way.

The car rumbled louder as Tom said, "O... kay" and accelerated toward the intersection.

Peterson had to imagine him gunning the engine as the noise of the engine hit its crescendo as it zoomed through the intersection like a race car passing through the finish line.

"WOO-HOO!" Tom yelled victoriously. "Oh yeah! Oh-ho-ho, my God, that was my first red light."

Peterson was relieved but still nervous. "Well, don't dwell on it, Tom, keep going if you want to save three goddamn lives tonight."

"I do," Tom said, then added, "Oh, God, another red light coming up."

"How's it look?"

"It looks, um...good. Uh, pretty clear." He chuckled. "No cop, no stop, right?"

Peterson was concerned, wide-eyed, but said "If you think you can make it, do it!"

Tom was excited and nervous and still sounded crazy. "Ohhhhhhh..." he started, almost emulating the engine. "I thiiiiiink...I can do iiiiiit!"

The engine revved again, and Peterson's jaw dropped open and his fist clenched as he listened intently.

The car sounded dangerously fast, building again to that crescendo.

He's gonna make it! Peterson thought. *The sonofabitch is gonna make it!*

Then, he heard Tom's tires screech, and the phone slide around the cab of the car. Peterson heard many car horns and squealing tires, as if a wreck was imminent.

He closed his eyes, waiting for the crash, and tightened his fist so hard it shook. Then, the car zoomed again, and the honking horns were far behind.

Tom shouted in ecstatic glee, "Ohhhhhh, my fucking GOD, that was fucking *sweet*!"

Peterson called loudly, knowing that with the dropped phone, he had more of the car to cover now to be heard, "Okay, Tom, I'm glad you're having fun, but maybe we should think about–"

"Oh, no, Anthony, I've got a sharp turn coming up! Am I supposed to brake or accelerate on sharp turns?"

"Tom, now, Tom!" Peterson called to him. Tom was playing with his own life as well as the lives of three others, including Anthony goddam Peterson's. "Tom, brake, please brake!" he shouted.

The tires screeched like angry birds of prey as Peterson heard the car spinning as if out of control.

"WOO-HOO! So sweet! Oh, my fucking God, I feel like a stock car racer!"

"Okay, Tom. Slow down. Listen to me."

"What? Hang on, I can't hear you. Let me slow down and get the phone."

Peterson sighed and shook his head. Of all the people to have your life in the hands of, he had to have his in the hands of Tom fucking Pocase.

"Okay, I'm here. The phone was on the floor," Tom said. "Aw shit!"

"What?"

"I almost hit a parked car. That would be bad, right?"

"Yes, Tom. That would be bad, but you didn't, did you? Now what's the GPS say?"

"Five minutes?"

"Okay, are you going to be okay now on your own?"

Tom sounded confident and even thrilled. "Hell yeah, I'm good. We're both good now. She's definitely breathing right now."

"Okay, Tom, that's fine, now, that's fine." Peterson felt again as if he were talking to a hyper child. "I'm going to hang up now and–"

"No! Why?"

"Tom? I need to call the doctor for you and tell him you're coming and that you've got a special package. Now, when you're done, you call me back after you've left her with him, you got that?"

"I will!"

"And Tom?"

"Yeah?"

"No more running red lights, and you slow down around those corners. If you die, I die, the girl dies, and Susan dies."

"No pressure," Tom mumbled. "But I'll be careful. I promise."

"I know you will," Peterson said, calmly pleased. "Thank you, Tom."

He could still hear the car speeding down the roadway as he hung up the line.

He put the phone over his heart and took a breath.

Jesus.

If the kidnappers didn't kill Anthony Peterson, Tom sure as hell might do it for them.

10 Unbound and Ungagged

Anthony Peterson's wife, Susan, was alone in the room, as planned.

Every so often she could almost feel someone looking in on her. It was that strange, universal feeling of being watched. Of course, she couldn't see who they were or hear much of anything. The blindfold they had tied (a bit too tightly) around her head also covered her ears and made everything sound muffled.

This further impacted the brief conversation she had had with her husband. From what she could hear, however, he sounded terrified and, for once, deeply in love with her.

The bastard.

Why hadn't he bothered to make her feel loved *before* this terrible day?

She was terribly uncomfortable. The ropes hurt, and the chair was hard. She couldn't even shift around for comfort in this horrible situation.

She didn't know who they were or how many they were. That made it all the more frightening. Her entire world was now darkness and muted noises. That, and the taste of the duct tape across her mouth.

She bowed her head and thought of trying to sleep again. She doubted she would. Every time she slept, she gained the comforting feeling that this was all a nightmare and that she could wake up and be free.

Then, she awoke and found that reality was worse than any nightmare.

Beneath the blindfold, her eyes widened as she heard a high-pitched noise. What was it? She couldn't place it at first.

It was…a creaky hinge. Someone was entering the room.

"MMM! MMMM!" she struggled to speak.

"I'm taking the tape off now. Don't scream, or I'll have to hurt you," a deep, emotionless male voice said. She stopped attempting to communicate. "Do you understand?"

Susan nodded twice and then raised her head to allow easy access to the tape. A rough hand slowly peeled off one edge, then ripped it off quickly.

"Gah!" Susan gasped at the stinging pain.

"Best to do it all at once," the cold male voice said.

"Are you freeing me? Did Anthony get the money?" she asked with hope in her voice.

"No, not yet. They needed someone to check on you. I was bored enough to volunteer."

Susan didn't respond, though the words caused her hope to sink. The voice was so cold and cruel. She knew it wasn't the voice of the kidnapper. The boss, or whoever he was, but the words proved that she didn't mean anything to this man. If Anthony failed to come through, then this man would probably be one of her rapists.

"Here, I'm going to give you some water," the man said and she felt a plastic rim touch her lips. "I'm squeezing now," he said, and she gave a slight nod as the water flowed into her mouth, slowly so that she didn't choke. She gulped it down with gusto. She felt as if she was dying of thirst. "That's enough," he then said and withdrew the bottle.

"Why are you doing this?" Susan asked pleadingly.

"No questions. I'm not here to talk," he said. "If I ask you a question, you answer. Aside from that, keep it shut."

She then felt his hands on her head. He felt around her long, light brown hair, almost tenderly, as if feeling for something. Was he going to skip the wait and rape her now?

"What are you doing?" Susan asked, timidly.

He stroked her around the eyes and ears, around where her blindfold was tied, and then withdrew his hands. "Do you have a headache?" he asked.

She nodded. "Splitting."

"I'm not surprised. You don't have any bumps that signify a concussion, but this damn thing is on too tight. I should've done it my damned self."

"You did this? You're the one who took me?"

He chuckled coldly. "One of them, yeah. But I'm not the one who put this on. I'm going to take it off of you and replace it," he said, and Susan felt that glimmer of optimism once more before he added "That is if, and only if, you promise to look straight ahead. If I see either one of your eyeballs, I'm going to pluck it out. You got it?"

Susan gasped loudly. It was almost a small scream. Then, she nodded. "I promise I won't look."

"Right," the man said and began to untie the blindfold.

It came off, and she felt immediate relief, as if blood was finally flowing properly throughout her head. She could hear a few small sounds in the distance, and she could see that she was in a dark, neatly organized storage room with olive-drab paint covering everything and a very small window in the door. Nothing on the floor but her chair and an unmarked, olive-green duffle bag propped up in the corner. Every shelf was meticulously organized, from what she could see.

"Where is this place?"

"No questions, Mrs. Anthony Peterson," the cold voice responded. "This isn't an interview we're doing here. You're a captive. Your life is on the line, and that's all you need to know. They put you in here because you wouldn't stop whining and crying, and nobody wanted to listen to it anymore. I gave you some water to keep you alive...for the time being."

Susan whimpered again and bowed her head.

"Do you need anything else?" he asked.

Susan scoffed, in spite of herself. "What difference does it make if you're going to kill me anyway?"

"Tell me what you need, and I will make that decision."

"I need to get up," she said, after thinking about it.

"You're not going anywhere."

"No, I need…" she thought about the best phrasing before saying, "I need to…to *pee*," in a demure whisper.

The man paused for a moment. "That, I can arrange," he said.

"What?" Susan was surprised. "That makes a difference?"

"Yes," the evil man responded. "The difference is why. You gave me a good reason."

"Well, that's kind of you," she said, halfway between sarcasm and genuine gratitude.

There was a rustling behind her before the man said calmly, "Now I'm going to put this over your head. It's a ski mask. I'm putting it on you backwards. You will be able to see some light, shapes and shadows, but you won't be able to make anything else out through the fabric. That'll be enough to get you to the head and back."

As the rough hands did just what the man said, she asked "I'm going alone?"

"Don't be stupid," came the response. The man didn't laugh.

"Oh, you're going to watch me?" Susan said, again with sarcasm, but this time mixed with fear.

There was a long pause before the man said, "Nah. Not me. How's this feel."

He changed the subject so quickly she almost couldn't keep up. "Do you care?"

"Bitch, answer the question, or you get nothing else."

"I can't really breathe," she said quickly, so as to not anger him further.

"All right," he said and rolled the bottom of the mask up over her nose. "There?"

"Better," she said.

"One moment."

She heard his heavy boots walk across the floor and saw his shadow envelop her. The man was huge. That's all she knew. She could hear some low murmurs from the hallway, and the door reopened. The sound of two pairs of boots followed.

"I'm going to release your feet," the man said and worked on the knots around her ankles. He paused for a moment and seemed to touch her left foot almost tenderly. She wore open-toed sandals, and her toes were hurt and probably bleeding from trying to kick the inside of the box they dragged her here in. If there was any tenderness in the action, it ceased quickly as the man continued.

"Kick me, and I cut one of your feet off. The arms stay bound. This isn't a charity. When I tell you to, you stand straight up, and the arms will clear the back of the chair. Got it?"

Susan nodded with an "Mmmm-Hmmm."

"Good," he continued. "Now, she's going to take you to the latrine. It's indoors. And don't make the mistake of thinking that because she's a woman she's going to help you. She's getting paid. She doesn't ask questions. Neither do the rest of us, so don't go asking her any questions. We don't care. We're doing our job only. You two are not going to make friends or share nail polish tips or chat about your favorite daytime soaps. Don't plead with her. You got that?"

Susan nodded again with another agreeable noise.

"Good," the hard man went on. "We're only doing this because none of us wants to smell your piss and shit. We sure as hell don't want to have to touch it when we move you around. This isn't an act of kindness, it's an act of selfishness. If you make us regret it, no amount of millions are going to keep us from butchering you as slowly and painfully as possible. Any escape attempt, any noise, any disagreeable movements and you are dying today. This is the last time I ask if you've got that."

"I've got it," she said, trying to sound agreeable, but feeling completely defeated.

"Good. Now stand up vertically, and I'll help you get…"

She had to pull her feet back under her hips to push up as he had instructed, but she did it, and he helped.

"Ugh!" she moaned at the soreness.

"There you go," he said. "Now, you keep being this good of a girl, and you'll be treated every bit as badly as you have been.

Disobey and things are going to get a hell of a lot worse for you. Now, she's taking you from here. Don't even thank her. Don't speak at all. She's not your friend."

Susan nodded as she was guided out of the room.

The man called after her, "And don't go getting Stockholm Syndrome either, Patty Hearst. This isn't kindness. Remember that. You have no friends here."

Tears came then. She tried to remain silent, but she felt the backwards ski mask soaking with tears of fear and frustration.

She was brought into a cramped bathroom, had her pants taken down by the silent woman who was guarding her (they had not unbound her arms from behind her back) and was watched the whole time. She wanted to thank the woman, but obeyed and remained silent as she was cleaned up with wet wipes. The woman also stayed silent, except for a few annoyed grunts.

Had this been a movie, this would be where she made her great escape. It wasn't. She was just going to obey and hope against hope that Anthony came through for her. For both of them.

She was dressed and guided through the halls again. The sounds around her felt intentionally muted. As if there was a lot going on, but they had to remain quiet while she was close enough to hear.

She kept her head bowed, though the tears had stopped.

"Good girl," the cold-voiced man said.

"I didn't sign up for this," came the voice of the woman. It struck Susan as strange that during that whole intimate procedure, the woman had not spoken once. She had the voice of a soldier. Stern and serious and without compassion. "Any more cleanup duty, and I'd better get the full ten million myself."

The woman helped her sit again, sliding the back of the chair through her bound arms then left the room, clicking her tongue in frustration.

The man knelt down to bind her ankles again, saying, "Remember, kick me and you get hurt."

"I won't."

"How's your vision?"

She paused to think and said, "Like you said, only shadows, but it's better than that blindfold. That thing hurt like hell."

The cold-voiced man paused to think for the moment, then said, "All right. I'll leave you the mask, then. Now, tell me, do I need to tape your mouth shut again?"

"No!"

"Why?"

"*Why?*"

"Why makes all the difference. Why?"

"Because I don't want you to have to hear me. I'll be quiet and good."

"Nice answer," he said and stood up.

"Can I ask why you're doing this?"

"I told you already you can't ask me anything and expect an answer."

"But you said the difference is why!"

He chuckled. "Smart little lady, aren't you? Well, you won't like my answer. I'm doing it for the money. That's all that matters to me. You're nothing more to me than a few numbers in a spreadsheet. Now, again, do I have to tape your mouth shut, or are you going to be good?"

"I'll be good," Susan whined.

"Like I said...smart lady. Now...I'm going to put this bag over your head. It's burlap. Plenty of air will get in, though it might not smell the best. That's not my concern."

"Then why–"

"Because it keeps you from rubbing your head against your shoulder to get the ski mask off, and it further impairs your vision. You'd be surprised what some people see by just peeking through the tiniest of holes."

"I won't get any ideas," she said, trying to sound reassuring.

"Don't," he said and started to walk out without a closing greeting.

"Wait!" Susan called, "How will I call you if I need something?"

"That's easy," he said, as cold as ever. "You don't. This isn't a hotel, and I'm not your concierge. If you're lucky, one of us might decide to come and check on you again before the end. If you're extremely lucky, your asshole husband might come through after all, and you might get out of this before we cut you to pieces."

She gave that muffled gasp-scream again and then whimpered, "Sir? Sir, I...how could you do this? How could you be a part of this?"

"I told you, no questions," the voice came from the far part of the small room as if he was just about to leave.

"But don't you have a family?"

She expected the big man to growl at her again, telling her to stop asking questions, but instead, she got only silence. He must have left, she thought.

Then, his voice came again and cut through the velvet darkness like a blade of ice. "No. I don't. Not anymore. The last person I cared about...died...several months ago. There's not a person alive who matters to me anymore, except me."

"Oh, sir, I really–"

He chuckled again mirthlessly. "No, no, no, lady, don't you try to bond with me. Me having nobody doesn't make things better for you. It makes them worse. I don't have a damn thing to lose. I've done a thousand other jobs like this, and I don't remember a single name of a single one of you. You will never matter to me."

She bowed her head and tried to think of something sweet to say, but there was nothing left.

"Now not another sound, or you get the tape," he said, opening the door with a creak.

Before he was gone, Susan let out a meek, quiet, "Thank you."

The big, cold man scoffed as he left. "Fucking thanking me," he muttered.

And Susan was alone again in the darkness, surrounded by muffled sounds. And Susan Peterson was very, very terrified.

11 Dead Man Talking

4:44 AM

Anthony Peterson tried to force himself not to pace about his confined space to preserve the air, but he found suppressing that urge to be difficult. He hated waiting. When he sat against the wall, he found himself banging his head again, so he tried lying down to see if it would calm him.

That hadn't worked either.

He idly wished for a ball to bounce across the eight-foot span. He considered throwing the phone but decided against it, no matter what the stupid commercial claimed.

Instead, he just stood there with the phone hanging by his side and thought. And he thought. And thought.

So many things had led him to this specific juncture in his life. This unpredictable fucking mess where he was (and he still could not believe this) trapped in a metal cargo container, being extorted by these kidnappers, with his wife God knew where, enduring God knew what.

He sighed. He wondered silently how many single little events in life might have been changed to lead him to another path… with any destination but this one.

The phone rang again, and Peterson looked down at it. It must have been having problems as the screen remained black. Cheap phone. His little lifeline had better not be breaking on him.

He hit the spot on the screen where the talk button had been and it worked, thankfully. He hoped this was a fluke and would not recur.

"Hello?" he answered, warily, not sure who it was. The line remained silent. Maybe the phone was broken after all or maybe it was just randomly ringing.

To Peterson, however, it sounded like there might have been someone on the line.

"Hello?" he said again.

"Hello, Anthony," came the voice. It was an older man's voice. Accomplished, wise and dignified, yet somehow it sounded sinister...and maybe a little bit familiar.

"Who is this?" Peterson asked, suspiciously.

"It's so good to talk to you after all these years. I'm glad to hear your voice," the man said back.

"Who are you?" he asked, more forcefully.

"Oh, I think you know exactly who this is, Anthony," the other man said, patiently.

"The hell I do. Who the hell *is* this?"

The man seemed to chuckle a little and said, "All right, if you want to play it that way...it's me."

"You?"

"Me." He laughed. "Oh, come on, it's *me*, your oldest friend!"

Anthony was silent as his jaw worked, searching for the right words to say.

"Your mentor."

Anthony couldn't speak. This was impossible.

"Aw, come on! Your idol? Your hero?"

Peterson was not amused. "You certainly have a very high opinion of yourself."

The voice sighed and said, "Anthony, it's Sully!"

Peterson immediately felt rage again. Was it Sully this whole time? Was he behind all of this? "Sully? What the–? You think this is funny?" he stammered in anger. "You think...you think this is fucking funny?"

"Now calm down, calm down," the all-too-familiar voice said soothingly. "I just want to talk, that's all."

Peterson bit back his words and shook as he listened.

"How are you?" Sully's voice asked. "How have you been? Long time, no talk."

Peterson pinched the bridge of his nose and breathed. He leaned against the wall and slid down to the floor. "No," he said. "No, no, no. No, this isn't Sully."

"Oh, but it *is*." Sully laughed.

"No, no," Peterson responded, exasperated. "That's not true. That's impossible."

"And why is that, Anthony? What makes this impossible?"

Peterson sighed, composed himself and finally said, "Because Sully has been dead almost two years."

"*That's* right," Sully's voice responded as if just remembering that crucial little fact was true. He then added with menace, "Thanks to you."

"Thanks to me?" Peterson scoffed. "I had nothing to do with it."

"Oh, I know all about what you had to do with, buddy. I'm your oldest friend. I knew everything about you, Anthony. Hell, I still do. I've been watching you ever since then."

Peterson scoffed and paused. "Are you trying to tell me…that Sully didn't die?"

Another chuckle. "Oh, Sully died all right. You saw to that."

Peterson shouted into the phone, "I don't know what the fuck you're talking about."

"Why of course you know," Sully said. "You know and I know."

"Who the fuck is this?"

"Sully."

"No, no, no, you're…you're some imposter hired to fuck with me." He stood up again and paced, involuntarily, nervously. "What are you-? Working with the kidnappers to drive me crazy?"

"Oh, Anthony…do you even realize you're talking to a dead phone right now?" Sully said, and Peterson jerked.

He looked down at the phone and saw the screen was still blank. What the fuck kind of trick was this? How did they do that?

"Anthony?"

"Yeah?"

"The phone didn't even ring. I never called you. It's all in your head."

Peterson recognized the tone of Sully's voice. It was the same tone Peterson himself had used with Tom while patronizing the idiot. That's what Sully was doing just then…patronizing Peterson as if he were a small, dull child.

He pulled the phone back and tapped the power button. The goddam thing was in sleep mode. Shit. He really was cracking up, wasn't he?

"Well, then if you're not real, then you can just fuck off! I haven't got time for this bullshit!" he shouted and let the phone drop to his side limply. "You're not real," he said to nobody. "You're not real."

He sweated and thought deeply. Either he was going insane or he was in hell.

The phone rang again, and he jerked it to his face. It was still black. "What?" he demanded impatiently.

"Hello-o!" Sully giggled in his singsong voice. "Dead man talk-ing!"

Peterson brooded "What the fuck do you want from me… whoever you are?"

Sully paused and then asked, "You've stopped taking your medication, haven't you?" Sully taunted him in his cruel, joking way.

What medication? Peterson was scared. He felt the color drain from his face. He must have been losing his mind. What other explanation could there be?

Could Sully have survived? Was he the one behind all of this? It would be a hell of a revenge if so.

"You're not really there. You're not real, you're not real," he said. But at this point, Peterson was unsure whether he truly believed that or not.

"Oh, I'm real all right," Sully chuckled. "I'm as real as you. As real as the smile you show the world. That 'tapestry' as you call it. As real as that little voice that pops up in your head when things really start to head south."

South again? Anthony thought.

"No…you're dead."

"Thaaaaaaat's right," Sully confirmed almost soothingly. "Courtesy of Anthony Peterson himself. One of the many. Now, what would you want to go and do a thing like that for, huh? After all I've done for you?"

Peterson shook his fist and growled, "I don't…*know*…what you're talking about!"

"That's the old Anthony Peterson defense mechanism right there. Always a rationalization for everything, no matter how serious. You buy into your own bullshit. You're still doing it. It's gotten so bad that you even fool yourself."

Peterson ground his teeth together. Who the fuck was this guy, and what right did he have to fuck with Anthony Peterson? And if this was Sully, Peterson was the one who should be angry, not him. "You want to know what I believe?" he demanded through clenched teeth and curled lips. "I be*lieve* I remember you having an affair with my wife, Sully!"

Sully laughed again. It was the laugh of a man who held all the cards. "Oh, ho, ho, Anthony. Is that what this is all about? Me fuckin' your wife? Well, hell, brother, somebody sure had to. You certainly couldn't be bothered for most of your marriage. At least the last half of it. And then, after everything, you left the poor gal on her deathbed. Oh, A.P."

"Because you took her away from me. Of course I left her, goddamn it. You did that… You…you were a piece of shit!"

"Oh, and what're you, then?"

Peterson had one card to play.

"*Alive!*" he barked. "I'm fucking alive, unlike you, asshole!"

He jerked the phone away from his ear and tapped the part of the screen where the red disconnect button should be.

12 Reunions

5:17 AM

Anthony Peterson tried not to think about Sully. Sully was proof of insanity.

Or was Sully a genius who faked his death and set all this up for revenge?

Peterson ran his hand over his hair and sighed. No, no, no. That was absurd, at best. He was just having an episode.

It was the real world he needed to worry about. It was the money.

If he didn't get every cent of that ransom together, Sully would kill Susan and–

He froze again.

Sully? Was he beginning to believe that? No. Not Sully. He was already thinking of Sully as being real and behind this. That was impossible.

Focus on the real world. Focus on reality.

The money. Where could he get the rest?

He sighed. He had the answer, but he didn't like it. He wished he could have relied on Tom to make this call, but Tom was occupied with his own drama and…for once, Peterson needed to do something like a man…on his own.

He was still nervous, giddy, almost hopped up on his endorphins as he lifted the phone, took it out of sleep mode, and dialed one of the other numbers he knew by heart.

"Yes?"

Peterson was silently relieved to hear the voice of his son. He had grown up to be a man, mostly while Peterson was looking the other way. Regrets.

"Evan," he said, quietly. "How are you, my son?"

"Son?" Evan scoffed, sounding amused and taken aback. "You all right, old man? That sounded almost endearing."

The warm feeling he had at the sound of his son's voice evaporated quickly.

"Actually, no, son, I'm not all right. It's been a bit of a clusterfuck over here."

"Ah, I get it. You *need* something." Evan laughed. Peterson hadn't expected Evan to sound so much like Sully had. "You know, it's late. Maybe we can talk more about this in the morning. Wait, what time is it? Later in the morning when decent people are awake. Goodbye–"

Peterson panicked. He was terrified that his son might hang up. "No, no, no, please…wait. Don't go. We need to talk about this *now*."

"Dad?" Evan said, seeming to realize the old man was serious. At the sound of his son calling him 'Dad' again, he brightened ever so slightly. Then, Evan's voice went back to business. "I see. What's up?"

"I've been kidnapped," he said abruptly.

"Pardon?" Evan responded, chuckling in disbelief.

Peterson swallowed, dryly. "This is not a joke, Evan. I'm trapped somewhere in a metal shipping container. I've been talking to the kidnappers. They tell me I've got air for twenty-four hours and no more. And that leaves me, now…" Anthony tried to do the math in his head and gave it up. "I don't know. Well, less than twenty."

"What is this? Really?" Evan stammered.

Anthony laid out the last straw. "If I don't pay them a ransom, I'm a dead man."

"Jesus Christ!" Evan said, shaken.

"And…they've kidnapped your mother too."

Anthony realized his mistake as soon as the words left his lips. Time slowed down as he silently cursed his choice of words. Peterson had touched a sore spot that he should have known better than to even approach.

Evan's voice changed immediately. "No, my mother is *here*!" Evan spat back.

"Now, now, Evan–"

"You mean Susan, don't you? That bitch is barely older than I am. She's not my fucking mother!"

"Evan, please, I didn't–"

"So, what you're *really* saying is that someone has kidnapped you and your fucking trophy wife, right? You know, if this is some kind of sick fucking joke, it's already not fucking funny."

"Evan, I told you this is not a joke!"

"Then you've got a phone. Call the goddamn police!"

"Evan, if I call the police, they'll kill her. If I call the police, they'll kill me, or let me die in here. You don't know these people. They're crazy! I…" Anthony paused and changed his tone to more of a whisper. "If I don't pay them the ransom within twenty-four hours, we're both dead!"

"So why are you calling me?"

Peterson was shocked. How much had his son changed over the years. He went from thinking his dear old dad hung the moon to hating the elder Peterson with a white-hot intensity.

"Why am I…" he trailed off in disbelief. "Because I'm your *father*!"

Evan paused as if mulling this over to the same extent that Peterson himself had mulled over whether Sully was really real. "I don't know, Anthony!" Evan said, using the first name for maximum hurt. "Sometimes I feel like I should say to you, 'Hey, thanks for the sperm!' and just leave it at that."

Peterson closed his eyes to try to calm himself. He knew better. He had never been the best father, but he had given the kids much more than just life. They were millionaires because of him…but he couldn't get into that just now.

"Son, I…I need your help."

Instead of responding, Evan just sighed, heavily as if to urge Peterson to just get it over with.

"I'm…I'm short on the ransom," Peterson said, pained. "I need every penny of what they're asking for to save my life. Both our lives."

"So clear out some of your–"

"I've cleared out everything!" Peterson said, perhaps too aggressively. "It's all gone because of this. I even tried selling off the properties, but they're mortgaged beyond belief."

"What's this got to do with me, then?" Evan asked, and Peterson could hear the sneer in his voice.

Carefully, he continued. "I gave you and your sister…your mother and I…gave you and your sister trust funds…and I need to borrow back that money."

"Then, why the hell didn't you call and ask her?" Evan was angry, and Peterson couldn't grasp why. This was his life they were talking about.

Peterson tried to respond calmly and plainly and honestly. "Because…Elena hates me," he said. It gave Anthony Peterson no pleasure to admit that fact, but it was the truth. If Evan had grown cold to his father, Elena despised him even more passionately. "She hates me more than you do. More than even your mother does."

Evan scoffed. "No, no, no. That's impossible. No one hates you more than my mother does."

Peterson felt defeated. Completely beaten down. Evan was his last chance at salvation and the boy was pulling that lifeline away. "Son…I need some help here."

"Don't 'son' me, Anthony. We're not close. We're barely on a first name basis, you and I."

"I need…help," he repeated, hurting.

Evan sighed and paused. "How much do you need?"

Peterson ripped off the bandage. "All of it," he said softly, regretfully. "Both accounts."

"All of it?" Evan shouted. "What the fuck?"

"Evan, please!"

"What the fuck are we supposed to live on?"

"Son, it's only money compared to your father's life!"

"Only money? Only?" Evan scoffed indignantly. "No, Anthony, if I learned anything from you, I learned that there is no such thing as 'only money.' I was raised by Ebenezer fucking Scrooge."

Peterson winced. He *had* taught his son that. He was hearing his own words fired back at him.

"Son, I'll be alive, we can make more money. I can pay it back!"

"I can't believe this, Anthony!" Evan shouted.

Peterson gave his son a moment and then said, "We're talking about your father's life here."

Evan was quiet. It was as if he was thinking long and hard about it, then he answered, wearily yet angrily, "You made your filthy fucking bed, Anthony! Fluff up that pillow and lie the fuck down in it."

Peterson flinched from the phone again. His sorrow quickly changed to rage. What did this greedy little shit think he was doing putting money over the life of his father and his step-mother?

Fuck this kid. Fuck him! Fuck both his kids. Fuck Elena. Fuck Evan.

"Yeah?" Peterson growled back at his son. "Well, maybe so, but, full disclosure, this was meant to be a courtesy call more than anything else."

"What?" Evan gasped, terrified.

"Yeah, see, technically I don't need your permission, or your sister's, to access both accounts. I wanted to call to talk to you. I thought, stupidly, that you might value your father's life. You know, maybe sympathize just a tiny bit with the danger I'm in, but I can see that's not going to happen. So, I'm notifying you now, anyway! I'm pulling the money out of your accounts."

"You…can't…do…that!" Evan insisted after a shocked pause.

"Actually, I can. Read the fine print, son, my name is still on both accounts."

Evan exploded. He had never heard such fury from his son, even in the teen years. He shouted like a rampaging animal so loudly at his father that his voice distorted over the phone line.

"YOU FILTHY FUCKING DEGENERATE PIG-FUCKER COCKSUCKER!"

Peterson flinched away from the vitriol pouring out of the phone. His eyes snapped shut, and he pulled the phone away to save his ear from this torrent of abuse. Evan hung up before Peterson could respond.

In spite of Evan's reaction, the call really had been a courtesy.

Peterson's life was at stake. Could Evan not see the importance of this? Did Anthony Peterson mean so little, even to his own children?

No, no, no! Nobody hung up on Anthony Peterson. He was not about to leave it like this. Not like this. Not with his son.

His...son.

That was who this was after all. He should never have let his anger get the best of him. Evan was his legacy. Elena too. How could he be so cold to them...again?

Mental pictures shuffled through his consciousness like quickly dealt cards. He recalled one photo Marie had taken of Peterson walking with Elena when she was only seven years old. She was holding her daddy's hand and looking up at him for guidance. Evan was there, too, a little older, trying to look cool in the corner of the photo in his leather jacket and torn jeans.

Another image flashed of Marie, still healthy at the time, holding both the kids behind a flaming birthday cake. Anthony himself had just made it into the background of the photo before the timer snapped the photo for him.

Another had Peterson posing on the shiny new motorbike he had bought himself with his growing wealth. He thought he looked like a young Brando, except for the fact that Evan was perched on the bike's tank in front of his dad, wearing a cheap, plastic toy helmet and trying to look tough as a frustrated Elena tried to climb up on the seat behind Anthony. She just perched there with her chest on the seat and paused with a big smile as Marie had taken the photo.

They really had been a happy family once, hadn't they? Marie and Evan and Elena and Anthony, the breadwinner.

Where had that all gone wrong?

His heart skipped a beat. He didn't need another electric shock for that or for the realization of the truth. He had gone wrong. Anthony Peterson and his greed had killed the family. He knew this now.

No, no, no. He could still die even now. He needed to try to make things right with Evan to start with. Then, Elena would be next after the money was transferred. At least Evan would talk to him. Wouldn't he?

He shakily dialed the phone again and let it ring and ring until Evan finally picked it back up.

It was as if the deluge of curses hadn't stopped, and Peterson had only tuned back in to the continuation. "Why did you leave? Why? *Why* did you leave us? Your children? Our mother. Your own wife?"

He prepared himself to tell Evan of his mother's infidelity. How she had cheated on him with his own best friend. The day he figured it out because she was the only one who ever called Sully by his first name. But before the words could come out of his mouth, he swallowed them.

No. Don't denigrate Evan's mother. He'll only hate you more. Stay on topic.

"Your mother was an invalid," Peterson explained patiently, if on edge. "She was very, very sick. I couldn't live the rest of my life married to an invalid." The second the words were out of his mouth, he realized they were the wrong ones. If anything, those words would have alienated his son even more than telling him about Sully would have.

"Oh, I get it. Well, that makes it all better, doesn't it? So, you're saying that you left our mother just when she needed you the most. Just when she was at her worst you left her so you could get yourself some cunt trophy wife?" Evan continued angrily and sarcastically. "Oh, and now, now, you're calling me as a *courtesy*? A *courtesy* to tell us that you're taking everything to save the life of that same cunt trophy wife you left our dying mother for?"

Peterson listened to every single word and cringed inside. He couldn't answer because that was exactly what he was doing.

"Just…just…" Evan started softly, sounding sad and too tired to keep fighting, "Go to hell."

With those words, he hung up again.

Peterson leaned sadly against the wall of his prison again, feeling beaten and stung by those words. All of the words.

And all of the memories.

And the old man was acutely aware that these might well be the last words he and his son ever shared before his death…and they were not good.

13 Climbing Hedera

5:41 AM

Anthony Peterson was not currently on the mind of one Tom Pocase.

He had made it to the Doctor's house, appropriately covered in ivy, and had banged on the door.

Doctor Ivy had shushed him, pointing both directions as if to say, 'shut up for the neighbors' and then motioned to the garage.

Smart. The doctor didn't want to bring a body in through the front door. "Oh, I get it," Tom said as the Doctor slammed the door.

When the garage door had opened, Tom drove in quickly, and he and the Doctor carried the girl in to try to revive her.

Tom couldn't even remember the girl's name. He supposed he should feel really bad about that, but he figured there was time for guilt and reintroductions later. He just wanted to get this done... somehow.

Maybe.

Hopefully with her alive.

Ugh, and then, there was that whole Anthony thing. Was that even real? How the hell could two things this bad happen on the same night?

Tom leaned in the doorway watching the Doctor work his magic on the immobile girl.

"Aw, man, I'm gonna lose my job," Tom said aloud.

Doctor Ivy looked up at Tom for a second, as if disbelieving he had said anything so ridiculous at a time like that, then got back to work.

Then, he realized something. *Oh, yeah...I'm still working! I'm, like, at work right now.*

He had an alibi. And it was getting close to dawn.

"Hey, just you let me know if I can do anything to help!" Tom called out to the Doctor who simply nodded and gave the girl another shot through her IV.

Tom texted his wife and spoke the words aloud, stupidly, as he did. "Honey, Anthony's...got...me...working...all...night. I know... Typical... Anyway...be...back...soon, I hope. Will... explain...later... You...know...how...he gets...when...he... thinks...it's...life...or...death."

He considered adding something about not being with an overdosing girl he had picked up, but deduced that might be a bad idea.

"Love...you," he added in a second text.

"Hey, that was easy. Convenient, really. At first, I thought my luck was terrible with all this happening on the same day, but you know, Doc? First, there's you, and now, my wife doesn't suspect a thing. Sometimes, things work out just–"

"Dude, do you mind shutting the fuck up here?" Doctor Ivy demanded as he checked the girl's eyes.

"Oh, oh, right. The...the saving the day thing. Right." Tom nodded and fought to stay quiet.

Tom paced back and forth, saying, "Please let her be all right, please let her be all right. Please let me still have a job tomorrow. Please let me have a wife tomorrow. Please let her be all right, please let her be all riiiiight..."

The Doctor was frantically working and shouted back at him, "Dude, do you mind? I can't hear myself think here."

Tom idly realized that he had never once heard a doctor say, 'dude,' and that was really funny to him. "You think it's because of all that beeping that machine's doing?" he asked.

The Doctor sighed and said, "No, joker, I don't. That beeping signifies her heartbeat. That's what I need to be listening for. Now, if you don't mind, push that table over to me with the instruments on it. Slowly."

"Oh, sure, sure," Tom said, delighted to be helpful. He started to push the cart, then noticed a certain object glimmering up at him. "Oh, hey, do you mind if I keep this Bluetooth you've got here?"

Doctor Ivy jerked the wheeled table from Tom and said, "If that's what it takes to get you to shut up, sure. It's all charged up, it's yours, just don't say another goddam word, dude."

"Fine," Tom said. "Nice Bluetooth."

The Doctor scoffed and kept working.

"Okay," Ivy said at last. "I think that does it. She's got adrenaline and a few–" The Doctor looked at Tom for a second and decided he wouldn't understand a single word he said, so he moved on. "–a few things that counteract the drugs you said she's taken. I can't promise there won't be any brain damage, but I am hoping."

"What happens now?" Tom asked, excitedly.

"Well, I just gave her the charcoal solution, so she should be puking her guts out into that bucket pretty soon. When that happens, you can either wait here with her to take her home, or she can stay with me, and I'll drop her off somewhere tomorrow. That, of course, will cost Anthony a few more bucks."

"You want her to throw up on purpose?"

"To clear out her system, yes. She has overdosed, after all," the Doctor reminded Tom, then mumbled, "On just about every drug in the book from what you said. Goddamn."

"Right, Right. Damn, that's really gross." Tom looked down at the girl's bare breasts with the electrodes stuck on them. "Such a hot girl, too. Damn."

The Doctor rolled his eyes.

"Gross," Tom said again. "So, when's she supposed to start barfing?"

The Doctor looked at the clock. "Any second now, we should see Old Faithful erupting."

"Old Faithful!" Tom exclaimed, surprised that the formerly stern Doctor was making a joke now. "Oh, man, that's funny. You're a regular guy, you know that? Strange. You almost seemed like Superman in here. It's like you can do anything."

Doctor Ivy laughed and shrugged. "That's why they pay me the big bucks," the Doctor said, finally relaxing. "I reattached a guy's hand in a makeshift clinic once."

Tom's eyes widened. "Did you? I'll bet that would make a great—"

Just then, the beeping stopped and was replaced by one long streaming blast of that same note.

"Aw, hell, what does THAT beeping mean?" Tom asked. "Does that mean she's all better now?"

Doctor Ivy had already raced to the girl and started pumping her chest and breathing into her mouth. "No, you idiot, that means she's gone into cardiac arrest. Get me the crash cart!"

"The what?"

"The defibrillator! That…" The Doctor struggled to find words the idiot Tom might understand. "… thing over there that looks like two…fucking…irons attached to a computer."

"Oh, sure. Neat," Tom said and did as he was told.

"Would you hurry, man. This girl just stopped breathing!"

It was right about the time the gravity of the situation hit Tom like a ton of bricks of hashish that his phone rang.

"Oh, man, oh, man, it's Anthony," Tom moaned in dejection. He fumbled for his phone, swore under his breath and gave a confident, "Yo!"

14 The Heart of the Matter

6:01 AM

Anthony Peterson scarcely had the luxury of licking his wounds after the verbal assault his son had laid on him, deserved or not. Time and air were both running out, and he wanted to live.

Secondarily, he wanted payback.

Some little voice in the back of his head said he wanted to change and start over and make up for all the wrong he had done.

But first…he had to make sure he lived. Then, he would decide on the rest.

He dialed Tom and waited for the younger man to answer. His heart and mind hurt almost as much as his body did. He could use a drink right about then. A drink of anything, really. Even water.

When the line finally connected, Anthony heard sounds of chaos in the back and Tom fumbling with the phone, swearing under his breath and saying, "Yo!"

Tom sounded hyper and probably high, but trying to cover for himself and the anarchy surrounding him.

Peterson felt suspicious, but remained calm. "Tom? How is everything?"

"Great!" Tom half-laughed. His voice sounded panicked as if he was actually saying that everything was fucked, but trying to fake it. "Just, uh, finishing up with the doc right now!"

Peterson was dubious and listened to the background noise. It sounded like a defibrillator charging. "Clear!" he heard another voice shout. He knew the voice. It was that of Doctor Ivy.

Then, he heard the violent sound of an electric shock followed by the thump of a body on a metal table.

"Tom…what was that?"

"Nothin'!" Tom said and laughed a high-voiced, nervous laugh.

"Tom?"

"The, uh…" he laughed again. "The Doctor is just giving her a little jump start is all! It'll be all right…in a minute."

Peterson listened again. Ugh, the Doctor was shocking her to life just as Peterson himself had almost been shocked to death. The very sound of the charge made him nauseous.

He heard the defibrillator charge again to the point that a high, mechanical whining sound filled his cell, making him feel sicker. Then, he heard the jolt of the electricity into the body and another thump.

And then, there was silence. No beep of the heartbeat on the monitor. No shouts of relief. Nothing.

Peterson's eyes widened. Had this girl died? Tom would be no use to him in jail. With Tom in jail, Susan was gang-raped first, then killed, and Peterson himself would starve or suffocate to death. In his present physical state, he was unsure which would come first.

"Tom?" he said, cautiously. "What's happening?"

Tom laughed again in that nervous titter, but this time he sounded like he was crying at the same time.

"Well…" he started. "She's not…breathing…and she's not…moving…so…my guess is she's…"

Peterson slowly started to form the word "Dead?" with his shocked lips.

Before he could speak, he was interrupted by the most blood curdling scream he had ever heard. It was the scream of a woman who had suffered a cardiac arrest, died, and then been dragged back to the land of the living by a very skilled, very unscrupulous physician.

Heaven could wait.

Peterson smiled and allowed himself to relax even as his ear was filled with the sound of coughing and vomit splattering all over the floor.

"Well, that's going to stain," he heard Doctor Ivy say in the background.

"Heyyyyyyyyyyyy!" Tom shouted with glee. "She's back! She's…vomiting up a hell of a lot of blood…but she's alive." Tom took a moment to say a few muffled words to the girl with what sounded like the phone against his chest, then he came back. "The Doctor's got blood all over his face now, but that's not important, is it? She looks like she's going be all right now. Oh, wait!"

Peterson heard more hacking and coughing and retching blast out of the phone. When it subsided, he finally said, "Tom?"

"Yeah?" Tom sounded almost pleasant, an inappropriate tone for this situation.

"Is she all right?"

In between sickly vomiting sounds, Tom responded, "Oh, suuuuure." Clearly, Tom knew the girl was pretty fucking far from being all right, but at least she was alive.

Peterson waited for a beat and then, politely as he was able, told Tom, "Well, then I need you to get the hell out of there, Tom, and get your laptop open!"

Tom stammered as if his mind was racing, then finally agreed. "Uhhh…yeah!"

Peterson waited as Tom quickly finalized things with the Doctor in a series of faraway muffled sounds. He then heard Tom stumbling at speed out of the Doctor's in-house clinic.

Tom raised the phone again and said, "Hey, you were right, that doctor was incredible. Oh, and hey!"

"What?"

"He gave me a Bluetooth!"

Peterson almost laughed. "That's great, Tom, that's great. Let me know when you're back in the car and then fire up your laptop!"

Peterson closed his eyes and winced as he heard Tom accidentally run into the side of his own car, swear, and drop his keys. He fumbled with them, managed to get the door open, and then slammed it once inside. "Man, this guy has a big garage. It's nice!"

"Come *on*, Tom!"

Tom didn't hear. He hadn't put the Bluetooth on yet. Instead, Peterson heard him fumbling around in his car for what seemed like an eternity, trying to get his laptop up and running.

"Okay!" Tom said, a little too loudly. He seemed to be a bundle of energy, but was trying hard to remain cool. "We are good to go!"

Peterson told him the good news. "I think we have the last of the money," he said, leaving out how he got it and what that money cost him.

"Really? That's great!" Tom responded, gleefully.

"Yes, yes, yes," Peterson said impatiently. "We just need to make the transfer."

"It's not in your account yet?"

"No, Tom, the banks aren't open, I can't make overseas calls, and I don't have internet on this goddam phone."

"Oh!"

"But we have to move fast!" he said. His fear was that Evan or Elena or both might liquidate the accounts as fast as they could to prevent him from getting the money.

He gave Tom the account numbers and told him to initiate the transfers and illustrated that time was of the essence.

Peterson realized that he somehow had a better memory for bank account and routing numbers than he even did for phone numbers. If the stakes weren't so high, he might have found that amusing. Or depressing.

He waited patiently while Tom clicked and typed and then heard him exclaim, "Holy *fuck*!"

Tom laughed in shock and Peterson feared that something had gone wrong.

"What, Tom, what?"

"It's all there, now, Anthony!" Tom said. "Well, it's gonna be when everything else comes in. All of it's gonna be there. With interest!"

Peterson sighed in relief and felt the tension leave his body, at least for the moment.

Tom continued to laugh. "Whoo-hoo-hoo-hoo!" he shouted, impressed. "Damn, you're good, son! How did you come up with the rest of the money?"

"Those accounts."

"What were they?"

He paused, not proud of himself. "My children's trust funds."

Tom inhaled, painfully, expressing what Peterson was feeling, that it must have hurt to do so. "Damn!" he said. "And if you think they didn't hate you already…"

"So, listen," Peterson said, interrupting him. "Once the other returns come in, I need you to wire this money—"

But Tom interrupted him back. "Whoa, whoa, whoa, let's not be too hasty here." Tom sounded like he finally had a chance to share an idea he had been incubating. "Are you *sure* this is the way you wanna play this?"

Peterson was taken aback.

This shit again? Tom was repeating himself, and lives were on the line, including his own.

"What exactly are you saying, Tom?"

Tom coughed and said happily, "I ain't sayin' nothin'! All I'm saying is there are opportunities that come around in life, you know? Opportunities that you should think very hard and long about before deciding your course of action."

Peterson went cold, and the tension returned. "Tom? You told me you were clean. Are you high, Tom?"

"High? No!" he responded, sounding amused. "I just dropped some low-grade blotter acid to mellow me out is all."

"Tom, I need you lucid for this. It's a matter of life and death, and you're supposed to be clean!"

"You want me to go back in and see if the doc has some coke?"

Peterson rolled his eyes. "No, Tom, no!"

"Are you sure? Cocaine should even me out if you want–"

"Goddamn it, Tom, no! I need to know you're *clean*. I can't have my life and my wife's life in the hands of a goddamn junkie!" Peterson almost screamed those last words.

"Oh, no, don't worry. This isn't a twelve steps violation, man. LSD isn't addictive." Then, he giggled the way only inebriated people do, sounding a bit emotionally punch drunk.

Mostly, Tom sounded pathetically, uselessly inebriated.

"Tom, you need to focus here," Peterson said. Apparently, the meaning of life and death was lost on Tom at the worst possible time. Peterson dreaded what was coming.

"Look," Tom said, "all I'm saying is that we should consider… *consider*, now…all possible options before we proceed."

Peterson tried to stay calm. "Did you just say 'we'? Tom, this is my wife's life *we* are talking about here."

Tom laughed sarcastically. "Well, come on, man, let's get real. She's a *trophy* wife."

Peterson tried to reason with Tom and stay sane and calm, but it wasn't easy. "She is my *wife*, Tom!"

"Yeah, yeah, yeah, I know, she's your wife, but is she really worth it?"

Peterson shook. He could feel his scream rising to the top of his throat, but he pushed it back down again, clenching his fists to calm himself. He hated Tom, but he needed Tom.

"I mean, *ten million dollars*?" Tom continued. "That's kinda overkill, don't you think? Is any wife worth that much? Really? Hell, is any *person* worth that much?"

Tom waited for Peterson's response, but Peterson was still fighting back his rage. The acid might not have caused Tom to hallucinate, but it certainly emboldened him to a point of false stature.

"Oh, you think I'm kidding?" Tom continued his litany. "Let's take my old man. If someone was ransoming me for ten million, hell, three million dollars, he'd just say screw it! Sayonara, Tom, Junior! I'll just make another one that looks just like him!"

Peterson breathed angrily and said, "Your father is eighty-six, Tom!"

"Yeah, but my point is, Anthony, you can get another trophy wife who looks just like her. She just ain't worth it, buddy!"

Peterson was shaking more than ever and fought to sound reasonable. "This is my wife, Tom. My...*wife*!"

"And you heard what I said about her."

Oh, yeah, Peterson heard all right, and if he lived through this, Sully was going to have a roommate.

"And, Tom? Might I remind you that this is also *my* life! There is no half-off deal for saving one of us. They are going to *kill* me if I don't get—"

Tom interrupted him. "Yeah, you know? About that... I've been thinking. You know, like I said, how much is anyone's life worth? Even yours? I mean, really? Mine? Yours? Life is cheap, not expensive."

Peterson honestly believed that his situation couldn't possibly get any worse, but Tom had just made sure it did. There would be hell to pay if Peterson survived this. And because of this bullshit, Peterson had one more vengeful reason to survive.

With every bit of patience he could muster, Peterson said, "What...exactly...are you pro*pos*ing...*Tom*?"

"Proposing?" Tom chuckled. "Hey, I'm not making a proposal, my old friend! I'm just sayin'. I mean, the situation as it stands now, you really are at my mercy, right?"

Wrong thing to say to me right now, Tom! Peterson thought. He was going to enjoy his revenge.

"I mean, you trust me to do the right thing, to care about you, your trophy wife, especially with you locked away somewhere, who knows where, left to slowly die for who knows what reason? All alone, no trace, never to be seen again. And here's me, good old Uncle Tommy, with access to literally all of your accounts now?" The son of a bitch paused to let that sink in before he finished twisting the knife. "I mean, theoretically I could just... hang up this phone and go on my merry way."

Peterson shook his fist and tried to sound reasonable. "Listen, Tom, we're...*friends*!"

"Yeah, *friends*!" Tom interrupted him sarcastically. "Everybody needs *friends* when they're down and out, don't they? In desperate times with desperate measures? But what about...*employees*? That's right, *employees*!"

Peterson licked his lips and waited for Tom to finish his bullshit diatribe. It was damnable what he was going through with this man. Never again would he put so much trust in another person.

"Employees. Let's talk about long suffering employees who are bitter about being passed over for promotion after promotion," Tom continued.

"Tom, no! You're my most trusted man. I haven't passed you–"

"Oh, but Anthony, baby...I'm just being hypothetical here, you know? Talking about those poor working stiffs who get snubbed again and again when it comes time to hand out the year's bonuses." He chuckled slightly and continued. "Bitter and angry employees with a serious grudge against their employer of many, *many* years. Employees who've had to *eat...shit* over and over and over again."

Peterson waited for him to finish.

"You know, Anthony? Hypothetically."

Fighting back his fury, Peterson pronounced his words carefully "What...do you *want*...Tom?"

"Well, ya know, internet gambling looks mighty good right about now."

"Tom!" Peterson bit his tongue.

Tom paused, calculating in his head, then responded casually, "Tell ya what. I said it was all there? Or soon would be? With interest? I take the interest, wire the rest to whoever you say. We're done. Consider it, I don't know, an overdue annual bonus. Or a severance package, if you prefer."

Peterson stared straight forward like a man possessed. He now sympathized with his angry son and wanted to shout at Tom the way Evan had shouted at him.

But he couldn't.

He couldn't!

Because Tom was right. Anthony really was at Tom's mercy.

But Tom was also right when he had observed that Peterson had trusted him.

No more. Never again would this happen. Peterson trusted so few people and one of the last remaining had betrayed him.

"I'll take that silence as a yes, then?"

Peterson didn't answer. He did not trust himself to speak politely. And he still needed Tom to rescue him.

On the edge of rage, Peterson listened as Tom typed out the transactions on his laptop.

And at last...there was silence.

"Finito," Tom said proudly. "Thank you, Anthony. You've finally made me rich."

And with that, Tom hung up.

Peterson was a bundle of raw nerves as he lowered his cell phone arm.

He felt like a girl who got fucked on the first date without the courtesy of dinner first or even an orgasm. The whole thing was exhausting. Not even his fury was invigorating. But he had a new reason for payback, it would seem. A new reason named Tom Pocase.

Perhaps the fact that the money transfer was, in fact, 'finito,' at least into his own accounts, his brain was telling him it was okay to rest. He felt drowsiness finally take him over again.

But that Tom, that goddamn Tom, after all Anthony Peterson had done for him? The anger chased away his sleepiness for the moment. Oh, yes, he would be dreaming up some payback, that was for sure.

Before he could plan out the rest of his revenge against Tom, in wakefulness or dreams, the phone rang again.

"Yes?" he answered, expectantly.

"Hey, it's Tom."

"I realize that."

"Just wondering how it tastes."

"How what tastes?"

"My shit, Anthony. *You* just ate *my* shit for a goddamn change."

Peterson scowled as Tom hung up again.

15 Mourning has Broken

6:43 AM

Anthony Peterson's son Evan was angry and rightfully so.

He stepped outside onto his porch holding a bottle of Irish whiskey, which he tipped back over his mouth and took two big glugs from.

His father...that bastard. All of the money. Gone. The one good thing that Anthony had ever done for him. Gone.

Oh, but he loved the old man, didn't he, still?

No. Not after this and never as much as he loved his mother.

He drunkenly watched as the sun struggled to rise. The sun dragged its way up the sky lazily just as the son was hating the old man with all the fire he had. As the sky began to light, Evan staggered back inside the colonial home and prepared his mother a wakeup drink.

He didn't want to be alone in his hatred and anger. There is no telling what he might just do in that state.

*

"Mom?" he shook the older lady in her bed and she didn't stir. "Mom!" he said again with a heavier shake.

"Mmm? Sully?"

Sully again?

Sully. His father's former best friend and business partner. He had become his mother's best friend and became more than that after his father had left. Fucking asshole that his father was. Who could blame them?

"No, Mom, it's not Sully. It's...it's me. It's Evan."

Her eyes flickered open, and she smiled. "Oh, my baby boy! Has morning broken?"

He leaned in and handed her the hot drink he had made for her. "Yes, ma'am. Just now. It's day time, and here's your coffee."

"Where's Sully?" she asked impatiently.

In his mother's present state, the state she had been hanging on to for years now, she was not quite right in the head.

His father had described her as being 'on her deathbed' and 'an invalid.' That was bullshit. Unbelievable bullshit. She wasn't on her deathbed. Not even today. But she wasn't quite right either.

"Mom, try...try to remember. Try to understand. Mr. Sullivan is dead," Evan told her. "He died a few years ago."

Mom's continued delusions were not going to make his day any better. Somewhere in his heart, he also knew this wasn't healthy for her. Believing Sully was still alive prevented her from properly mourning the man.

The old lady scoffed, "Oh, now, of course he's not dead, goddamn it!" she said and almost laughed. "Why would you say a horrible thing like that?"

Evan sighed. He was still angry. He didn't want to take his anger out on his mother, whether or not she could accept that Sully was long dead.

"Drink, Ma," Evan said. "I put a little Irish in your coffee."

She looked up at him in the slowly lightening room and said, "Why how thoughtful of you." She took a sip and then looked back up at him. "That's my boy!"

Evan giggled like a kid again, but his mirth was short-lived. His thoughts turned back to Anthony, and immediately, Evan looked out the window, dejected again.

"Oh, my boy, what's so wrong with you this morning?" his mother asked with sweet concern.

Evan coughed and shook his head. "Nothing...a lot...a whole lot."

Evan's mother giggled. "You sound a bit more than conflicted."

Evan looked at her and then took a pull from the bottle.

"What is it, son?"

Evan coughed slightly and took in a deep breath. "It's…it's the prick. He's finally getting what he deserves."

"Getting what he deserves?"

"Yeah."

"You really hate your father, don't you?"

"I hate that prick. He was never much of a father to me, was he?"

She made up a face as if deep in thought. She had her very thoughtful moments still. Sometimes, she was downright lucid, but other times, she was still lost.

"I suppose not," she agreed. "Sully was more of a daddy to you than Anthony ever was, wasn't he?"

"Yeah, I guess," he said, not truly agreeing. As far as Evan could remember, he was already in his late teens by the time Sully became more than a friend to his mother.

"Where is he, by the way?"

"That's what I need to tell you. Dad's in a… Dad's been–"

"No, no, not your father! I don't give a shit about him. Where's Harry?"

"Harry?" Evan asked. She must be confused.

His mother scoffed, then corrected herself. "Sully!"

This again? Evan thought. Some days, she really couldn't understand. She would ask for her mother, she would ask for her brother. Once, she even asked for Marilyn Monroe and then James Dean. She couldn't accept when someone was dead.

It was bad for her, mourning. She never moved on.

But when it came to Mr. Sullivan, Mom was different somehow. The other assertions of the dead rising were clearly the products of dementia. Somehow, when she talked about Sully, she didn't actually seem demented. She seemed…self-assured. Almost clear-minded. That was the worst part of this disease. The very worst goddamn part. Sometimes, she didn't seem senile, even when Evan knew goddamn well that she was.

"I'm sorry, Mom. I have to tell you again, please try to understand. Sully is dead. He died a long time ago."

Mom laughed. "You keep saying that, but it's not true." She sipped her Irish coffee again and shook her head. "Sully isn't dead, darlin'."

"You're sure about that?"

"Yes."

"Even though you went to the funeral?"

"No, no, no. It wasn't a real funeral. Sully is alive."

"Mom?"

She patted his hand and said "He is. Trust me."

"What makes you so sure?"

She looked past his shoulder at the sunrise and smiled. "Because he promised he would always take good care of us. And *Mis*ter Sullivan…" she said, with mock reverence, "… was never the kind of man to make idle promises. He's alive."

Evan shook his head and took another pull from the bottle. He decided to leave it alone. There was no convincing her of this any more than she believed him when he assured her that Abraham Lincoln had, in fact, not visited her a few months ago.

Thus, Evan decided to move on. "So, about the prick."

"Your father?"

"My father."

"The prick." Now, it was Mom's turn to giggle like a kid.

"The same," he said and took another swig.

"What about him?"

"He's finally gotten what he deserves…I guess."

"What do you mean?"

"He's…ah…" Unexpectedly, Evan's eyes welled up with tears, but he kept his voice as steady as he could. "He's been kidnapped, apparently. His bitch of a wife, too."

"That young thing?"

"That young bitch."

Evan's mother drank deeply and then looked back at her son. "That's terrible," she said matter-of-factly. Then, she narrowed her eyes in confusion. "Isn't it?"

Evan drank. The buzz was going to his head. He felt a tingling like his skull was filled with bees. "I guess, yeah. But to try to get out of this mess he got himself into, he's…he's…he's cleared out my trust fund."

"He thinks he can save his own ass by stealing your money?"

"Elena's too."

She hissed in air through her teeth and looked out the window, as if deep in thought. "Can I have some of your whiskey?" she finally asked him.

"That Irish isn't enough for you?"

She laughed. "It's finished," she said and held up the empty cup for him to see into.

Evan leaned forward and prepared to pour a few shots into his mother's cup.

"Are you sure?" she asked. "I'm not supposed to be drinking, you know. With the medication?"

Evan paused. This was the reality of living with the former Mrs. Peterson. She would often forget her very stance on a subject and switch sides completely.

"Uh…" Evan said, then poured a bit more. "How about just this once? You know, I hate to drink alone."

"That's true," she said with excitement. "I remember that."

"Well, good. Then it'll be our little secret."

And they sipped together.

"So, he's in jail?"

"No, Mom, no, Dad is…Anthony is…he took our money. He says he's in a cargo container somewhere, and he'll die if anyone interferes."

"That's awful."

"I don't know. I'm going back and forth. I mean, I hate him, but I…he's still my–"

"Evan. I mean, it's horrible that he took your money."

Evan almost laughed, but sipped instead. She sounded so innocent, as if unaware she had just said something so cold.

His mother continued. "And I could kill him for taking Elena's money."

"She might find and kill him herself when she finds out."

"You haven't told her yet?"

"It's six something AM. You're the first to know."

She narrowed her eyes and nodded. "So, someone has him?"

"And his bitch of a–" he sighed. "And his wife."

His mother sipped her whiskey from the coffee cup and smiled. "Then, you need to help him."

"What?"

"Help him. He's your father."

"No, Mom, I can't."

"You can, Evan. Even if you hate him, you have to understand, he is still your father, and you must be the bigger person. Remember that's what Sully always tells you. Be the better person."

Sully again? Evan sighed and nodded. "I can't do that, Mom, I'm sorry. Dad says that if the police get involved, he's dead. They'll kill him at any sign of police."

"Oh, my."

"Yeah."

She made up a face and looked out the window again. The rising sun lit her face up like a golden angel's. She was truly beautiful in her old lady way.

"I wonder if Sully knows."

Evan sighed. He couldn't convince her, so he joined her. "Why don't you ask him next time you see him?"

"I haven't seen him lately," she asserted.

"I wonder if that's because the man is fucking dead!" Evan spat at her angrily. His mood was shifting as quickly as her reality, thanks to the booze.

"Still on that, are you?" she said calmly, with a laugh in her voice.

Evan grinded his teeth and laughed. "How is it that you remember that I've told you that Sully is dead, but you can't remember that Sully is dead?"

"You'll see. He's taking good care of us," she smiled.

"Yeah, whatever."

"Don't you whatever me." Mom laughed. "Remember what he told you. Be the better man. Always be the bigger person."

"It's not hard to be better than Anthony Peterson."

"So, what do you do now?"

Evan sucked in air through his teeth and felt that whiskey sting on his throat. "Nothing. He's always held all the cards. Do you know what he said to me? He said he was just calling as a goddamn courtesy. He didn't have to ask me to make me destitute. He just... took it."

"How awful of him," Mother said. "So, what happens now?"

"I...I don't know. I know I fucking hate him."

"Evan."

"You should too. After all he did to you?"

"And Sully has always been here for us."

"No, Mom, I...goddamn it." Evan was too drunk to reason with her, and he couldn't deal with this Sully bullshit.

"What does your heart tell you?"

He paused. That was a stupid question. Fucking stupid. Who the fuck cared? Who asks a question like that? "I don't know, Mom." Evan said impatiently. "What the hell would you do?"

Mom nodded several times as she thought about the situation. "That's a good question. Well, he is your father, taken for all with all," she said and nodded again at him. "So, yes. I would help him."

"You would? After all of this? All he did? All we've been through? You would actually help that man?"

"Why of course I would," Mom said.

"After all he did?"

"Yes," she said and drank some more. "This is some really good scotch."

"That's Irish whiskey."

"That."

Evan sighed. "After all he did...after all he did..." he repeated. He felt he couldn't say the futile phrase enough.

"Be the bigger person."

"But, Mom, nobody knows where he is. And he might even get out on his own with all our money."

"That *was* a lot of money," she agreed.

"And I can't help him anyway," Evan insisted. "Don't you remember? Don't you understand? If I call the police, the kidnappers will kill him and his...his...his fucking trophy wife."

"Evan! Language."

"Sorry, Mom."

"Besides..." she said with a laugh. "I fucking remember. And yes... After all of this...after all he's done...I think it's very clear that you should be the bigger person."

"Mom, I can't."

"Oh, I heard you," she said, with an innocent smile. "I believe... that considering all...there is no other option. You've *got* to help him."

Senility. Dementia. Even with a buzz like this, Evan had already gotten his fill of his mother's bullshit.

"Mom, try to understand, they will kill him!"

"Evan? Help...him!" she said as she darted her face from the window back to her son and locked eyes with him. Her smile and her eyes had a determined, serious look as if she was trying to make something very clear. Was that right, or was she in her cloud of dementia again?

"Mom?"

"Help...him. The way you know he deserves." She kept that same look on her face and stared him directly in the eyes without blinking. Without looking away. This was not dementia. This was lucidity. Marie Peterson knew exactly what she was saying at that moment.

Finally, Evan reached into his breast pocket and retrieved his phone. Was this what she was urging him to do? Even if she didn't realize what she was saying, Evan did. He nodded, then took a deep breath, and then a deep pull from the bottle. "I have to go," he said.

"And what are you going to do, Evan?" she asked boldly.

He sighed. "I'm going to help Dad."

Her smile faded, then returned in a friendlier, less intense grin. "That's...my boy."

And with that, Evan Peterson left the room and made one incredibly important phone call.

16 The Raggedy Man

7:28 AM

Anthony Peterson dreamed he was a toy. More specifically, Anthony Peterson dreamed of himself as a nice, handmade, stuffed male doll that someone had been careless enough to shove into a small – too small for him – cardboard box.

Who would have been so ungrateful as to do such a thing for a doll so grand?

He was alone, but he felt something painful. He, the doll, was being held in place by a long, red pin straight through the forehead.

A beam through the forehead again! How careless.

Then, he saw his owner. He stood over Anthony Peterson like a god and laughed at him. Although Anthony Peterson could not see the face, he instinctively knew who it was… It was the cocksucker motherfucker who had kidnapped him in the first place and stuffed him in here.

He hated that person, but he tried reaching up to him for help anyway.

And to Anthony Peterson's surprise, the owner did indeed reach down to him, but instead of taking him out and helping him, he ripped a piece of him off.

His leg. The right one.

The pain was excruciating, and Anthony Peterson wanted to scream out, but he realized with horror that his mouth was only painted on.

How could he then scream? It was very unfair!

Then, the owner reached back down and yanked out a bit of fluff from where his leg used to be.

Had Anthony Peterson blood to shed, he surely would have bled profusely. But Anthony Peterson was a dry, cotton toy.

Then, the figure moved on, but another took his place. Someone he did recognize. It was Sully. This time, Sully came to him and ripped off another piece of him. His foot from the other side.

Then, Evan came to him and ripped out part of his middle. Then, Elena. He recognized his daughter as she came and grabbed a string and pulled and pulled until much more of him was gone.

Then, Tom. Tom would help him, wouldn't he? No. Tom took another piece of him, then came back for more. Then, the original assailant returned and reached down to grab and pull at another thread.

And Anthony Peterson knew that he would soon be no more.

The box would be empty, and the doll would be destroyed.

*

A ringing awoke him from this new, terrible nightmare. He had already been through hell since he woke up the first time, and he had reached a level of depression like he had never felt before.

When he was depressed, he wanted to sleep. He hadn't slept yet since the kidnappers awoke him, not really…but he drifted off after Tom's insult-to-injury extortion.

Now, his whole life was a nightmare, and his dreams were no consolation.

And there was that ringing. But Anthony was groggy, and his mind wasn't clicking properly. What was that weird sound, and where was it coming from? Who could help him get rid of that noise?

Oh…it was this small, glowing box. How did he make it stop, he wondered?

Wakefulness was slow to come to him, but whatever it was that caused that ringing sound was certainly persistent. If it stopped for a few seconds it returned soon.

It was called a 'phone.' He remembered that now. But how did he make it stop that noise? What stopped the ringing?

At last, he realized he needed to touch it, so he did.

Finally, he felt himself lock fully into a phase he could safely describe as 'awake,' and Anthony Peterson felt ridiculous for his confusion.

"Hello?" he answered tiredly.

No one was there.

He felt angered for his sleep being interrupted, though that nightmare had been his worst yet. At least nightmares ended, though.

"Hello?" he answered again, feeling spooked.

Slowly, Peterson started to hear laughter. Quiet at first, then louder and louder to the point that it became maniacal, yet pained. Peterson pictured a psychotic clown coming for him with a knife.

Was he still dreaming?

Was 'Sully' calling him back?

"He-he-he-he-hey-hey there!" the voice said.

It took Peterson a few seconds to place the voice. It was familiar, but sounded different. Distorted. Odd.

"Evan?" he finally said.

"Yeah! How's it goin'?" Evan sounded out of it. Inebriated. Crazy. "I just called…to tell you…that you…were the *shittiest* father *ever*!"

Peterson responded tiredly, "Evan, have you been drinking?"

In response, Evan just laughed again, that same mad clown laugh. Peterson could tell by the sound of the laugh that Evan was just that…drunk.

Evan sighed heavily. "But ya know something?" He paused and then added as if speaking a great truth, "I was never much of a son, anyway."

"That's *not* true!" Peterson responded with no thought whatsoever. Evan had been a wonderful boy once. The pride of his daddy's life, and little Elena had been his little princess. He had failed them, not the other way around, and he knew that, deep down inside. "Actually, you were a great son," Peterson said, trying to sound reassuring and loving. It was his chance to make nice with his firstborn. "It was my fault. I let you down. I didn't teach you to be self-sufficient. I should have–"

"Naaaaaaaaah!" Evan spat back, still seeming to relish the comedy of their situation. "My whole life has been like that. No responsibility. Spoiled, pampered, weak. Just this...rich... *prick*...living off his parents' money. So much to say about that. I suppose...maybe I should be apologizing for being so shitty now."

Peterson heard his son shaking his head as if trying to agitate his brain into sobriety.

"But...now...right now...what I wanted to do...was call... to say goodbye."

Peterson was concerned. "Goodbye?"

Evan laughed again, then cut to silence, like a radio switching stations. "I did something..."

"What?" Peterson demanded. His dry throat locked up. Was Evan in danger? Had the thought of losing all the money made him suicidal? Had he taken something? "Evan, what did you do?" Peterson pleaded.

"Something..." Evan started, then shook his head again "... maybe I shouldn't have done."

Peterson's lower lip quivered as he listened to his sorrow-filled son. "Evan? What did you do?"

"Iiiiiiiiiiiiiiiii, um...I, uh...I called the cops."

Peterson's concern turned to absolute terror. "Son, you, you didn't! Please tell me you didn't!"

"I did, though," he said, still sounding like he was on the edge of laughter. "I know you said I shouldn't, since your *friends* might be listening." Then, the humor left his voice, and he tried to sound reassuring. "Don't worry, though. I didn't give them your number or anything. I'm not sure they even believed me, even."

Peterson was shocked and distraught. It was like the dream Evan had come back to pull off another part of him. "Evan, I...I told you...if I called the police they would *kill* me."

"That's the idea," the drunken Evan replied sinisterly.

Peterson recoiled in shock, but was speechless. It was as if a coin had flipped in Evan's head and he had become someone else. Someone different from the son who had just called him.

"After everything you've done to me over my entire shitty life... after all you did to Elena, and...for fuck's sake, everything you did to my *mother*...you taking away my trust fund was the last...*straw* in a long line of indignities."

Evan paused, seeming to take another drink. He heard the drinker's hissing exhale and knew that Evan was hitting the hard stuff.

"I figured with you and the... step... *bitch*... out of the way, everything would just inherit on back to *me* anyway."

Peterson trembled as he listened to these evil, uncaring words.

"That's way too much money to blow on ransoming a slutty little trophy wife and a dried up old man suffocating in a metal box."

Peterson was petrified and in disbelief. "Oh, Jesus! Oh, Jesus, Evan...you've *killed* me!"

"*Really?*" Evan mocked, sounding like an expectant child hearing the best news of his life, mockingly wracked with emotion and tears of joy. "Oh...I hope *so*, Daddy!"

And then, Peterson's son hung up on him amid more wild laughter.

17 The Price

Anthony Peterson pulled the phone to his face the second it started ringing. He prayed that it was Evan calling to tell him he had been joking and maybe even to apologize. But before he could even answer, his head rocked back again as electricity coursed through his body.

He shook and his muscles contracted, the phone still pressed against his face.

"Mr. Peterson, didn't anyone ever tell you that rules aren't made to be *broken*?" the kidnapper growled, angrily.

Peterson just shook.

"And this is, by the way, this excruciating torture you're going through is far from the highest setting. We've been going easy on you up until now." He laughed cruelly and proved his point by increasing the voltage. "You're going to *die*, Mr. Peterson. You're going to feel your brains boiling inside your head as you *die*, Mr. Peterson. Then when that's done, your eyeballs are going to explode from their sockets and paint the walls like modern art… and then…your head is going to explode like a *fucking volcano* as you *die*, Mr. Peterson!"

As the voltage intensified, the accompanied buzz increased to a deafening level. If the energy didn't electrocute him, the sound would surely kill him. It felt like an earthquake. Blood leaked from the corners of his eyes and from his ears, but finally, with great pain, he managed the words "*It…wasn't…me!*"

With that, the voltage was suddenly cut, causing Peterson to fall to the floor, bloodied and breathless.

The phone landed next to his head again.

He felt drained of life. As if his blood had taken the last of his fluids and he was now a dry husk of a man or...perhaps...a raggedy man. A doll.

"Yes, Mr. Peterson, it wasn't you."

If he had breath, he would have sighed in relief at the knowledge that he had been spared for the time being. Instead he continued gasping for breath and staring at the phone.

"Yes, your son called the police. We know. But don't get your hopes up too high, Mr. Peterson. No one is coming to save you. The information your son gave to the police was sketchy at best."

"Then I...I..." he breathed hard and tried to catch a breath to speak with "I...didn't...break...your rules... Ah."

"Regardless of who did, Mr. Peterson, the rules of the game *have* been broken. And you must, therefore, pay the penalty."

Peterson sat up and brought the phone to his bloodied ear, baffled at what the penalty might be, and angry at the unfairness of having to pay for a crime he didn't commit. "Penalty? Penalty?" He was indignant. "What the fuck are you talking about? You've already taken everything from me. What more could you possibly–"

"*Twenty* million."

His heart sank. "Wha-what?"

He hadn't realized he had any further to sink, or that he had coveted a tiny bit of hope after his last call with Tom, but he sank further and felt his hopes dash.

"The ransom has now doubled. Twenty million or you both die."

Peterson shook his head in disbelief. For once, Anthony Peterson told the whole truth. "It's...it's just not possible!"

"Hmmm, you know, I'm staring at your wife's sweet mouth right now wondering how good it feels. Maybe I'll slit her throat while fucking her mouth. Live streamed." The kidnapper laughed.

"No, no! You can't be serious! I barely scraped this together. There's no way I could get twice that much, no matter how much time you gave me."

"No time extensions."

He looked up to the ceiling as if there was some overlord who might help him.

"Then…then I *can't* pay you. There's just no way."

He heard an electric hum, and he automatically flinched at the sound. This time, the room didn't electrify. Instead, he heard what sounded like a door opening. Was he being freed? Was this big, sick prank finally over?

No. The sound came from the far end of the container. A small compartment did open, and a heavy object fell and rebounded off of the floor with a metallic clang. He could barely make out what it was in the dim light.

"What's that?" Peterson asked. There was only silence on the line. Not even laughter. "What is that?"

"A little gift for you, Mr. Peterson. A gift delivered by remote control, so don't get too excited. But it is a gift that might just save your life. Or, at least, your money."

Peterson walked slowly, tentatively over to where he heard the noise and then stopped. His eyes focused as he blinked the blood from them, and he saw a particularly nasty pair of pliers glimmering up at him.

He recoiled in horror. "What the hell is this?" he asked, terrified.

"Compromise, Mr. Peterson."

"Com-compromise?" he stammered in horror.

"Call it, ha-ha, human trafficking, Mr. Peterson. Piecemeal human trafficking, if you will."

"I don't–"

"You're selling your body, old man. A little at a time. Each body part costs a certain number of dollars. You remove one body part, we remove part of the ransom. It's really quite a deal."

Peterson felt like he was going to piss his pants again. "You've *got* to be shitting me."

"No, I don't think so."

"Go fuck yourself!"

"Fuck myself? When your wife's sweet mouth looks so inviting? Oh, we won't stop with her mouth." He laughed. "I want to hear her screaming as we–"

"No, Christ, no, don't touch her!"

"Then, it's time to make a payment, Mr. Peterson."

"I...I can't."

"It's really very simple, Mr. Peterson." The kidnapper then patiently explained in a disturbingly normal voice, as if he were reciting the rules to a board game. "Each body part has its own monetary value. One toe, one million. One finger, *two* million. One foot, four million. One hand, *five* million. One arm, eight million. One leg, *ten* million. But let me clarify! You can only remove up to ten million in ransom. The original price. No discounts."

Peterson shook with rage, fear and dread. "You are fucking crazy!"

The kidnapper paused again in that chilling way, leaving the metal coffin silent for the moment. When he finally spoke again, Peterson almost jumped.

"Relax, Mr. Peterson. We don't really expect you to sever a limb with a pair of pliers. Although...I admit that would be fun to watch."

Peterson's head jerked around. Watch? Did they have this thing wired up with cameras too? He didn't respond. He waited and...wondered.

"I'll tell you what, Mr. Peterson," the kidnapper said with a mock-friendly tone. It was the same voice Peterson himself often used when sealing deals. It was the crooked salesman's voice. "Since you're such a valued customer, we'll make it nice and easy for you. I'll let you in on a special we're running this hour only. It's a one-for-one deal."

"One-for–"

"One tooth? One million."

Anthony Peterson cringed. His teeth? That was the worst thought of them all. He couldn't! The pain. And not his teeth. Not that. He considered it for a few seconds then morbidly remembered how much money he had spent on his teeth over the years. That bright smile he flashed to seal the deal each time had not come cheap.

Then, his darkest side reminded him what a great deal he was actually getting. Surely he had not spent a million bucks a tooth over the years. Maybe the kidnapper was right. What a bargain this actually was.

He couldn't laugh. The very thought made him sicker. "I'm not doing it."

A quick, sharp jolt of electricity ran through the box, and he screamed both in pain and anticipation of more pain. "Have a seat, Mr. Peterson," the kidnapper commanded. But Anthony Peterson was already on the floor.

He had fallen heavily, and the phone, then the pliers fell and clanged next to him. After a moment, he sat up, cross-legged and looked at the pliers with dread.

"Now, put me on speaker phone and set the phone down, face up so the case can accept the shock. You recognize the brand, I'm sure. Now you know why we chose it." Peterson rolled his eyes. "I'll bet you wish you were shockproof right about now."

He did not laugh or move. Another quick jolt hit him to remind him of who the boss was. He put the phone down as ordered and prepared to sit, roll over, play dead, and self-mutilate.

He eyed the pliers in agonized hesitation, then slowly reached for them. Another jolt caused him to cry out.

"Fuck! I'm *doing it!*"

He reached quickly for the pliers, but handled them the way he would a viper, fumbling around with them until the jaws faced him. Slowly, he opened his mouth and inserted the pliers. They tasted bad, not that it mattered. They seemed like the cheap kind of tool. The kind they sold in cheap chain hardware stores. The kind that broke after a month or so. The kind made of metal that always stank because it was degrading right in front of you, much like the walls of this coffin only worse.

Jesus, GOD, just get on with it. he thought. *Get this over with.*

He clamped reeking talons around one of his backmost teeth and hesitated there, in that humbled position, breathing awkwardly, and hating the taste as he built up the courage to rip pieces of himself off of his body.

He sealed his eyes shut to hold back the tears he knew were coming.

And he was right.

With a hideous crunch, his tooth came out at the root, and he screamed in pain. It was worse than any feeling he had ever had, even worse than the goddamn electric shocks. But the tooth didn't come out clean. It was stuck there. He fought with it. What the hell was keeping it held on? He didn't know, he just pulled and pulled as his mouth filled with blood that flowed down over his chin.

He coughed wildly as he inhaled blood, and that violent cough dislodged the rest of the tooth. It snapped loose, excruciatingly, with a sickly wet crunching sound.

He sagged down, holding the plier-bound tooth in one hand. He bled and trembled and felt like passing out.

"Very good, Mr. Peterson," the kidnapper mocked. "Why you're a pro at this! I think you missed your calling as a dentist."

"Fuck you."

"Now, don't you worry! Every tooth costs the same amount. Keep the ones in the front for aesthetics, the ones in the back for function. Make your choices wisely." The kidnapper laughed again. "That's one down, nine to go."

Peterson thought the bastard was enjoying this a little too much. Was the guy yanking his cock imagining Peterson's suffering?

He put the pliers back into his bloody maw and gripped another of his third molars. He gagged at the pliers and the blood and hesitated for a moment, then closed his eyes and pulled again. He screamed in misery and fell to the floor. This one was easier to yank out, though it drained him of blood and energy even more.

The tooth made a sickly sound as it bounced on the metal floor.

Queasy, he lifted the pliers again, and they slipped in his fingers because of the blood. He had to stop to dry his hands before he tried again.

Another tooth. This one was really stuck in there. He had gone for a bottom one this time. He found it was much more difficult to pull up than it had been to pull down. He thought of switching, but then reconsidered.

How many teeth did a person have? Thirty something. Thirty-two? Or was it twenty-six? Maybe there were twenty-six letters of the alphabet and thirty-two teeth. Or did he have that backwards?

It was a ridiculously stupid thing to think about, but it worked. It distracted him enough to finish the job without obsession. It still hurt severely, and he needed a moment to recover.

He was going to bleed to death from his mouth, wasn't he?

No, no, no…he couldn't think about it. He needed to focus on something else as he had done last time. The pain would be there.

So, he focused on his wife. Each tooth, this pound of flesh, was for Susan. He was unimportant in this. He might as well really be the raggedy man with pieces of him coming off. He was not Anthony Peterson, even.

And from that point, it was as if he was outside of his own body, connected only by a painful invisible thread from his forehead to the real world, watching some other poor bastard hunched over, crossed legged on the floor of some fucking goddam toy box, hurting himself for the amusement of the person he hated most in the world. Getting mind raped and destroyed by someone who redefined evil.

Someone worse, even, than Anthony Peterson.

He just watched as the poor bastard tore himself to pieces. He would help him if he could, but he was just a raggedy man in a box, was he not?

Another piece of the prisoner was ripped away. He never realized how long it took to pull a tooth. This poor bastard was torturing himself for a long, long time.

How many was that? How many were left?

Something told him he could stop at ten, but...then, if he stopped, wouldn't he be him again? Wouldn't Anthony Peterson have to face his pain again? The pain. So much pain.

Who *was* that poor bastard bleeding on the floor there?

*

When his vision cleared again, he saw a hideous little bloody circle of ten freshly-pulled back teeth.

He cocked his head to the side. Whose teeth were these? Why were they here? Was it a gift? Should he try to put them back? Some were broken.

The blood. The teeth. His vision blurred again, and he watched as these bloody teeth turned into another one of those mocking, accusatory skulls that continually invaded his mind all that day. Something about South America? He couldn't remember. All he knew now was pain and weakness. Whose skull was this? Whose teeth were those?

Then, he felt the gory pliers slip from his red, wet hand, and he looked over at them drunkenly. He focused on the pliers as his head swam, then looked up a little to the hand.

That was his own hand was it not? If so, that meant... probably...that was his own blood his hand...and putting those facts together...those must have been his own teeth.

His eyes widened, and he looked back to that hideous circle. The skull faded away, as if back through the invisible wound in the center of his forehead, and he saw clearly again the circle consisted, in fact, of blood and teeth.

His own blood. His own teeth.

He had done this to himself…because they had made him. He shook with tears, clenching his eyes closed as tight as he possibly could to hold them back. Nobody did this to Anthony Peterson.

Did they not know who they were fucking with?

But that very thought brought the skulls floating back up to gape at him in the darkness of his closed eyes. Not his skulls, but his responsibility.

His swimming head slowly tuned back in to reality.

No. Not his responsibility. Someone was doing this to him, and nobody fucked with Anthony Peterson.

That was true.

He was not the raggedy man. He was real.

He was Anthony Peterson, and nobody made him do anything. He was doing this to survive. He was a survivor, and playing the game was his only way to make sure he lived to make them pay. He spat a mouthful of blood sideways, then began to clean himself up.

Tears and blood. They would get no more of either from Anthony Peterson, goddamn it.

He held his pocket handkerchief up to his mouth to soak up the gore as he slowly took control of the pain. He would win. He always won.

Pain was just a feeling. Pain could be controlled. It wouldn't control him.

Peterson breathed and shook as he suffered. His nerve endings felt like they were on fire. He was terrified. So, he let himself feel it all for a few seconds and deliberately began to compartmentalize.

Pain was just an emotion, right? It's the way we react to the physical feelings that matters. Change the reaction and the pain goes away.

Fear is just a state of mind. Control it. Put it away.

It worked. It had to work. Peterson was all business. Peterson was going to stay alive. He swallowed his blood. It was the closest thing to nourishment he had had all day. He wondered darkly how long he could feed on himself until he was gone.

He shook his head and fought back the pain again. He was not going to bleed to death from his mouth.

Compartmentalize. The positive? He was drinking something. His parched mouth and throat were appreciating the drink he was getting now, as disgusting and self-destructive as that was. Ironically, he now needed to dry his once parched mouth to stay alive.

He had to stop the bleeding. He glanced at the phone and shrugged his shoulders. Let them wait.

The toothless wonder carefully untied his tie and began to unravel the tail.

This was why he was going to win. He was smarter than they were.

He tore the slip stitch, which allowed him to separate the fine silk all the way down to the blade of the necktie.

Then, he retrieved the interlining. The interlining of his tie, like many ties, was a woven wool-like material that managed to simulate a gauze pad pretty damn well. It was an expensive designer tie, but it was not worth his life. He needed what it could provide.

He tore the interlining into equal segments and rolled four of them to make pads for his erupting sockets. He placed them in his mouth and bit down for the pressure. It hurt, but he was controlling the pain. He was not about to bleed to death. He was going to use his brain to stay alive and get his precious payback.

This was why he was going to win. He was smarter than they were.

He was surviving.

And when he was done, Anthony Peterson picked up the phone, still on speaker and noticed blood spatters across its screen. "Harrumph!" was the noise he made into the phone to let them know he was there.

"Can you talk, Mr. Peterson?" the kidnapper asked after a pause. He sounded almost concerned. Almost.

It took him great effort and he slurred his words at first. It was as if he was retraining himself to talk with a new mouth. "Yeth... yeth." He swallowed a mouthful of blood, painfully cleared his throat, and forced himself into the calmness he had just created. But it wasn't easy.

"Yes," he said finally.

"Ten teeth. Ten million," the kidnapper said as if to make official the completion of the deal.

"Ngo...nnnnngo..." Peterson steadied himself again, then defiantly said, "Go...fuck...yourself."

And as the kidnapper laughed that horrible laugh again, Anthony Peterson lost the battle he had been fighting and finally passed out from the pain.

18 Smoke and Reflections

8:06 AM

Anthony Peterson was possibly the farthest thing from Calderon's mind at that particular moment.

The mercenary had stopped listening in right around the time he caused the pliers to drop and got up to stretch his legs as the self-mutilation continued. He didn't need to listen while the boss was on the line. Besides, this was going to take forever. Calderon had pulled a few teeth in his day, both for safety in the field and for torture. The fastest a tooth was ever pulled was probably around three minutes. The slowest took around fifteen. Ten teeth? Calderon had some time, so he put Anthony Peterson out of his mind.

Instead, he thought a good bit about Susan Peterson. Why was she here? The reason she was here was very different from the reason her husband was in such a predicament. It was the difference of why, the difference between these two whys that exercised Calderon's brain.

Calderon still wished he didn't care.

He opened the door to the room where they were keeping her, but didn't talk to her this time. Instead, he squatted down to his backpack, next to his oversized duffle bag and fumbled around for some cigarettes.

"Hello?" Susan Peterson said. "Is that you?"

He shook his head. Silly question, wasn't it?

He looked around the clean floor of the organized storeroom for a moment, not wanting to actually look at the woman. He thought about reminding her that she had no friends here and not to start thinking that she did, but decided not to respond. She either got the message or did not.

She wouldn't be there all that much longer, come what may.

Calderon exited the room and trod his way down the stairs, feeling wistful. It was his past that kept coming back to him.

This was still his kind of place. Off the grid. Hole in the map.

He carefully opened the door, waited for his eyes to adjust to the sunlight, and walked in the preordained path under the shadows to his tree and lit a cigarette.

In this modern world, everyone was watching everyone. Calderon would know. He was one of those watchers. He was recording all the calls on this particular mission without Peterson or that Pocase guy or anybody else knowing about it, just as he had a thousand other times.

But this place…nobody was watching this place. And he liked that because it was so rare.

A man could get lost out here, he thought, then frowned because the thought had surprised him.

That was true. Places like this were the very kinds of places where people could easily get lost. Maybe never found.

For a guy thinking about leaving it all behind, that thought, perhaps, should have given him comfort, but it didn't.

Instead, it gave him a chill.

Knock-knock…that was the sound Mrs. Peterson had made as she kicked the inside of the coffin. He saw how one of her feet was bloodied, injured as she knock-knocked on that coffin. Why? Did she think they didn't know she was in there? As if they had made one stupid mistake by grabbing the wrong box? Did she think that she could kick her way out?

Calderon shrugged and puffed.

No.

She was doing that because it was better than doing nothing.

Calderon was sure that was the reason. Not because he had the greatest insight into human nature, but because he had reasoned out such a thought over the months.

Since that day…

He hadn't lied to the woman when he told her the last person he cared about had died a few months before.

It was his nephew.

He didn't like to think about it, but that is what happened, and that was what was still haunting him.

His brother had made a son with a beautiful wife and, well, that had let Calderon off the hook as it were. To the extent that Calderon could care about family tradition, he no longer had to worry about it. The name would now continue. He didn't need to have a kid of his own now.

That was good because Calderon knew he was not a very good man. He would surely make a terrible father. He would be absent all of the time, and when he was home, he could scarcely imagine being terribly loving. He might even have been abusive.

But that was only a concern if he had a kid at all, which was never in the cards for those same reasons.

But then, he had this nephew, and maybe that kid was the very thing he needed. It wasn't just that he was off the hook.

No. This was perfect for him. Justin was perfect for him.

Calderon was gone all of the time on missions. With Justin, he always had someone excited to see him when he visited. And visit he did. They spent camping trips together, went to batting cages. Target shot. Hunted.

His brother turned out to be an excellent father, but it was Calderon, the 'awesome uncle,' who taught Justin how to shoot and fish. Man stuff.

Of course, that was when Calderon visited, which was not always terribly often. Thus, Justin grew up quick as Calderon missed a summer here, a year there.

Justin was a teenager. He would be fifteen now...had he lived.

His brother had asked for a loan, and Calderon had come through. Why not? He always got paid, and what else mattered?

Thus, his brother had surprised the family by buying a nice homestead on the outskirts of the suburbs of Houston, Texas. Far enough away from the city to be affordable. Close enough to still offer anything they needed.

Plus, there was a big forest behind the place. Everything a boy could dream of.

He was an adventurous kid. Maybe that had something to do with his uncle, Calderon himself. Though Calderon discouraged Justin from military pursuits, he clearly craved the adventures they had shared.

Justin rode his bike, scouted the area, climbed trees, and blazed new trails with his machete. He asked for a dirt bike for his birthday but Calderon had said he might send him a hunting rifle instead. He didn't think much of it at the time. That was the last time they spoke.

Months ago…

Justin had gone out exploring like any other day. He was late for dinner. Not that strange for an adventurous boy.

But then, he missed dinner altogether. His parents discussed grounding him. Then, swore he would never leave the fence surrounding their house again. Then, they called the police and started bargaining, hoping somehow Justin would be found.

Justin was found…about a week later.

Calderon had been away on a mission. He couldn't be reached. When he called in for a visit, his brother had relayed the story to him.

Justin was dead.

He had been out exploring, and apparently had come across an abandoned well. He probably hadn't even seen it. It was no wider than a large pizza. More of a vertical pipeline than a full well and nothing above ground. Just a hole.

Goddamn whoever had left that death trap out there.

Justin was just skinny enough to slide all the way in to the bottom once he fell in. The well was just tight enough that, doctors said, he probably was unable to shout for help. Not enough breath.

It took him days to die.

Calderon was sure Justin had fought as hard as possible. He was a tough boy, Justin. He could imagine him fighting for life, fighting to be heard.

The search parties must have missed him. Couldn't hear him. Didn't go near that particular spot. Simple bad luck.

That tight prison where he died. It must have been horrible. In Calderon's nightmares, he imagined Justin screaming and fighting to get out. Terrified. Hoping to be heard. Slowly giving up hope as he slowly gave up life.

They had not buried him yet when Calderon learned what had happened.

He flew to Texas as quickly as possible in a state of disbelief.

He asked to see the body, and the request was granted. The coroner was just about to transfer Justin's remains to the funeral home when he arrived.

The investigation was complete. It was nobody's fault. No man's land. Whoever the hell had left that vertical pipe in the ground like that, they were long gone. It was just an accident.

Calderon had approached the dead body, still in shock. He had seen dead bodies before. Hell, he had long ago lost count of how many people he himself had killed. Those he had tortured were an even larger number. Those he had hurt constituted an even greater number. Calderon was not a good person at all, and he knew that.

But Justin had been...Justin had been very good. And Calderon had never before seen the dead body of someone he had loved.

Justin was so pale. So cut up. So...wrong. He was fucked up beyond belief.

Calderon, the tough soldier, never once cried. He just looked at his nephew and wished he had not been somewhere else when Justin had needed him.

He had reached for the white sheet, the shroud that covered Justin, and although the morgue attendant objected, he threw it aside.

There was Justin, naked, skinny, and dead.

Calderon looked down at the kid's presumably still unused penis. He was sure Justin would have told him if he had lost his virginity. It didn't matter, of course. That was just sex, but... somehow that penis, at least as a metaphor, was exactly what took over Calderon's mind. As he stared down at the small thing, he couldn't help thinking of all Justin would never experience. His first time with a girl, working hot summers for low wages, finishing high school, seeing his favorite team win the Super Bowl, watching classic movies rereleased on the big screen, finding a wife, buying a peaceful home, having kids of his own.

Calderon looked away abruptly. He would never have many of those things either. Just as his brother had gotten him off the hook for continuing the name, Justin himself was going to live the calm life Calderon himself never had. And Justin would have done just that... had he lived.

When his eyes refocused, he found himself staring at Justin's right foot. It was bloodied. The nails torn off, the toes broken.

He had cuts and scratches in many places, including his face, but that foot was absolutely mangled.

Once he had sadly left the morgue, Calderon talked to his brother about the foot, and he got the story.

Apparently at the bottom, due to rainfall or an animal burrowing or rust or something, there was just enough room for Justin to move his leg, just a little, and kick the wall of the well.

And that's what he did...for days and days on end.

Justin couldn't scream and couldn't climb out so he kicked and kicked and kicked and kicked, hoping to be heard.

Knock-knock. Knock-knock. Knock-knock.

Calderon had thought about that desperate, futile move for these months. That had probably stuck in his mind more than anything else had. Kicking with broken bones.

Knock-knock. Knock-knock. Knock-knock.

Justin must have been so sure someone would come. They would rescue them. They would hear. They would save him. It was worth kicking like that. That was his way of signaling so he could be saved.

But no one ever came. No one fixed his foot. No one found him. Not before he died. Not even his favorite uncle.

At some point, he had to have given up. Surrendered to death.

Calderon had seen that surrender in the eyes of many people he had killed over the years. He never thought his nephew Justin would have to surrender like that.

Knock-knock. Knock-knock. Knock-knock.

Calderon never had cried, he just moved on while the thoughts ate away at him from the inside.

He could have gotten past it, eventually and, in fact, he hadn't been obsessing over it during this job, but...

But then, he heard Susan Peterson's desperate kicks.

Knock-knock. Knock-knock. Knock-knock.

He had seen the shape of her foot afterward.

Knock-knock. Knock-knock. Knock-knock.

She was doing what she could.

Maybe they would hear her and release her.

Knock-knock. Knock-knock. Knock-knock.

Just like her "Is that you?" It was all she could do at that time. It was better than nothing, even if that something was...nothing.

Knock-knock. Knock-knock. Knock-knock.

No, lady. I'm sorry, he thought. *Nobody was listening for him. Nobody is listening to you now.*

Knock-knock. Knock-knock. Knock-knock.

Calderon dropped the cigarette, crushed it, and started to walk inside.

The *knock-knock* sound was so strong in his head, he almost knocked on the door before shaking his head and laughing it off.

He went back inside to check his equipment and put it all out of his mind.

Calderon never cried. He had his work. He had his money and what else was there?

He listened in as Peterson's phone went off again.

And he still couldn't help but think of retiring.

19 Bad Luck Tom

8:31 AM

Anthony Peterson was startled awake from visions of the bleached white skulls of children surfacing in filthy canals filled with blood. The phone rang and buzzed near his head again. He was not dreaming this time, but when he awoke, he idly hoped that the unnecessary dental extraction he remembered was only a nightmare.

A quick, yet excruciating, check with his tongue proved that was not the case.

He fought with the expensive makeshift gauze and worked it to the side so it could do its job while still allowing him to speak.

"Yeah?" he answered, acutely aware that pain was dulling his voice.

"Hey, hey, boss man!" came Tom's voice, sounding far too genial. "It's your very own right-hand man."

Peterson sighed. Tom may not have been in on this, but he was helping them snip away at Anthony Peterson, raggedy man.

"Tom..." Peterson growled in frustration. "What do you want?"

"Well, before I head out the door, I wanted to call to let you know you're still about a million and change short of the ten mil."

Shocked, Peterson forgot his injured mouth for a moment and shouted "What? But you said–" and then winced at the pain his agitation caused to his wounded maw.

"Yeah, I know what I said but here's the deal, daddy-o. I was estimating based on the expected return. I just found out that some of your investments we sold off didn't get nearly the returns we expected. Chalk it up to bad luck."

Peterson rolled his eyes. The nightmare never ended

"Bad luck?" Peterson scoffed. "Then give back the interest you stole."

"Stole? Moi?" Tom chuckled. "Not a chance. If I do that, and this still fails, I get nothing."

"But the lives of two people–"

"We've been through that! Now, I'm willing to keep helping you, Anthony, I am…but believe me when I tell you that my help is out of gratitude for the fact that you just made me a millionaire."

Peterson stood up and paced around the room for a moment. It was all he knew to do anymore. He hated Tom passionately for what he was doing, but still needed Tom for what he could do for him.

And a piece of him, just a tiny little piece, realized that Anthony Peterson had taught Tom well. Tom was a remarkable protégé. This was Anthony Peterson's own reflection shining back at him. His own greedy, guilty reflection.

He thought hard and then twisted his face as a crazy idea came to him. It was as if the scant nourishment he had received had caused his brain to work in high gear again. His own blood had given him the blood sugar he needed to formulate a plan as insane a plan as it might have been.

"Okay, bad luck, Tom. We're going to try it this way. I own a small business."

"You own a few of them, but I already told you we can't sell them off in enough time, even if they weren't mortgaged to the balls."

"No, no, no, listen. This specific business is one I rarely visit. It's over on Fairfax."

Tom raced through his memory.

"The…sex boutique?"

Peterson shook his head. "No, Tom. It's the jeweler."

"Jewelry store? Oh, yeah. Yeah, you bought that place on the cheap, right?"

"Yeah, you remember right. The owner got twenty-to-life for wholesaling fake stones, so his family had to unload all his assets." For a second, Peterson forgot himself and just laughed with Tom.

Naturally, Tom Pocase had to ruin the moment by saying "You mean kind of like you're doing now?"

Peterson's bloody smile faded. "Yeah. Pleased you remember the place," he said, regretfully. "Listen. I'm gonna need you to rob the jewelry store for me."

There was a very pregnant pause on the other end of the line. Tom was absorbing this in shock. Then, he burst into laughter.

"Oh, maaaaaaan! You *can't* be serious."

Peterson nodded. "Serious as a ripped-out tooth."

"What?"

"I'm serious, Tom, unless you've got some better idea of how to save my fucking life."

Tom scoffed. "But Anthony, that's *crazy*. I know you're under a hell of a lot of stress right now, but be reasonable. It's broad daylight, and I'm no heist man."

"Under a lot of stress, Tom? Tom!"

"Yeah?"

"Listen to me. That time we went to Vegas and I was in that high stakes poker game? I was under a hell of a lot of stress then. When we negotiated that deal to buy that chain of Buick dealerships, I was under a hell of a lot of stress. When my children were born, I was under a hell of a lot of stress. When Marie got sick, I was under a hell of a lot of stress! Right now, I am trapped in a goddam Rubik's Cube about to *die* after listening to my wife get gang-raped and murdered. You know, the wife whose life you recently tried to convince me didn't matter? So, no, Tom, no, you fucking asshole, right now I am far, far beyond being under a hell of a lot of stress. Okay?"

"Okay."

"All right?"

"All right. I'm sorry." Tom sounded actually contrite and sincere, but Peterson didn't let up.

"So, I suggest that *you* be fucking reasonable and listen to me, Mr. Millionaire."

Tom paused for a moment, then said, "All ears." Perhaps there was some loyalty left in Tom after all.

"Good. Now, it's going to be easy. I'm going to tell you where to get the keys, I'll give you the alarm codes, I'll talk you through the whole thing. You'll be in and out in five minutes flat."

"Sounds like having sex."

Peterson smiled at last, knowing he was getting through to Tom. "Easier than that. We can do this. *You* can do this." He paused, feeling the agony in his mouth and added, "You've *got* to do this."

Tom sighed and nervously said, "It's just too crazy. I could go to jail."

"You think I don't know that? You think I don't know this could be the end for me if you get caught? That's why I'm going to make absolutely goddamn sure you don't get caught."

"Fifty thousand," Tom said, without missing a beat.

"What?"

"Fifty *thousand*," Tom repeated.

"On top of the fucking…severance…you already took from me?" Peterson was incredulous. He resorted to trying to make another deal. "Look, put that severance you stole back in the pot, send it to the kidnappers, and save us this misery, and I'll repay you every penny you took plus a *hundred* thousand."

Peterson could actually hear Tom shaking his head. "Hell no, buddy. What's mine is mine now. You keep thinking about yourself, your own life, your wife's life, and you know? I can't blame you. I can't. But I gotta think about me. If you die anyway, I lose everything. My job goes, my wife goes, my–"

"Fine, Tom, fuck it, you've made your point. But then you're going to have to keep helping me if you keep that. I need that money. I need to survive." Peterson did his best to sound kind and giving as he said, "Tom? If you save our lives, then you not only keep the million plus you just…" he wanted to say extorted, but instead chose "…just earned, but you keep your job and, hey, bonuses and everything to come. Your boss will owe you."

Tom seemed to think about that for a moment, then said, "Make it a hundred thousand more this time, and we've got a deal. I'll break into your store."

Peterson scoffed. "Don't push your luck, Tom. You just said fifty."

"Hey, the clock is ticking, Anthony, isn't it?"

Peterson squeezed his eyes shut again. Every time he got close to not hating Tom today, he pulled another of these fucking stunts.

"Done," he muttered sadly. "Are you in your car?"

"Negative."

"Well, where the hell are you?"

"Actually, I'm still in the doctor's house," Tom explained at a pace just the wrong side of frustrating. "See, I had to work on these transactions and the rest of the sales and returns. And the clock is ticking, so I didn't want to go home yet, right? The wife thinks I'm working with you, which is true, really, and the Doctor is still with the girl, but he kept checking on me."

"Tom? Tom?"

"After a while, he said I might as well come in, so I've been charging my phone and the Bluetooth and the laptop, and you know what? This Doctor Ivy guy has some *killer* wi-fi!"

"Tom, seriously–"

"It's fast! Have you been to his place? He's got a water filter that–"

"Goddammit, Tom, who gives a shit about Ivy's house? I need your help, goddamn it!"

"Right. Damn. You're right, Anthony. Sorry. My car's in the garage."

"Well then get in the damn thing, then, pronto. Like you said, twice, the clock is ticking!"

Peterson listened while Tom exited the room, slammed the door and started his car.

Tom then said, "Shit," got back out, hit the button to open the garage door, and promptly began burning rubber down the road.

"Where to?"

"You got your Bluetooth on?"

"Yeah. Wait…" After two beeps, Tom repeated, "Yeah."

"Okay, good. Now, first, you go to my place. You're going to need the jewelry keys."

"Yeah, golden. I'm not far away. Luckily, you and the doc live close to each other. You got a gate code or entry key?"

"Yeah, Tom, it's six, six, six."

"Six, six, six? Subtle."

"Don't be a critic."

"Hey, it suits you." Tom chuckled. "It's not very secure, but it does suit you."

Peterson listened to the car skid to a halt and heard Tom running. Then, a loud crash. "Uh, I tripped over the garbage cans," he said, offhandedly and embarrassed. "You didn't tell me it was garbage day."

"Well, you know? I've had a lot on my mind, Tom!"

"Right. Back up and running. Heading around back to be safe."

"Around back?" Peterson started with unpleasant surprise. "No, no, no, the front. It's not safe."

Peterson heard Tom's running feet stop, and the growling of a large dog filled the phone's speaker. Peterson cringed, knowing what was coming.

"Uh, Anthony?" Tom muttered, sounding scared but trying to remain calm. "When did you get a mean-looking dog?"

"That's what I was trying to tell you. He was a gift from Susan."

"Wuh-what's his name?"

"Satan."

"Well, of course it is! Why do I *ask* these questions?" he scoffed, in spite of himself. "Is…is he friendly?"

"He's an attack dog named after the motherfucking Prince of Darkness. Does he sound friendly to you?"

"Then, I'd better make a run for it."

"Tom…" Peterson called warningly.

Rabid, insane barking followed as Satan lunged after Tom.

Peterson could only hear what was happening, but it was enough to give him some very terrifying mental pictures. If Tom died, Anthony was as good as dead.

"Oh shit!" Tom screamed as he ran away.

Peterson could only hear running footsteps and the sound of Satan's collar jingling. Then, Peterson heard the terrible sound of teeth on meat.

Tom screamed in pain. "Oh, shit! He's got my fucking leg!"

A scuffle erupted through the phone, and Peterson insanely almost warned Tom to be careful with his dog. The thought of Satan trying to rob a jewelry store gave Tom an awful lot of leeway.

Finally, Peterson heard the dog crying out in pain.

"I got him off me. Kicked him in the face. I think he's done."

"Tom? He's not done!"

"Shit!"

Barking followed footfalls and Tom's frantic breathing.

"If you can run, run to the house, we keep a key in the planter there."

"Not much of a choice, man!" Tom hustled, and Peterson heard the pain in his voice as he ran. He fumbled with the backdoor lock, fighting to get the key in the hole in time. "Come on, come *on!*" he grunted.

At last, the back door clicked open as the growling increased and the door slammed. Lastly, Peterson heard his dog's face running smack dab into the glass of the door and after a pause more growling and barking to be let in.

Tom panted and caught his breath, trying to calm down.

"You better hit that alarm code fast, Tom," he said and heard Tom scrambling to the panel.

"Yeah, yeah, number of the beast," Tom said, and Peterson heard the beeps, followed by a tone signaling disarmament. "It's done," he whispered above his heavy breathing. "I'm in."

"Can you walk?" Peterson asked.

"Well, I just ran all that way, so I guess so!" he panted. "Where to?"

Peterson closed his eyes tightly and imagined his home. "Upstairs, master bedroom. Try not to kill yourself on the stairs."

"You got a bathroom up there?"

"You have to piss at a time like this?"

"No, asshole, but I could use some Bactine. Your dog almost took my leg off, you know?"

"Yeah, right off the master bedroom. Keep time in mind."

"Roger wilco." Tom said and ran up the stairs. "Whereabouts? What am I looking for?"

"It's in the medicine cabinet, genius."

"Not that. The...the fucking keys and shit!"

Peterson started pacing again. "Top dresser drawer."

"Well there are two dressers!"

"Tom..." Peterson patiently explained, "...the one with the Jake Slater novel on top of it is mine, the one with all the pink shit on top is obviously Susan's!"

"Right, right, I'll go to yours."

"Top drawer...under the porno mags...there should be a... ring of keys and a pocket notebook. Get both!"

Tom rustled around until Peterson heard keys shaking. "Got 'em. I'm out!"

"No, no, wait. Go into the closet. You'll find a bag with my ski trip gear in there. You're going to need a ski mask and gloves, unless you've already got some in the car."

"Not something I just keep with me."

"Then grab them and come out of the closet, boy."

Peterson listened to Tom running, then a strange whooshing sound caused Peterson to ask, "Tom, did you just slide down the banister?"

"Yep! Sidesaddle. Old school!" he said, pleased with himself, as if on an adrenaline rush. Peterson rolled his eyes, but they shot wide open when he heard the front door open with a crash. "Anyway, back outside now. All good and...oh what the FUCK?"

"What, Tom, what?" Peterson asked as he heard Satan's growls and barks.

"Your fucking dog must have jumped the fence."

"Well, get the fuck out of there, right now!"

"Shit!" Tom yelled and ran as Satan chased him, snarling.

Peterson listened to the car door open and slam shut as Satan scratched and bit at the glass to be let in.

"Tom? You all right?"

"Yeah! I'm in the car now."

"Well, boy, drive, dammit, drive!"

"Yeah!" Tom panted, agreeing. He turned the key and gunned the engine, and Peterson smiled painfully as he heard the tires screech to a start. "You know, you really got your money's worth for that dog!"

"Sounds like it."

"He's out now. Your neighbors are going to hate you."

"They aaaaaaaaaaaaaalready do, Tommy-boy."

"Yeah, well, I hate that dog. My leg is bleeding like fuck. I feel like going back and running him over."

"You get me and Susan out of this alive, and we just might let you do that, but we ain't got time right now!"

20 The Cavalry

8:51 AM

Anthony Peterson. Those were the words scrawled across the lined notebook paper Detective Gilley dropped in front of the desk sergeant.

"What about him?" Sergeant Burns asked.

"That's the name you gave me?" Gilley asked with some annoyance.

"That's the name the kid said over the phone. It mean something to you?"

"Yeah. Businessman. Real estate mostly. Investments. Really rich guy. Snake in the grass, too. I'm surprised he hasn't run for office yet."

"So?" Burns asked without laughing.

"So, how do you know this isn't a prank?"

"I don't know a damn thing, except that his kid, Evan, called and said he was missing," Burns reminded him. "Also, it's not my damn job to know if it's a prank: it's your job to find that out after an investigation."

"Oh, right, right, right, that's my job. But you didn't say he was just missing. Read that back to me."

Burns sighed and looked up at the Detective. He was a fit man in his thirties, prone to wearing jeans with his badge on the belt with cowboy boots and checkered, western style shirts to go with the getup. He also wore his hair in a tightly curled, bushy afro which he matched with a firm mustache and a pair of sideburns reaching down toward it. Burns often wondered why Gilley bothered being a plainclothes detective, if he was going to look like someone who just woke up from the mid-1970s. Wasn't the point, supposedly, to blend in?

Still, Burns generally liked the man, and he had little better to do, so he indulged Gilley. "Uh, kidnapped, kept in a metal cargo container or something, and he didn't know where he was, but if they didn't get ten million bucks to some offshore account, they were going to kill the guy and his wife."

Burns half-expected his detective pal to respond with something anachronistic like, "Dy-No-MITE!!" or "Far out!" to match his look, but instead, Gilley leaned in and asked, "And that didn't sound odd to you?"

"Well, of course it sounded fucking odd, that's why I gave it to you *dicks,* instead of just sending a car out there."

"But you did send a car, right?"

"They haven't radioed in yet."

"I think this is a joke. I think the kid is pissed off at daddy and wants to cause some trouble. This sounds like a horror movie plot," Gilley said.

Burns nodded. "I thought the same thing. And you can't find anything?"

"Not a damn thing," Gilley confirmed for his friend. "But then, he hasn't been missing that long, it seems. Maybe the kid is just paranoid and didn't get some going out drinkin' money from daddy."

Burns chuckled. "Yeah, I don't think that's much of a problem."

"Meaning what?"

"The kid was clearly blitzed on the phone. Yeah, at this time of day. Slurred speech and everything. He either got started real early, or he just got in from a night out," Burns said.

"Further proof this is bullshit, then," Gilley said.

"So, we just drop it?"

Gilley leaned in on the tall desk and drummed his fingers. "No. No, too high profile a name to just forget about it. If it turns out to be something, and it's probably not, we don't want to have to answer to the Chief on it."

"Not the reporters, either," Burns said.

"Thing is, it could be anywhere. That's just not enough information, man," Gilley said, drumming harder and shaking his head. "Anything else you can tell me?"

"Uh…he said his dad had taken his trust fund. So, yeah, you could be right. Could be a family spat over money."

Gilley blew air out through his lips. "Hell of an elaborate story to make up because you're pissed off at daddy."

"Well, he seemed happy about it, somehow."

"Happy his dad got kidnapped?"

"*If* his dad got kidnapped."

"Hell of a thing," Gilley chuckled.

"Hell of a thing," Burns agreed.

"Well, unless you expect me to bang on every cargo container from the port at Long Beach to…what, every storage facility in the county, I'm out of ideas," Gilley said, still not quite taking it seriously.

Burns shrugged. "Well, sure, you could just wait for the squad car to call in, but at the risk of telling you how to do your job, which again, ain't my job, could I make a suggestion?"

Gilley looked up at his friend and raised his eyebrows. "Shoot."

"Go see the kid."

"Come again?"

Burns tapped his pencil on his steno pad to make the point. "Go get a statement from the kid in person. See if he cracks. Hell, bring him in and tell him you want an official police report filed."

"You didn't ask him to come in?"

"I didn't want a guy that drunk on the streets." Gilley laughed, so Burns continued. "If it's a prank or publicity stunt, or if he just called it in for the hell of it or to piss off daddy, you arrest the little bastard for filing a false police report."

"Damn good idea." Gilley sighed. "I guess I'll do just that. You know, it's a little too early in the goddamn day for this shit."

"I'll say," Burns agreed.

"Any fucking way…good chat. I'm out."

"Later," Sergeant Burns called after him and picked up the ringing phone on his desk. "LAPD. Yeah, it's Burns. Yeah? You don't say. You... Aw, holy shit. Charlie! Stop, Gilley, there, quick!"

Gilley came jogging back to see what Burns wanted. "Where's the fire, Burnsy?"

"You're not gonna believe this. There's a break-in over in Bel Air."

"Yeah?"

"And it's Anthony Peterson's house. His attack dog is running around the streets, terrorizing the neighborhood. Big, bad, black, spiked collar and everything. Rottweiler. Their exact words were that it looked like that monster Zuul from *Ghostbusters.*"

"Lovely. And?"

"Well, and Peterson's front door is hanging wide open. Streaked tire tracks on the pavement out front, too."

"Aw...fuck," Gilley said.

"So, what's the plan?"

Gilley slapped his hand on Burns' desk and thought. "Get backup out to Peterson's place. I'm going to go talk to the kid."

"Right. Good thinkin'." Burns laughed without humor.

"Tell the Lieutenant, too."

"On it."

"Oh, and for God's sake..."

"Yeah?"

"Call animal control, OK?"

21 Smash and Grab

9:20 AM

Anthony Peterson heard the car skid to a stop again just a few minutes after Tom had called him back. Fairfax was not Bel Air, so Tom had had a drive ahead of him. A drive Peterson didn't have the battery life (or desire) to sit through.

"All right, I'm here."

"Where's here?"

"Alley behind the Fairfax store. It looks deserted."

"Good. The place doesn't open 'til ten. Now get dressed for the occasion, because we've got to work fast."

"Okay, I put my black jacket on al*ready*. Got your gloves. Hey, flexible!" Peterson heard a cloth rustling just before Tom asked, "Can you hear me with the ski mask on?"

Peterson paused. "Well, it's...it's muffled if you've got it on over the Bluetooth."

"Well, I can't very well wear the Bluetooth outside the mask."

"Right. Uh. You're going to have to go one-handed for this part. Leave big blue in the car."

Peterson heard two beeps, then the car door opened and shut in the distance. He felt, and not for the first time this bizarre day, as if he was listening to a radio program.

"Okay, what now?"

"Check if the coast is clear and head on inside the back!"

Tom paused. "Can't I just go in the front this time?" he asked, clearly hating the idea.

"Back's safer. Trust me. How's the leg?"

Tom crunched across the gravel in the alley, saying, "Well, I fucking forgot to patch it up in your bathroom, thanks to all your instructions. But I will survive, I guess."

"Good." Peterson resisted the urge to call Tom an idiot and said, "The key you need is the big silver one."

Tom approached the back door, unlocked the heavy door, and went in.

"I'm in."

"Alright, now I just need you to head to the–" Peterson paused. Something was wrong. "Tom, are you there?"

"Uh…"

Peterson listened intently. Was that a gun cocking?

He heard the distinctive sound of the phone dropping to the floor.

Then muffled conversation and clear sounds of a violent struggle filled Peterson's ears.

"Tom?"

He heard muffled threats, and Tom shouting responses as the argument and fight escalated to an explosive point.

Peterson had to jerk the phone away from his ear as a blast was heard, more loudly than he had ever heard anything through a telephone before.

How was that even possible?

Things went in slow motion for him as he tentatively pulled the phone closer to his ringing ear. Much more of that, and he would go deaf.

"Tom?" he demanded, but realized he couldn't even hear himself over the ringing, so he switched ears. "T-Tom?"

He was met only with heavy breathing on the other end of the line.

"Tom? Who is this?"

"He's dead." It took Peterson a moment to realize that was indeed Tom's voice coming through the line. The crazy-go-lucky man Tom had become over this long night was no longer with him, replaced by a stern, serious and distressed doppelganger.

"What? Who? Who's dead?"

"The security guard, rent-a-cop…something."

Peterson was aghast. "Since when the fuck did they hire a goddamn security guard?"

"Right, Anthony," Tom said, still coldly, but with sarcasm. "Because there's *no* chance anyone would rob the place."

Peterson wanted to argue that it wasn't stealing if he stole from himself, but this wasn't the time. "Well, did you have to kill him?"

"He had a fucking gun to my head. A goddamn hand cannon."

"Why didn't you just tell him to stay calm?"

"He! Didn't! Speak! English!" Tom said, each word its own exclamation.

"Well, why the fuck didn't *you* stay calm, Tom?"

"Anthony, a giant crazy-ass Mexican guy who spoke zero English had a .357 Magnum pointed at my head about to shoot me in the fucking face and you expected me to stay calm?"

Peterson panted. This was bad…this could get worse…but what other way did he have to get out of this mess? Peterson looked upward again and shook his head. He would have to remember to send a care package to the man's family once he got out of this goddamn box.

Anthony Peterson was, after all, a good man.

He composed himself and got back to his mode of cheerleader and coach all in one.

"Okay, Tom, I understand. Are you going to be okay now?"

"Am I going–? I just *killed* a man, Anthony!"

"I know…I…I know."

Tom panted. "I didn't want to kill him, I just wanted to fight him off. I used to be a boxer, you know?"

"I remember, Tom, I remember. Golden Gloves. Undefeated for seasons on end," Peterson said, but needed to hurry things up. This wasn't the time for Tom to ramble and reminisce.

"Yeah. I just meant to hit him, not…" he thought for a moment while panting. "Maybe, I…I mean, we were both struggling with the gun and it went off, I guess, really, he kind of shot himself through the chest, but…but…"

"Tom," Peterson said reassuringly, "it isn't your fault."

"You believe that?"

"Of course I do," Peterson said, not entirely convinced. Tom was a loose cannon tonight, it was true, but Peterson also knew that putting a gun to the head of an intruder was an extreme measure. Still, none of this would be happening were it not for this situation. If anyone was to blame, it was the kidnappers.

Even the extortion Tom had partaken in was only because the kidnappers had created this situation. It was damnable. Damnable!

"I'll be okay," Tom said, as if trying to focus once again. "Just tell me what to do next."

Peterson thought quickly. The distraction of the regrettable death may have caused major issues. "Is the alarm going off? I don't hear it, but…any flashing? Any sign of a silent alarm?"

"N-nuh…no," Tom said, still shaken.

"Okay, grab the notebook and punch in the code you see for the place." Peterson listened to the beeps as Tom punched in the code. "Do you think anyone heard the shot?" he asked cautiously.

"Shit, I don't know. Maybe. It's pretty quiet."

"Okay…no news is good news."

"No cop, no stop?"

Peterson's lips parted into a bloody smile. He might have Tom back after all. "That's right, Tom, that's right. Okay, use the small gold-colored key with the letters, uh, CB stamped on it to open the black lock box on the wall."

He heard Tom jingle the keys and say "Got it," as the hinge squeaked open.

"Okay, inside there, you'll find the kill switch to disable the cameras, security, weight sensitive systems, everything."

A click, then "Done."

Peterson smiled, and his voice rang out like a game show host. "Well, time to go shopping, baby!"

"Right!" Tom said, almost like a veteran thief.

Moments like this excited him, and he realized that even today in these perilous situations, he was thrilled when he was doing what he did best, pulling the strings.

He had felt this way with the South America job, too. That caused him to pause, sadly, and swallow, but that only served to fill his stomach with more blood so he spat.

The South America job. La Aldea. How casually he had thought of that. His vision filled up with blood blossoms and gaping skulls again at the very memory.

He forced himself to forget it for the time being and took on that carnival barker tone again. "Head on out to the main showroom where all the glass cases are. Use the hammer and the bag."

"I'm in the main showroom with the glass cases."

"Then, do it to it! *Smash and grab! Smash…and…grab!*"

Peterson heard the cases shatter one by one as Tom greedily and excitedly emptied each one with hyperactive laughter.

"Yeah, that's it! Grab everything!" Peterson shouted, egging him on as he paced.

"Okay, that's done. Safe?"

"Safe's in the back office, combination is in the notebook. Hurry, boy, hurry!"

"That is, if they haven't changed the combination yet," Tom said over the sound of his feet crunching over broken glass.

"Ah, yeah," Peterson said, his shoulders sagging. "We need that shit. That's the most valuable stuff this place has. If the combination's been changed, somebody is getting fired when I get out of this."

"You mean *if* you–" Tom began but let the chilling thought dissolve into a mumble.

He gritted what was left of his teeth and listened closely as Tom flipped through some pages and mumbled as he dialed. Then, there was a solid click.

"Open!"

"YYYYYYYYYYYYES!" Peterson cried.

"Lookin' *good*, boss man!" Tom said as he emptied the entire content into the bag.

"Good. Just grab and go, grab and go! We're cutting it close as it is. The manager could show up to open the store any minute now."

"Got it. This shit must be worth a fortune!" Tom said. "Got it all. I'm out of here. Ah, shit!"

"What?"

"Ah, just...stepped in some blood there. Almost slipped. Never mind. Fuck it!" And after a few more sounds, the car door slammed and Tom yelled, "Hell yeah! We made it!"

"Good, but listen, Tom!" Peterson said, remembering the fun but dangerous red light running from earlier. "Just drive carefully. Don't attract attention."

"Right, right, gotcha," Tom said, clearly trying to remain calm. "So, where we headed?"

"Just head on over to the Southland first," Peterson said, then rolled through his memory for precise directions. "It's a good drive. Outskirts of town. On the corner of Booth and Lincoln, you'll find an old army surplus store. It's also a pawn shop. There's a reliable fence there whose available twenty-four-seven. His name's Dino. Lives above the shop. Shop's named after him, too. Dino's. He can get us fifty cents on the dollar for most any kind of merchandize."

"Up to a million?"

"Up to and over. You'd be surprised, Tommy. Dino has connections."

"Sounds perfecto, then, boss m–...oh."

"Tom?"

"Oh, no, oh shit!"

"What, what is it, Tom?"

"Uhhhmmmm... There's a cop behind me."

And Anthony Peterson bowed his head, wondering just how in ever-loving Hades this already horrible day could possibly have gotten any worse.

22 Truth or Consequences

9:37 AM

Anthony Peterson. Who the hell was that man after all?

He was nobody. Just another rich son of a bitch who treated the world like his own little sandbox. If things didn't go his way, he was going to take his toys and go home.

That's pretty much what Peterson had done in the past, wasn't it?

Calderon had heard every word passed between Peterson and the boss. He knew neither was a good man. Then again, Calderon wasn't a good man either.

Justin could probably attest to that now.

And, of course, he had to think of Justin again.

Knock-knock. Knock-knock. Knock-knock.

Again, as always, though, the difference was why.

Why was Calderon a cold-blooded killer? That was how he was trained. That was what he was good at. That became his job, and ultimately, it was too late to do anything else. Guys like Calderon didn't become pet shop owners. They died on the job, or they did the job forever.

Why had the boss become a cold-blooded killer? Calderon imagined it was much the same thing. He didn't know this boss prior to this job, but he could tell the man knew what he was doing. Military background. He knew just what to ask for and demanded nothing less than the best.

The boss must have been trained to kill, too, and that part of him had taken over his entire life.

But why had Anthony Peterson become a cold-blooded killer?

If that South America story was proven to be 100 percent true, that is, why?

Peterson was privileged, white, rich, spoiled, pampered, and comfortable. Even in debt, he was richer than most people could dream of. He wasn't a billionaire, but he was incredibly wealthy by the standards of most anyone on earth.

What did Peterson want for? Nothing.

Yet, someone in that village had wronged him in his little sandbox, and Anthony took his toys and went home. Worse, he decided to break all of their toys, too. Scores of people had died because mad little Anthony Peterson had a temper tantrum.

Peterson had not been trained to be a killer. He didn't kill to survive or eat. No. In fact, this Peterson son of a bitch didn't even do the killing himself. He just had other people do it to keep his hands clean.

Oh, but they weren't clean, were they?

So, what caused that? What caused Peterson to become what he became?

Calderon knew. It was just greed.

Sure, Calderon loved getting paid for what he did. He always said nothing mattered more than money. But in truth, that was simply the way he rationalized doing his dirty work.

Peterson, though? He didn't have to kill anyone. He just did it because he wanted to. As if some dark part of himself needed that power. The power of killing something. And if that dark part of him didn't get that powerful satisfaction, it would keep kicking its way through his psyche until it broke its way out of him.

Knock-knock. Knock-knock. Knock-knock.

Calderon and Peterson were not that different.

The only difference was why.

But was that 'why' good enough? Calderon wondered about that. Peterson had kids killed. Kids Justin's age and younger. So had many mercenaries killed children in the past. Did the 'why' of it really matter at all?

They were just as dead.

As dead as Justin when he finally stopped kicking.

Knock-knock. Knock-knock. Knock-knock.

As dead as pretty little Susan Peterson was going to be, if her husband didn't come through for her.

Knock-knock. Knock-knock. Knock-knock.

The *knock-knock*ing kept echoing in his head.

Was Calderon finally cracking up? What the hell?

All of these missions. All of this killing. All of the times he almost died himself. And the only thing that had ever given him PTSD was the death of his nephew.

Knock-knock. Knock-knock. Knock-knock.

They were just as dead...and Calderon still didn't feel the slightest bit bad about it. But that one little thing kept wearing at him over these months, and finally, he wanted to quit. Justin.

Maybe now was the time to retire to that island full of naked women and eat and drink until he got fat, happy and laughing, and he'd never think about the past. Not the killing. Not Justin's death. Not ever again.

Just leave the blood to someone else and retire.

Knock-knock. Knock-knock. Knock-knock.

"Knock-knock?"

The voice came from behind him, and he turned around quickly.

"You're not used to being snuck up on, are you?" one of the female mercenaries asked with a light laugh. It was Keeler, the woman who had taken Susan to the head earlier.

"This would probably be the first time ever," Calderon agreed.

"What were you thinking about?" the woman asked casually, not really interested.

Calderon took a puff from the cigarette, dropped it, and crushed it out. He took a deep breath before turning back to her and saying, "Retiring."

"Retiring, huh?" the gruff woman responded with a laugh. "Well, let's hope you're not abandoning your listening post 'til the job's done."

"Not at all," Calderon said. "When I go, I'm taking that shit with me."

"Ha-ha. That makes sense now."

"Well, that shit's expensive," Calderon added. "I'm still listening, actually," he said and pointed to his ear.

"Ah, Bluetooth. Anything good?"

Calderon laughed. "Sometimes, it's interesting. Like listening to an old radio show or something. This Pocase guy is certifiably insane." He shook his head in thought. "But most of the time, I'm just making sure everything gets recorded, and if anything important happens, I can cue the boss."

"Anything important happening now?"

Calderon cocked his head and said "Uh, yeah, sounds like that Pocase fella is getting stopped by a cop."

"Ouch. Looks like we might be slicing up that bitch after all, then."

Calderon narrowed his eyes. This woman, Keeler, was cold as ice.

He changed the subject. "The rest of the time I'm just watching that old TV to pass the time."

"TV, huh?"

"Yeah, the boss didn't ask for video monitoring."

"No? How do we know the prisoner really ripped out his teeth, then?"

Calderon chuckled. "You'd be amazed what people will do when they think they're being watched. I left a couple of button cameras in there. Not much. The boss hasn't had much interest. Peterson's not being watched. The TV is, though."

"I'm surprised you get a signal out here," Keeler laughed.

"Oh, just barely. One local station. Looks like they just have a lot of old reruns licensed. You're welcome to watch with me."

She scoffed. "I believe I'll pass. Shouldn't you be monitoring the device up there, though?"

"I multitask. I'm good at my job," Calderon informed her.

"So I hear from the boss. He said he demanded you."

Calderon coughed and then asked, "Is that why you came out here? Check to make sure I'm doing my job?"

"Not exactly." She smiled. "Actually, I just wanted a cigarette, and I don't have any."

"Ah," Calderon said.

"Can I have one of yours?"

Calderon was already reaching for the pack. He lit one for each of them, then handed one to her.

"Thank you," she said.

"Yeah," he responded in his usual uninvolved way. "Uh, hell, I'm, uh, Calderon by the way. You're Keeler?"

"I am Keeler," the woman confirmed, offering her hand. She was a sporty type woman. Lots of energy. Cute in her own dangerous way. Something didn't feel right quite about her though. Something felt...off. It was as if Keeler was just a few steps removed from humanity. And that was a hell of a thing for someone like Calderon to think, considering his own background.

They shook hands and Calderon asked, "Do you know the boss?" It was an attempt at friendliness and also at figuring the younger woman out.

"Somewhat," Keeler answered. "We've worked on a few things before. And I've been training at this compound for the past few weeks. I'm not supposed to say his name, though."

"Yeah, my contract said to just call him 'Boss.'"

"Well, it works. Beats codenames." Then, without even a beat, she looked at Calderon and asked, "So, do you think we're going to have to gut the bitch?"

Calderon blinked for a moment. Even in their line of work, such casual reference to butchering another person seemed odd. "What do you think?"

She laughed. "It doesn't bother me much either way, as long as I don't have to clean it up afterward."

Keeler took a long drag and exhaled one long white streak of smoke.

"Yeah, it's just a job," Calderon said.

"Just a job. Hey, are you really retiring?"

"Seems so."

"Why?"

"My business."

"Of course, Mr. Mystery." She laughed and coughed out smoke. "Truth is, I kinda hope she does die. One less crazy rich bitch in the world. She probably hasn't worked a day in her sad little life."

"Does that bother you?"

"Not really," Keeler said. "Just a good reason not to care if she does die."

Calderon chuckled a bit, then said, "But you said you actually do want her to die."

Keeler snickered and finished her smoke. "Yeah, I kind of do. I'll do it if the boss wants me to. I've done jobs like that before. Torture. Executions."

"And you like it?"

She laughed and gave him a playful, almost seductive smile. Was she flirting with him? "I get off on it."

"Killing?"

"It's just a job," she echoed him. "But what a job it is! I can't believe you'd want to retire from these thrills."

"How do you mean?"

She took a deep puff, then looked at him again with that seductive, yet silly, grin. "You know, it takes a very special kind of person to do what we do. Not just the skills, but that too. I mean it takes a really special kind of person to do our work *well*. Practice it, you know? Love it enthusiastically!"

Calderon studied her up and down, sizing her up. "And you love it enthusiastically?"

"Most of it. The thrill of it." She seemed to think for a moment, though Calderon got the impression she didn't really have to think about her answer. "Yeah, I do. I get off on that 'I am become death' feeling, like I said."

With that, Keeler let out a joyful laugh. It was childlike for such a tough woman. She really did love the thrill, didn't she?

Any other day, Calderon might laugh with her, just to keep up the appearance of camaraderie. She wasn't his type of person. She wasn't professional, it seemed. Oh, well-trained, sure, or she wouldn't be there, but she didn't take the job professionally. She took the wrong parts seriously and the wrong parts as funny. He would have laughed with her and moved on any other day, never to work with her again.

This day, however, he was decidedly annoyed.

"So, it wouldn't bother you if this innocent woman got raped and murdered, just because her husband couldn't come up with all that money?"

She thought about it for a moment, then turned to look Calderon in the eye. She was a relatively pretty girl. Short, practical brown hair, brown eyes, no makeup. She didn't need makeup to be attractive, but she didn't seem to care if she was attractive either. She looked like a soldier. She simply, and this was nothing to do with her gender, didn't strike Calderon as a professional soldier.

Instead of answering after that moment, she said, "Can I have another one of your cigarettes?"

"Uh, sure." He nodded and pulled two more out. "So, it doesn't bother you?" he asked as he handed her a lit cancer stick.

"What, like you've never killed anyone innocent before?" she mocked.

"Oh, I have, yeah," he said. "I'm not an angel."

"Neither am I."

"I can tell. But maybe, I've been thinking, maybe we're not all that different from the Petersons," Calderon admitted.

Keeler pushed him backwards playfully and said, "If they're like us, they deserve to die for sure."

Calderon didn't laugh. Instead, he was careful to stay in the shade as he had trained himself.

"I'm serious, though," Calderon said. "I mean, look at her. Different background, sure, but she's about your height and weight and build and even age. You two probably think the same way about a lot of things. You know, had things been different, you could be in her same situation right now."

"Strapped to a chair about to be cut up by mercenaries?" Keeler joked.

"You know what I mean."

She sighed and shook her head. That half-smile never left her face. "Yeah, I know. And, ha-ha, you're right. We are a lot the same. Physically, at least. We have the same body type. I noticed that while I was wiping the bitch's ass."

"Uh-huh."

She laughed again. "But, no. I wouldn't want her life. I like what I'm doing now. Look at us, okay? Why do we have the same body? I'm constantly working on my training. She's probably taking yoga and wasting her time on a Stairmaster watching reality shows."

This time, Calderon did chuckle. "The difference is why," he said.

Keeler laughed back. "Yeah, exactly that. We're completely different. Her life doesn't offer any thrills for me. Besides, I don't have any sympathy for bitches like her who don't think about anybody but themselves."

"Did she say something to give you that impression?"

Keeler laughed again. "Nah, just like you, I won't talk to her. But I know the type. Spoiled princess. Rich beau. Thinks everyone else is trash. She'd probably look down on me for staying fit by training instead of, you know, her way. The easy, pristine way." Keeler took a puff and made a sour face as she analyzed Susan Peterson. "You know, if I knew for sure she was going to die in the end, I'd probably do this job for free, you know it?"

"Really?"

Keeler scoffed, "Well, yeah, why not? We get plenty of money to do what we love. I started out doing it for free anyway."

"You started out as a mercenary for free?" Calderon asked, skeptically.

She laughed to herself. "No, not that. Mercenary work is just the wrapper around the real job. *Mercenary* is just the nice word we use instead of *killer for hire.*"

Calderon narrowed his eyes. What she was saying was not accurate. Mercenaries did more than their fair share of killing, and sometimes, it got ugly like this job, but killing was hardly the only part of the job. Often, it was peacekeeping, guarding, threatening violence to prevent violence. There was training, espionage, listening.

Killing was the outcome, often, and many mercenaries such as Calderon himself had grown numb and emotionless to the killing, but Keeler...she seemed to be suggesting she was in it for the killing above all else. As if the money was even secondary to her enjoyment of that death. No life mattered to her more than her love of ending life. Yet, Keeler had accused Mrs. Peterson of thinking only of herself. Irony.

"You're saying you kill for free outside of the job?" Calderon asked, genuinely curious, but chilled inside.

She looked up at him with her brown eyes. She no longer looked tough and badass, but like an innocent young woman or even girl.

"Can you keep a secret?" she asked.

"That's a big part of our job," Calderon said.

"Yeah, it is. But this one...I don't know. I feel like you'd understand." She looked up at his face, studying it. Her speech slowed, and she moved to a more thoughtful tone. "I think maybe you retiring has to do with you losing something. I think maybe I can help you get it back. I think maybe I can trust you."

He exhaled and tried to hide how much this woman disturbed him. She read him right, mostly, but maybe she didn't quite understand the difference of why. He said, "Trust me. I'm listening."

She sighed an exhale of smoke as if to prepare herself for this speech. "It started, for me, with the kill. I started doing it as soon as I could lift a gun. Junkyard near my dad's place? Rats everywhere. I started going down there all the time to shoot them with my old twenty-two, and I'd just leave them there, or I'd take the bodies and put them into lots of cool shapes and hope I freaked somebody out. Even spelled out a few threats here and there in rat bodies, you know, just for fun. That's how I ended up being a sharpshooter, practicing on rats, you know?"

"That's a good start," Calderon agreed, and he meant it. The ability to hit small, moving targets was a coveted skill in this line of work.

"Then, later on, I used to take pets from the neighbors, bring them there, and hunt them. Dogs. Cats. Even a rabbit once. Guinea pigs are no fun, though. They're just fatter, slower rats."

Calderon was starting to get to a new level of discomfort. Up until now, he had been satisfied talking to Keeler because she kept his mind off of Justin. But now…if the difference was why, her 'why' was disturbing.

"You killed a lot of pets that way?"

"Sometimes. But the problem there was I ended up having to hide the pets, and I usually hate cleanup. See, if they never find the pets, then they just ran away, right? If they find a big pile of dead pets, then somebody out there is killing them, so they find me. Not worth it. You know the expression, 'truth or consequences'? Well, the truth is, I hate consequences, so I ended up hunting other shit after a while."

"Like what?" Calderon said, eyes narrowed.

"Deer. With my dad, you know?"

"Uh-huh."

"Squirrels."

"Right."

"Armadillos."

"Interesting."

"Even a razorback or two."

"Wow," Calderon said, impressed but without mirth.

"And all of them were all the same to me, you know?" She finished her cigarette, stomped it, and then put both arms up, flexing them in an intentionally comical, victorious way as she sang out "The thrill of the kill!"

"The thrill of the kill indeed," Calderon chuckled, hiding his disgust as he listened to her.

"That's what I think people miss. 'I am become death.' It's all about the thrill of the kill. Any kill. It's all the same," she said.

"No matter what it is?"

"No matter what you kill. And then…well…" she whispered that next part, "I graduated."

"From high school?"

She laughed and slugged him in the arm. "No, fool! Well, I mean, yes, I did, but that's not what I meant. I meant I graduated to the next level of hunting. I started killing people."

"Really?"

"Oh, yeah. Bums. Homeless guys. Hobos. Drifters. The people nobody ever would miss. Some of them were strong, so I ended up using them for knife practice. I got real good too," she said, with excitement.

"Bums."

"Yeah, bums. And I'm a cutie, too, so getting them to follow me was never hard. A lot of the time, they even thought it was their idea." Keeler affected a deep voice and thicker southern accent to get her point across. "Look at the cute tomboy girl over there. I gotta get me some of *that*."

"And you killed them," Calderon said.

"It wasn't always easy, but I didn't want it easy. I wanted the challenge. That was my thrill. I learned to fight, use knives, different guns. So, by the time I joined the army, I was real good. They gave me the training I needed, sent me off to Afghanistan, and I had myself a time."

"Lots of killing, huh?" Calderon asked.

"Some. Rules of engagement, though." She nodded, then took another cigarette he offered her. As he lit it for her, she continued. "Can't kill willy-nilly. I did a few and just hid them. Did my time, discharged, went soldier of fortune. Natural outcome, I guess."

"I guess," Calderon said, still unnerved. "I'll bet you've got some stories."

"Oh, not as good as yours, I'll bet, old man," Keeler laughed, playfully, still looking Calderon up and down.

Calderon faked a laugh and lit his own cigarette. "I do get around," he admitted.

"That!" Keeler said. "Exactly that. That's my very favorite thing about doing these jobs?"

"Getting around?"

"Yeah, sort of," she said.

"More than the killing?"

"Well, it all goes back to that, right? We travel, we keep training, we learn the right tools for the right jobs." She looked at Calderon and he nodded, so she continued. "See, my favorite way to test my equipment is in public. On the streets, you know?"

He shrugged. "Not really."

She pouted for a second and then said, "Okay, so when you get a new weapon, you probably like to go out to a shooting range and test it out, right?"

"Right. Target shooting. Adjust your sights, get used to the trigger."

"See, I do that, but I prefer to do it on the streets. Like, if I get a new sniper rifle, I like to go to a public park or something." Her eyes got wider, more excited, more insane the more she described it. "Then, I climb way up in a tree and I take aim. It's much more like what we do for a living." She smiled, puffed, and went on with her story. "Moving targets, right? And completely unexpected. Nobody expects that!"

Calderon narrowed his eyes. "You shoot at people?"

"Sometimes. Sometimes, I just pick off a dog while its owner is walking it. Sometimes, I'll take out half a couple. The other one doesn't know what happened at first. They just freak out."

Calderon was suddenly not feeling well, which was strange because he was far from squeamish. "So, you actually are randomly killing on the street?"

"'I am become death,' Calderon! I told you I'd do it for free if I wasn't getting paid." She laughed. "Oh, I killed two gay guys fucking in a park once. That was my two for one. They died happy, at least. Once I caught a guy sneaking a smoke behind the bathrooms. Boom. His family kept searching for him for hours."

"I see," Calderon mumbled.

"And one time…" She leaned in with a conspiratorial whisper. "I took out a baby in a carriage."

"A baby?" Calderon said, attempting to mask his horror. It wasn't appropriate to be unprofessional, even when faced with this.

"Well, it wasn't my first kid," she chuckled. "Just the only baby so far. In one side of the carriage, out the other. They didn't even know the kid was dead for a while."

Calderon quickly lit a cigarette with shaking fingers. The more she spoke, the more he thought of Justin.

"Just right through the carriage. The mom didn't even realize something was wrong for several minutes." Keeler paused and looked back at Calderon's sweat-beaded face with concern. "Hey, are you all right?" Keeler asked.

"Oh, I'm fine," Calderon lied quickly. "Just wondering what your story has to do with getting around."

She laughed again and said, "Oh, right. Well, that's the best part. If you get a bunch of kills like that in one city, you've got a serial killer, right? Big public outcry and a manhunt. Remember the DC Beltway Sniper?"

"I do," Calderon said.

"But, see, I travel all over the world, and anywhere in the world I go, I practice that. I become death. One shot. Only one. A dog, a girlfriend, a husband, a kid at play, a lonely old man playing chess. I watch the reactions for a while, then I scramble back down and drive away. I monitor the news in that city for the next few days. They're always clueless, and nobody's ever put my kills together. They're all so random and far apart No consequences."

"That's…that's…you must be very skilled," Calderon said, searching for the right words. He no longer felt like looking Keeler in the eye, so he just looked down at her body.

"I like to think so," she said cheerfully. "Oh, uh, you like what you see?" she asked, misinterpreting his gaze at her body. She then gave a playful model pose with her hands on her hips.

"It's…very nice. You're very fit, you're right," he said, but stayed on topic. "So, that's why you don't care if Mrs. Peterson dies? Even though you admit you're not much different?"

"I said we're physically similar. Only. But what do you mean? What reason?"

"Well, you're talking about killing innocent people as a hobby. Your hobby."

"Right."

"You're saying since you love doing that, you also love the idea of Mrs. Peterson getting cut to bits?"

Keeler shrugged. "Not exactly. But you're close." She held her hand out for another cigarette and waited until he handed her one. "What I'm saying is that it's all the same. It's *all* random. These people…they never get an answer as to how or why some stray bullet came out of nowhere and killed their greyhound mid-walk. The couple in Dusseldorf, they had no reason to expect one bullet to go through both their hearts. It's senseless, isn't it? The family looking for the dad? They will never know who shot him or why. Because there *is* no why. There *are* no answers. It's just random craziness." She took a step closer and leaned in to say, "It's just…life."

"It's just life?" Calderon asked, looking up at her.

"Well, yeah. You get it, don't you? I can tell you've had your history, and it's something else. How many kills?"

"I've lost count," he said, truthfully.

"I knew it," she agreed. "You get it. Just like me, you become death. It's our living. The randomness, the killing."

"The baby?"

"His or her parents will *never* know," Keeler said, missing any thought of morality. "And for the rest of their lives, they'll wonder.

They'll wonder who did it. They'll demand answers. They'll need to know why. They'll question themselves. What if they had gone down a different street? What if they hadn't gone out that day at all? They'll want to know why police weren't patrolling. In a weird way, I gave them purpose."

"I guess you did."

"And you've done the same."

"I haven't sniped strangers for no reason."

"Well, not yet, anyway." Keeler giggled in that wide-eyed, playful murderer way. "But that's the thing. There are no reasons. You do it for money, you do it for the thrill, you do it because you're pissed off. It doesn't matter. There is no difference. They're just as dead, no matter the rationale."

Her words hit him hard. What was Keeler, a mind-reader?

"Hey, you keep looking at my body," she giggled.

"Uh, you're very fit," Calderon responded casually.

"No, I don't mind. I've been looking at yours!" she laughed "You, uh, maybe want to get together later? After this, I mean?"

Calderon narrowed his eyes and looked up at her face. Yes, she was cute and fit, that was true. Hopefully, his discomfort managed to come off as sexy. His mind reeled. New ideas, new pictures were developing from the puzzle pieces all around him. Justin, Mrs. Peterson, the boss, the job, the retirement, the blood.

And Keeler's words might have been providing the very means to finishing this new concept. The final missing piece, as it were. Keeler was the key, wasn't she?

"Yes!" Calderon said, suddenly happy and excited as Keeler had just been. "Yes, actually, I think that's an excellent idea. You might be just what I'm looking for." He looked back down at her body and gave her a once-over. "Yeah, you might just be what I'm looking for."

"Nice," she said, running her forefinger down his chest to hitch on his belt, playfully, sexily, then fall away. She looked up at him again with her brown eyes, now inquisitive and hopeful. "You do get it, don't you? The randomness? Every death is the same. The thrill of the kill. I can't talk to just anybody about this, you know? I am become death, you know? I figured you'd get it."

"It's all random," Calderon muttered. "Death is all the same. So, you're saying you think it doesn't matter if she lives or dies?"

"Is it any different from shooting a rabbit or swatting a fly?" she asked, her eyes wide and childlike. "It's all just one death. And maybe she dies, and someone else lives later, you know? I mean, really, who cares? It's just death. Does it matter in the overall scheme of things? Besides, you know, making people like us happy."

And as he considered that incredibly absurd question, suddenly everything started to feel better and calmer. He felt enlightened in a strange unnatural way.

It was like an incomplete puzzle was finally getting its missing piece. The elements settled into place, and he rather liked the image he was seeing.

"I get it," Calderon said and gave her a smile, not forced this time.

"It doesn't matter who or what you kill. It's all the same. So, you can kill anything. When you become the truth of death, there are no consequences."

Calderon coughed and extinguished his cigarette. "That's amazing. That's pretty much exactly what I needed to hear."

"Yeah? So why retire?"

"You must be psychic."

She gave him a sexy look and got very close to him. "Well, maybe I am. And maybe I'm a lot of things."

He laughed and looked her up and down again. "Like I said, you might be just what I'm looking for."

"Now come on. Look at me in the eye, here. You don't *really* want to retire, do you? And miss all these thrills?"

He thought for a second as they turned back toward the building. "Well, I clearly have a job to do, after all."

"Yes, you do."

"For the first time in a while, I think I know exactly what to do next."

"Ah, good!" she laughed.

He followed her inside on his way back to the old television.

He had always said, "The difference is why."

Keeler had just told him that there was no difference because there was no reason. There was no why.

Hell of a philosophy. It was a new truth, and that new truth meant that with no more reasons there could be no more consequences.

He smiled, thinking of her words, her face, her crazy eyes, her body, and her stories. They all pointed to something. His next big step.

And for the moment, Calderon felt great. Absolutely great, even when he thought of Justin.

He knew just what to do.

The knocking had even left his head, and he was thinking clearly at last.

It was time for a new plan. No consequences.

23 Crash and Burn

Anthony Peterson clenched his eyes and his fist tight as he replayed Tom's words in his head. "There's a cop behind me."

"Oh shit…" was all Peterson could come up with to say back to Tom. He thought fast for a plan and the right words but all he could manage was "Just…just stay calm."

"I am," Tom replied nervously. "This cop just pulled up behind me out of nowhere."

"Do you think somebody called about the shot?"

"Maybe, but… Uh…" Tom sounded dumbstruck. "Well…I think I just figured out why he pulled out behind me."

"Why?"

"I just realized I'm still wearing my ski mask. He must have spotted me as I drove by."

Peterson cringed and immediately got angry. "Why the hell are you still wearing your ski mask?" He was finding it increasingly difficult to hold in his anger with Tom.

"I don't know, I don't know. I guess I just forgot in all the excitement. I didn't even realize it until I started watching him in the rear-view mirror and caught my–"

Peterson heard the siren break through the line as Tom continued to ramble "It's just they're so comfortable and– OH SHIT! He's stopping me!"

"Tom?" Peterson spoke in a calm and direct voice. "Get out of there, Tom!"

Tom revved the engine. Lucky for Peterson, Tom loved his muscle cars. Tires squealed, but Peterson could hear the siren keeping up as the cop gave chase.

Above the roar of the engine, Peterson heard Tom's voice saying something excitedly. Peterson couldn't understand him as he clearly had dropped the phone.

"Tom?" he said, then shouted "TOM! Put the Bluetooth on!"

"Oh yeah!" Tom said, barely audibly and after a couple of beeps he said "We're losing him, Anthony!"

Peterson paced and thought hard, like a mastermind. "What street are you on now?"

"Uh...comin' up on Main annnd...Gleason."

"Hang a hard right..." he said.

"Your wish, my command!" Tom said, exasperated but maintaining his humor.

The tires squealed on the pavement as Tom made the dangerous turn, and Peterson did wild calculations in his head. Tom's adrenaline pumped and got him high enough to laugh again. "Oh, yeah! Bat...meet...HELL!"

Peterson had an answer. "Tom, listen, coming up should be an old parking garage. Old burned out neon sign says 'Playa Parking.' I want you to go in through the *exit*. The bar won't be down and don't worry about the tires, the spikes haven't worked in years."

"You better be sure."

"I am! Just head in there and keep moving."

Another tire screech and engine roar.

"I'm in. Jesus, this place is like a maze."

Peterson nodded. "Slow it down and keep it quiet. Hopefully, he didn't make it in, but if he did..."

Peterson heard the siren go by in a Doppler effect accompanied by the sound of a revved-up engine.

"That was him," Tom laughed excitedly.

"Wait, wait!" Peterson cautioned him. "He's not an idiot. Keep it slow and low till we know he's not coming back."

Tom obeyed and drove around inside the garage for a little while.

After a time, Tom said, "No sign of the cop."

"Then no stop!" Peterson said, with a bloody grin. "Now, don't head out the main rear entrance, just look to your left, and take the side exit. It lets out into an alley you can follow to Main again."

"How do you know all this?" Tom asked in amazement. "You're like a human GPS."

Peterson smiled and said professionally, "I have quite a memory, young man. Alarm codes, account numbers…even phone numbers. It's safe to say I know this city like you know the feel of your right hand."

"Well, then you must know it pretty damn well," Tom said, honestly impressed. "Side exit is coming up."

The sounds of another sharp turn followed and Tom shouted victoriously "And we're clear! No sign of him."

"Nice driving, Tommy!"

"So, what's next, papa bear?" Tom laughed, sounding like Mr. Cool as he revved the engine once again and caused his tires to squeal in acceleration.

"Just keep going straight—" but Peterson was cut off by a new cacophonous mishap.

"Oh shit!" Tom shouted in panicked terror as Peterson heard Tom's wheels braking quickly and noisily followed by a loud crash.

Peterson's damaged mouth fell open as he listened to wheels swerving and a horrific crunch, followed by another and another. At last, the noises began to abate. It sounded like the car had flipped over.

"Tom? *Tom!*" Peterson was not a praying man, but he was willing to beg for Tom to be alive.

Metal screeches and scratching sounds continued before things went silent for a second…and Tom finally allowed himself to breathe.

"Tom!" Peterson said hopefully as he heard Tom's coughs.

"Yeah. Give me a second," he said in a strained voice as he crawled out of the wreckage. Peterson waited as he heard scratching sounds, gasps from Tom and broken glass hitting the pavement.

"Are you all right?"

"Yeah, I'm…I'm good!" Tom said, sounding almost as amazed as Peterson was. "I had those cross-ways professional seatbelts installed last year. It was a vanity thing at the time, but turns out they're really helpful."

Peterson exhaled and allowed himself to start pacing again. What to do next? "Are you sure you're all right?"

"I'm a little banged up," Tom said. "Got to love those seatbelts. Aw, but my car is totally *totaled*!"

"What the hell happened?" Peterson asked.

"Freak accident. Fuckin' other car came out of nowhere, and I had to swerve to keep from hittin' it. Ran right into a lamp post. Knocked the fucker down at the base like a lumberjack. The damn thing's just…lying across the road like a big old tree, man."

"And the other car?"

"I didn't hit 'em. But the lamp post fell and crushed it."

Peterson started. "And the people inside?"

"Hang on, shit."

Peterson heard cloth rustling again and asked, "Tom, what is it?"

"Can you hear me?"

"Not as well, but yeah, if you talk in that voice. Why?"

"There was a whole family in there. They're okay. A couple of cuts and scratches, but I saw they were all tweeting about it and taking selfies, so I had to pull down my ski mask again. I just had it up around my head like one of those old-style burglars, you know?"

"Tom, spare me the play-by-play, would ya?"

"Right, uh…yeah, so they're all sitting over there on the curb with their phones. Big family. Cousins, maybe. Doesn't sound like they speak English, either. How the hell did they fit so many of 'em in one damn car? Musta been a clown car."

Peterson was impatient. "Tom. Can you get the goods and get the hell out of there?"

With those words, Peterson heard a siren approaching, and he knew the answer was not going to be 'yes.'

"Uh…well, there's a new problem with that."

"What now?" Peterson whispered in exasperation.

"That same cop just drove up. Looks like he's calling the accident in on his radio."

"Tom, get out of there."

"I can't just get out of here; the stuff is still in the car. You know, the car that's registered to *me*?" Tom mumbled to keep from being heard.

"Does he see the license plate?"

"I don't think so," Tom mumbled some more. "It's bent in half, but…"

"I know! I know!" Peterson said, terrified. If Tom ran off, he could claim the car was stolen by the same people who robbed the store.

The problem with that was Peterson had no other ideas of how to get the money, and that meant his life and Susan's life were both forfeit. If Tom ran, Peterson was dead.

"Okay, just stay there but stay calm, Tom. You've already done so much today. You've proven you've got brass balls, kid. You can face this too."

"Shit, he's walking toward me. Looks like the goddamn Incredible Hulk."

"He's just a guy, Tom. How big can he be?"

"Huge," Tom said, and Peterson froze. "And he looks *seriously* pissed off."

How gigantic must that cop be for Tom to be intimidated? The guy boxed for years. "Okay, just run. We'll reformulate a plan, maybe get you to rob the impound lot."

"Shut…up…Anthony," Tom hissed in a terrified whisper. "His gun is drawn."

Peterson's eyes were the size of saucers now, and he pressed the phone to his ear, listening. He turned the volume up to hear all he could through the ski mask, but he was ready to throw the phone if there was more gunfire.

"Hands up! Drop what you're holding and put your hands in the air *now*!" he heard the agitated street cop command.

Peterson heard the phone drop, and he whispered, "Tom, are you there? What's happening."

Tom's only response was a light "Shh, shh, shh!"

"Down on your knees!" came the cop's voice again.

"You got it, officer, you got it!" Tom said reassuringly.

"Lace both hands behind your head."

"Okay! Okay! It's cool! It's cool!"

Peterson heard the mask rustle again against the microphone as Tom's breathing increased sharply.

Peterson heard the click of handcuffs, and Tom grunted while one of his arms was being pulled down. "Tom?"

"Argh!" Tom shouted, and Peterson heard a solid punch followed by sounds of a scuffle, the family shouting in surprise and something metal hitting the pavement.

"Get your mitts off me, motherfucker!" Tom growled, and Peterson heard three more punches, followed by the sound of a very heavy body hitting the ground and Tom's panting.

"Tom? Tom!"

"He's out," Tom panted. "I knocked…huh…huh…I knocked him out."

"You what?"

Tom hyperventilated and finally said, "Golden Gloves, remember? The man is down for the count."

"How?"

Tom gasped a few more times and said, "I waited 'til he had my wrist cuffed, and while he was concentrating on that arm, I swung around with the other and knocked the gun out of his… fucking enormous hand. Then a few body blows and…fuck this guy is strong… Anyway, I got a clear shot at his chin and knocked him out with one punch."

"Sounded like a lot more than one."

"One punch *to the chin*, Anthony."

"Right."

Tom laughed in surprise and triumph. "I can't believe I just did that."

"Neither can I, Tom, but as you so eloquently pointed out earlier, the clock is really ticking here. What else is happening?"

"The family is tweeting about it. I think they got some video. I better Google myself later. Good thing I pulled the ski mask down," he said, catching his breath and giggling.

Peterson thought fast. "Tom how much gasoline do you have?"

"Huh? I keep a spare tank in the trunk, why?"

Peterson smiled. "Can you get to it?"

"Uh, yeah, I think so," he said "Looks like the only part of the car that isn't wrecked. The rear license plate was knocked off, though."

"Can you find it?"

"It's right over there. I'm looking at it," Tom said.

"Get it and get the gas can too. Then, I need you to take off your front license plate."

"It's all bent down, why?"

"Because, Tom, I need you to torch the car."

Tom scoffed, "Torch my fucking Charger, are you fucking insane?"

"Tom? If you don't do this, you're going to jail, and if you go to jail, then I'm dead. That cop already called it in, and his buddy boys in blue will be there any second now. So, what I need you to do is get a screwdriver, rip off that license plate, get anything in the goddamn car that can be traced back to you, license, registration, pictures of your kids, and soak it in gasoline, then douse the rest of the car with gas and light it up."

"Well...okay," Tom said reluctantly but seeing the logic in Peterson's words.

"Put the license plates and anything you really need to keep in the bag with the jewels."

"You want me to get the bag of jewels out first?"

"*Yes, I want you to get the bag of jewels out first, Tom!*" Peterson shouted at possibly the stupidest question he had ever heard.

"Oh, right, because of the…right."

"And get the VIN number off of the dashboard, too."

"The what?"

"The little metal plate on the dashboard, rip it out with the screwdriver and take it with you. Once we all get out of this, you're going to report the car stolen. That'll fit the story. They'll be looking for the guy who did this forever while you sit back and laugh with your new Charger, courtesy of your insurance company."

"Oh, okay. That sounds good. Real good! I'm on it!"

Peterson listened to the sounds of metal on metal, followed by paper rustling, jewels hitting each other in the bag, and finally liquid pouring over Detroit steel.

"Okay, you ready?"

Peterson pumped his fist in nervous excitement. "Now handcuff the cop with his own cuffs. Hogtie the bastard and lock him face down in the backseat of his police car. No, better yet, the trunk."

"Okay," Tom said, and Peterson listened to him grunt and curse about how heavy the guy was. "Done," he gasped at last.

"Now, light it up, baby, light it up!"

Peterson listened to Tom whisper, "Bye-bye, baby!" before a Zippo lighter clicked, followed by the unmistakable whoosh of flame rushing over the car. "Burn, baby, burn!" Peterson heard Tom exclaim as the family shouted in surprise and fear.

Peterson continued, fist still clenched and pounding. "Now, quickly, get into that damned police car and drive the hell out of there!"

"Right!"

"Switch your ski mask for the cop's hat once you're on the road. And do it fast! Remember, that cop's backup is on the way."

Peterson could hear Tom hustling. The engine roared, and the siren blared. "What a rush! We're outta here!" Tom shouted.

"Kill the siren, Tom," Peterson said obviously.

"Oh, right, sorry," Tom responded, still slightly muffled, as the siren ceased.

"And Tom? Ski mask."

"Right, right," he said, removing the mask and throwing it in the back.

"Now, get your ass to the fence and cash out!" Peterson said and then repeated the directions.

"That's...wow, that's not a short drive, Anthony."

Peterson scoffed. "Two questions. One, do you have anything better to do, and two, do you think I'm stupid enough to send you in a stolen cop car with stolen jewelry to a fence close to where you stole all that shit?"

"Okay, I got it, I got it," Tom said. "So, this fence, do you trust him?"

"Implicitly," Peterson said. "You wouldn't believe the things he's moved for me. There's not a thing he can't buy or sell."

"Really?" Tom said, interested. "Well then, do you think he could fence this police car?"

Peterson was taken aback. He hadn't thought of that. "Definitely..." He considered for a moment, then added, "Maybe. Ask him."

"What about the pig hogtied in the back?"

"Strip him bare ass naked and leave him cuffed face down in an alley somewhere before you reach the fence. Odds are he'll be too embarrassed to include much in his report about it."

"Good, that's good," Tom laughed.

"Then, cash out, take your share, and deposit the rest to my account. Then, we've got to get the money to them."

Anthony felt the phone vibrate in his hand. He looked at the screen and immediately felt a chill. It was the kidnapper's telephone number. He had texted Peterson the account and routing numbers to transfer the ransom to.

They were ready.

That meant that time was of the essence. It was nowhere near one o'clock AM, the actual deadline. Hell, it wasn't even one o'clock PM yet, but neither the kidnappers nor Anthony himself wanted to race the clock. The sooner this was done, the better.

"Make it *fast*, Tom!" Anthony said, feeling a lump in his throat. "You've got a long drive ahead of you, and I'm almost out of time here. I will be soon, anyway."

"Done and done, Anthony. You sit tight. I'll keep you posted. I don't want to attract too much attention in this thing, for all of our sakes."

"Thank you, Tom," he smiled.

Peterson stayed on the line to make sure all went well.

It wasn't his preferred method for passing the time, but there was little chance he could get bored in this situation.

24 Loose Ends

Anthony Peterson eyed the battery level on the cheap phone with the expensive case. He didn't know how many hours it had been. He had stopped counting and inside this coffin of his, it was always night.

But he hung on the line. After all of this, the torture, the betrayal, the supplication to Tom's selfish will, this was probably the most important part of this entire affair. The collection of the last few dollars.

Anthony and Susan Peterson might well survive after all. But only if this went well, only if these constant disasters stopped happening and only if Tom didn't stab him in the back again.

Tom had dropped the now-stirring cop off in an alleyway a few miles from the fence. It took longer than planned, as the cop hadn't slept long and he sure as hell kept fighting. Tom couldn't get the cop's shirt off without un-cuffing him, so he settled for just taking everything he had from the waist down, plus his badge. Peterson laughed as he heard the cop cursing after the ski-masked Tom.

Dino Dennison, Peterson's implicitly trusted fence was, much like Doctor Ivy, a morally malleable citizen. Not actually a member of the Mafia, but happy to take mob money to keep the lifestyle extravagant. Anthony Peterson was no mobster, but he was starting to realize more and more that he was far from being a good man.

Peterson called ahead to get Dino ready for Tom's visit, but even then, he insisted on using the three-way calling instead of hanging up. He was going to keep Tom on the line, no matter what. This had to go right. It just had to.

"Aw, Jesus!" Tom said as the motor slowed.

"What?" Anthony said, wide-eyed and white-knuckled. "What is it now?"

"This place is a goddamn dive, man."

"Well, what were you expecting, the goddamn Piccadilly Circus? It's not just anywhere that you can sell stolen goods for fast cash. It's not going to be pretty."

"Okay, I get it, I get it. We're here."

Peterson's whisper was becoming a growl. "Tom, do what he said. Bring the car around back. He can't–"

"He can't have a stolen police car sitting out front, I know, I heard him as well as you did."

"Just do this by the book. I'm dead soon if you don't, millionaire," Anthony hissed.

Around back was a fenced-in lot with black nylon mesh lining the roof-tall chain link fence. Tom smiled and said, "Appropriate for a fence."

"No puns."

"Hey, there he is."

Dino Dennison waved Tom into the lot and pointed to a cleared-out area, just the right size for the car.

"Nice," Tom said and hopped out. "Tom Pocase."

"Dino," came the hoarse response. Dino was not a man of many words.

"Meetcha," Tom said.

"You wear gloves this whole time?" Dino asked.

"Yeah, and I had this ski mask over my hair the whole time," Tom said, sounding self-satisfied as a kid who brought home a C+ after a series of Fs.

"You ain't wearin' it now."

"Oh, right, I threw it in the back. I'm not balding, though, who cares?"

"I'll get it all cleaned up, anyway. It'll be stripped after that. Well, come on in."

Tom followed and did as Dino told. When haggling was needed, Peterson had the phone handed to Dino.

Peterson knew damn well that he wasn't going to get top dollar. Half of what the merch was worth, at best, but if it was enough to save Peterson's wife and life, that was good enough for him.

Besides, he'd had that jewelry place insured to the hilt, so he'd get it all back. Free money, baby!

He smiled to himself at the thought. He was already making a profit off of this whole thing. He'd be back, and he'd get his revenge.

After all was done, Tom was given a briefcase full of cash and sent on his merry way.

"Aw, wait, shit!" Tom said.

"What? What?" Peterson's heart could scarcely take another setback. The air was getting thin. How much time did he have?

"Well, you know how far away this place is?"

"Yeah, so?"

"So how the fuck am I supposed to get back?"

Peterson's eyes clenched tightly. Of course this was a problem. They had just sold the cop car.

"Goddamn it, Tom!" Peterson whispered. "Turn around and ask Dino if—"

"Oh, wow!" Tom interrupted.

"What? What now?"

"As soon as I turned around, Dino's standing there with a set of keys."

"Oh, thank GOD!" Peterson gasped.

Dino's voice took over. "Now, this is just a junker. Good trade-in. I factored that in to the cash I gave you. If you ain't gonna keep it, let me know where you leave it. I can always use it again."

"Ha-ha-ha! You got it. Thanks, Dino," Tom said.

"Tell Anthony I hope to see him soon."

"Anthony, he says—"

"I heard him, I heard him!"

"So long!" Tom chimed as he turned around.

"Uh, Tom?" Peterson asked as Tom left the building,

"Yeah, Anthony."

"Please tell me you didn't torch your laptop."

"Nope. As they say at the horse races, it's in the bag."

"Good. Glad you didn't fence that thing either."

They both laughed for a moment, and Tom said, "Dennison did offer me a good price for it."

Anthony said, "Well, we did it. Get in the jalopy, get that cash into the bank. ATM, late night teller, whatever it takes—"

"Anthony, the banks are open now, man," Tom said.

"Really?" The dark was taking its toll on Peterson. "Good, good, then, so then go ahead and wire that money into…hang on!" He flipped through his texts and then read off the account number.

"Got it. I got it. Consider it done."

"Text me when the transfer is complete."

"You got it."

"And Tom?" Peterson almost hated himself for what he was about to say, but his relief got the best of him. "Take an extra fifty Gs for your troubles."

"Hey, hey, the man is a tipper!" Tom laughed. "I'm on it. Oh, and boss man?"

"Yeah?"

"I'll see you at work on Monday," Tom said, with a confident smile in his voice.

Peterson grinned. He might live to see another day after all.

25 The Mounting Evidence

2:13 PM

Anthony Peterson was the subject of the day. The man was just rich enough, just powerful enough, and just well-known enough for the department to move as quickly as possible. In today's world, if the media got hold of a kidnapping story, and it looked like the cops were not doing enough, it could lead to complete and utter bedlam.

Detective Gilley didn't like this at all. It was about to become a circus, and Gilley would have vastly preferred to be on the streets looking for the guy than inside talking about it.

He stood in the back of the large conference room with a toothpick in his mouth. It was his little substitute for the cigarettes he had given up months before. He could use one now, especially after having dealt with that whiny, drunk, spoiled little Evan Peterson kid.

Detective Austen took his place beside Gilley as the rest of the team filed in.

"You believe this?" Austen asked.

Gilley shook his head. "Remember when that little black girl went missing, and it took everybody two days to get in gear? Ever seen anything this fast?"

"Hell no, man. They got court orders, search warrants, GPS, the works," Austen sneered.

Gilley bowed his head, pretended to scratch his nose to cover his mouth, and mumbled back to Austen, "Yeah, yeah, yeah. Seems like the only way a missing person's case gets any attention these days is if you happen to·be a rich white guy."

"Ain't that the truth?" Austen agreed. "They say this here is a 'special case,' which means…ah, well, let's just listen, then."

The detectives and the rest of the room silenced themselves as the Lieutenant took to the podium.

"All right, all right, boys and girls, let's get this shit-show on the road," Lieutenant James said.

The tall man looked like a throwback to a 1980s cop show and sounded like a throwback to a 1980s Nyquil ad. He wore out-of-date brown suits with vests. His hair, mustache, and sideburns were straight out of central casting for a *Hill Street Blues* flashback. Gilley often wondered what it was like to be out of style by decades. Lieutenant James always interrupted his own speech with a cough that never seemed to leave his voice, and he also consistently sounded as if he had just woken up with the mother of all hangovers.

"All right, that's enough, quiet," the Lieutenant boomed.

"How can he be so loud and still sound like he just got out of bed?" Gilley said quietly to Austen as the attendees quieted down.

"Something funny there, Austen?"

"Not a thing, Lieutenant. You've got our attention."

"Good, good. Let's keep it that way. Fring?" Lieutenant James leaned over to talk to an aid. "Is this the latest and the greatest?" he mumbled and then had a brief and muted discussion about whether or not the report he held in his hand was indeed the greatest in addition to being the latest.

Meanwhile, the four rows of seated cops waited in mild frustration at the delay. "More hurry up and wait," Austen muttered.

"Yeah, get your shit together and schedule the meeting after that," Gilley agreed.

"Okay, the latest and the greatest," James droned as he stood back up to the podium. As he flipped through the report, staring down through his reading glasses he repeated, "The laaaaaaaaaatest and the greatest. The latest…and…the greatest," a few times to Gilley's intense annoyance.

When the hell did people in management decide to start adding 'and the greatest' after the word 'latest'? And why did it have to be said every single time? It was intensely irritating to Gilley and anyone like him.

As if finally remembering he had an audience in front of him, the Lieutenant looked up and addressed his officers at last.

"All right, everyone. We are all here to discuss the *possible* kidnapping of this man." He nodded to Fring, who pushed a button on the remote control to bring up a decidedly unfriendly looking picture of the subject onto the screen behind the lieutenant. "Anthony Peterson," James said. "Local businessman. Missing since at least early this morning, possibly yesterday evening."

The cops in the room took notes and nodded as the droning lecture continued.

"Also, seemingly missing and possibly kidnapped is Peterson's wife, Susan." The button was pushed again, and Peterson's face was replaced by that of a very pretty woman in her thirties with long brown hair and green eyes. This resulted in mumbles and whistles throughout the crowd. "Right, right, right, she's good looking. Decorum, please," James said and coughed.

Officer Witrack waved a hand in the air and spoke before being recognized. "You keep saying 'possibly' and 'seemingly.' Are we really putting this much effort into looking for a guy who might just be out on another goddamn fishing trip?"

There were chuckles throughout the mostly controlled crowd, and Lieutenant James coughed a few more times before leaning in toward the podium microphone and continuing. "Right, right. We all remember the story of the actor from last year. Who was it?"

"Kent," Fring said, barely audibly.

"Right, Kurt Kent, the actor. For those of you who don't know, he was reported missing a year or so ago, and we all went hog wild on the search. By the time night rolled around, it turned out the guy had been on a thirteen-hour deep-sea fishing trip with his mistress, which is why his wife didn't know about it."

"He got a hell of a sunburn to go with his divorce, too," Gilley called from the back, causing more chuckling.

"That he did," Lieutenant James admitted. "And, yes, it might turn out to be exactly that way, but this is Los Angeles. You know how things are. If we don't act, we look bad. If we do act, we look—"

"Slightly less bad?" Austen offered from the back.

"Good enough. So, we're moving on this one under the assumption that this kidnapping is real." James said, then coughed a few times and continued. "Now, what do we know? Well, not much. Early this morning a call came from Anthony Peterson to his adult son Evan Peterson who, soon after, reported the father missing. Peterson and the step-mother, Susan. Detective Gilley went to see him and ultimately brought him in."

James nodded to Gilley who picked it up from there, speaking loudly over the crowd without a microphone. "Right. I've got him cooling his heels in one of the interrogation rooms with a big pot of coffee. He's not a suspect, but he's a material witness right now. Thing is, he's also drunk as hell and kind of belligerent, so it's hard to know if we can trust him as far as we can throw him."

James took back over. "True, so in the meantime, Burns sent out officers Riley and Gonzales to check out the Petersons' house." He turned the page in his report and looked back up. "Instead of finding Peterson playing lawn darts in his bathrobe, they found the front door wide open." The projector switched to a digital picture of the front of the house. "It seemed like someone was in a big hurry to leave because the door was thrown open hard enough to crack the window in it and bend the hinge. Whoever the hell it was is a strong guy."

James looked up at the crowd for any reaction or questions, then kept going.

"Around that same time, a call was coming in about a rampaging attack dog." The projector switched to an image of a mean-looking black dog. "Turns out the neighbors recognized the pooch as—" cough, cough "—get this, 'Satan,' the new guard dog purchased by the Petersons. The bad pooch was running around, terrorizing the neighbors until one of them gave him some leftover chicken. Now, he's putty in their hands."

"Good boy," Witrack called out, causing a few more chuckles.

Lieutenant James patted the air again and said, "Now, just sit back, people, because here's where it gets a lot more serious." The officers quieted themselves. "The alarm was shut off, so clearly the burglar had the code. We've got some blood on the stairs and the back porch that we're looking at, but aside from some apparent rummaging in the bedroom, it doesn't look like anything of value was taken. No real signs of struggle either. The Petersons apparently kept the place pretty damned clean. We're looking for fingerprints, but so far, we're coming up blank."

"And the blood?" Austen asked.

"Not sure. Still being analyzed. That might be the key, but it's too soon to tell."

"Yeah, they'll have it in a half hour," Austen said under his breath as Gilley nodded to him.

"Now, if that was all, it would still be enough to get us moving on this. We don't want the press to find out about this and start asking questions we can't answer." Lieutenant James coughed.

"Sir? Officer Hall," a young, female officer said. "Is he really that big a name?"

James nodded. "He's a well-known businessman. Enough that his picture on the front page is going to look bad. As far as we know, he's kind of a snake in the grass, but a single TV news story can turn him into a pillar of the community and everyone from Walt the postman to the Mayor himself will start screaming that one of our finest citizens is missing."

Fring leaned in toward the microphone and said, "And, officially, it doesn't matter how big a name he is. We treat all kidnappings the same." The officers groaned and chuckled at the bogus claim, so Fring continued, "We'll put a community liaison in front of the cameras when the time is right, but for now the most important thing is getting out in front of this."

As he leaned back out, Lieutenant James coughed a couple of times and added, "Whether this is actually a kidnapping or not."

"You said there's more?" Officer Nopke asked.

"Much," James affirmed, and the screen then showed a jewelry storefront. "This is Fairfax Unlimited Jewelers. It was broken into, also early this morning. From what we could tell from when the alarm code was entered, this was not too long after the Peterson place was hit."

A few hands went up, but James ignored them. "Tragically, this was no mere jewelry heist. The place was cleaned out, yes, and the thief or thieves also apparently killed–" the image on the screen changed again to a uniformed man in a pool of blood "–this man. Pedro Antonio Americano, security guard for FUJ."

The crowd responded with shocked murmurs and muted conversation as Lieutenant James continued.

"Naturally, and I hope this answers your questions–" Lieutenant James coughed a few times before shifting gears. "I'm guessing your next question was what the hell this has to do with Peterson?" He saw a few nods and adjusted his train of thought. "Homicide headed out there after the uniforms called it in. When they interviewed the store manager, he identified the owner of the place as one Anthony Peterson."

Murmurs rose again.

"True, we would've found it out anyway, but the guy was nervously trying to figure out how to tell 'Mr. Peterson' out loud. So–"

"So, it looks like someone is specifically going after Peterson and his wife and their properties?" Detective Austen asked.

"Detective Gilley?"

Gilley turned to Austen and said, "That's right–" before realizing he was talking too loudly to his friend who was right next to him. He shook his head and addressed the rest of the group together. "That's the assumption we're under right now. The son, drunk bastard that he is, tells us a hell of a story. Seems like daddy called to tell him he's being kept in a shipping container–" the crowd mumbled to each other "–yeah, that's what I said. He's got limited air and…and that's beside the point for this part of the case, because the reason he called was that the dad took away Junior's trust fund and his sister's too. Says he'd be dead without it. Ransom."

"How much are we talking about?" Hall asked.

Gilley nodded to her and rubbed his hands together nervously. He never really enjoyed public speaking much.

"Well, it's still hard to get a straight answer from this kid, but the trust funds total about three million. The son seems to be indicating the total ransom is around ten million."

More murmurs and whistles from the crowd served as his response.

Lieutenant James coughed a few times to get attention back on himself and went back into his monotone presentation. "So, we've got Homicide involved, we're looking for prints, but they're not finding any. Thing is, whoever hit this place also had the alarm codes, because everything was turned off including the cameras. We've got a dead security guard with a family and someone on the run with a lot of money. Plus, a smeared, size-twelve footprint – presumably of one of the perpetrator's – and that's about it."

"Inside job?" someone called out.

"Possible," Lieutenant James said. "They did have the alarm code. We haven't ruled anything out. Hang on, now, there's a lot more to cover, and time is running out. It's already been several hours, now and there's a lot more evidence to go over."

The room quieted again.

"Next up, one of our own, Officer Nash," Lieutenant James said as the screen went from smeared blood to a picture of a large, bald man in a blue uniform. "This guy called in a routine traffic stop not too far away from FUJ. Late model Dodge Charger, local plates," he droned even lower as he read. "Thing is, the driver wore a ski mask, which Nash rightfully thought was odd in this weather, so he tried pulling him over. But the Charger sped away, and Nash lost him."

"Must've been some driver," Austen mumbled.

"After Nash's call-in, the desk had the plates run, and they tell us the car is owned by this man."

The screen changed again, this time to a photo of a man with a ridiculously goofy look on his face. It looked like a selfie, perhaps pulled from a Facebook page. James turned around to look at the face, coughed twice, and turned back to the crowd. "This comedian here is one Tom Pocase. You can probably guess there would be some kind of connection by now. He's a high-level assistant of good old Anthony Peterson."

Gilley took over and said, "We don't think he's behind this, though, because, as it turns out, he's missing too."

James leaned in and said, "Pocase's wife called in early this morning, and the call didn't seem significant at the time for reasons that should be apparent. See, he reportedly texted her that morning, and she indicated the texts didn't seem like him. Plus, he hadn't been seen since the previous day. She said it sounded like someone was covering something up, but had no other evidence, so Burns gave the standard 'we'll look into it' response figuring the man would be home by breakfast."

"That is, until Nash had those plates run," Detective Reeves added.

"Right," James confirmed. "So, we met with the wife and... Reeves?"

Reeves stood on the side of the room and filled the group in on what he found. "We got the wife's permission and traced his credit cards. Turns out he checked into a pretty nice hotel room downtown, so we figured it was just an affair. Coincidence. But when the uniforms searched the room, he wasn't there. The place was trashed, Pocase was gone, and they found blood, cum, vomit, and a whole shitload of dope all over the place."

A few disgusted sounds came back, but mostly the crowed was quiet and looked back to James with rapt attention.

"Thank you, Detective Reeves," James said flatly. "We're trying to give you all of this in some sort of chronological order, but it's getting harder to pin down exactly what happened when."

"Well, where is Nash?" Officer Nopke asked. "Isn't he a witness?"

James sighed and nodded. "Right, Nopke, right. Uh…well, here's where it gets even worse. A car crash took place a few blocks from where Nash last saw Pocase's Charger, and Nash was the first on the scene. I won't keep you in suspense: it was the same year's black Charger. Knocked down a pole and almost killed a family, then the guy actually flips the Charger but survives."

"No shit?" Austen scoffed.

"The family got out, took some video and–" The screen changed again to the captured digital video from the phones. "We see this guy. Looks like a Caucasian male from the few seconds his mask is up. He pulled it down quick. No good look at his face. Then…"Lieutenant James narrated as one of the videos continued. "Nash goes to arrest the driver and…"

The police in the room gasped as the masked driver punched out Officer Nash.

"I'm going to save you the rest for good taste and time, but this son of a bitch then torched his own car, locked up Nash, threw him in the trunk, and then stole Nash's squad car."

Hall spoke up. "How the hell did he do that?" she asked, causing some more chuckles, this time with something of the gallows about them.

James nodded. "We were as surprised as you are. For any of you who don't know the man, Officer Nash is a very large, very strong cop. His nickname off and on has rightly been The Incredible Hulk for years, and the guy has earned it."

The crowd nodded and voiced their agreement in low voices. James went on. "Because he was able to take down Nash, we do know we're clearly dealing with someone who has training. Now, we're treading lightly because the license plates are missing, as is the VIN and the rest of the car is burned pretty damned well, but come on. How many guys in ski masks were driving around Fairfax in the same damn year, make, model, and color of a car?"

Light chuckles and agreement followed.

Gilley spoke back up, "Now, uh, that's the latest that we know of, right?"

The Lieutenant nodded and shrugged with his thumbs, indicating that was pretty much true.

Gilley continued, "Now we're running with the idea that whoever this…asshole…is, he's probably not keeping the police car for long, so we're working on tracing its GPS locator. But the problem with *that* is the database system had that bad upgrade six weeks ago, and we're still trying to match GPS locators with squad cars. IT is on it, and we've set a fire under their asses to get it done, stat."

"Good luck with that," Austen mumbled.

James took back over. "Okay, boys and girls, we're almost done here. With a court order, we've gotten access to some of Peterson's bank accounts just now and…" He turned a page and continued. "…it looks like a lot of money is moving around fast. This lends credence to the younger Peterson's ransom claims. We do know that all of this is connected to Anthony Peterson, but we're not sure how."

"In short," Gilley called out, "if this isn't a kidnapping like the kid said, something is going on here anyway."

"Right," Lieutenant James agreed. "So, we have to proceed with the assumption that this is a kidnapping perpetrated by someone with a grudge. We're running with that. Anthony Peterson and his wife have been kidnapped and are apparently being kept at separate locations. Peterson's friend and assistant Tom Pocase has also apparently been kidnapped, his car stolen, and his secrets used to rob certain Peterson properties, even as the same guys are extorting ransom from him."

Lieutenant James paused sorrowfully before continuing more slowly. "We've also got a homicide here. Security guard just doing his job. It's a real tragedy. We've got a stolen police car, and, maybe worst of all, one of our own has been assaulted, kidnapped, and could be in serious danger. We don't want our fellow policeman added to the homicide list. Needless to say, SWAT teams are on standby."

The crowd rapidly took notes.

"We're sending all of this to your mobile devices. Treat this as priority one. Do not talk to the press. Refer them back to us if you get any questions. Hopefully, you won't. Meantime, I want every storage facility checked. Get someone out to the docks. If you see a cargo crate in a backyard, knock on the door. Peterson could be anywhere in any container, and his wife could be anywhere else. Think outside the box, people. There's a kidnapper and killer out there. We need to find this guy and *anybody* he's working with and get the Petersons, Pocase, and Officer Nash home safe before they get popped like Americano."

The cops began closing their notebooks and readying themselves for duty.

"Okay, then, let's be careful out–"

And with that, the door swung open, and Sergeant Burns ran inside.

"What is it?"

"You've got a call you'd better take."

"We're almost done here–"

"Sir! It's Nash!"

Lieutenant James's eyes widened, and he ran to the nearest phone, followed by Gilley, Reeves, and Austen.

26 Transaction Transpires

4:47 PM

Anthony Peterson was winning like he knew he would. This would set him back by much more scratch than he could ever be comfortable with, but he would recover. He would make money again. He would find out who did this, and he would exact revenge. Someday, somehow.

Don't fuck with Anthony Peterson.

He sat, watching the clock on his phone, waiting for a text to come through. It had to come through before the last minute.

It was no longer 1 AM they were racing against. Now, Peterson knew it was the closing of the banks. Cash had to be confirmed and converted, and Tom had to explain a few things as to how he got it and why he needed it done so quickly. This wasn't a midnight cash drop. This had to be done during business hours and that took time.

Time had now passed. So, where was that text? Had Tom betrayed him after all, even after his generous 'tip'? Had Tom run off with the extra millions to live the life of Riley on some island off of Belize? And if not, where was that text?

And at last, there it was. The confirmation text from his assistant, Tom. Tom who still *was* his assistant and not just his backstabber.

Finally, Anthony could smile. Tom had come through for him after all. Anthony Peterson was going to win, and Susan Peterson was going to smile again.

He stood in triumph and dialed the phone.

"Mr. Peterson. Your time is almost up," came the kidnapper's now-familiar voice in its robotic tone. "How's the air in there?"

Peterson shook his head. The air comment was meant to intimidate him. The kidnapper knew as well as Peterson did that the real deadline was the closing of the banks.

"I've got the…" he paused in thought. Whether it was resigned acceptance or Stockholm Syndrome, he amended himself. "… *your* money. All of it."

"Send it to me now," the kidnapper commanded.

"I want to speak to my wife first."

The kidnapper rustled with the phone for a second. He heard the voice tell someone, "Quick talk," as he seemed to hand it over to a surrogate. Peterson heard boots echoing down what sounded like a short hallway, and just for a second, he heard a TV playing something annoying in the background. Then, a door opened, and her beautiful voice came through.

"Anthony?"

"It's me baby, it's me!" he said, relieved that she was alive.

"Please, help me, I'm scared."

"I will, baby, I promise. It's all gonna be over soon."

The phone rustled again, and that obnoxious TV was passed by in the background. He heard the faint noise of air rushing by followed by what sounded like a pair of hands catching the thrown phone.

"Now, Mr. Peterson?"

Peterson sighed and said, "Yeah." Then, he waited a moment as if to imply he was doing something. He didn't know why. There wasn't much he could do since Tom had completed the transaction, but it seemed appropriate for the moment. Finally, he said, "Check it now. It's all there."

Peterson listened to the kidnapper tapping on a keyboard and clicking on a mouse. He thought he could still vaguely hear Susan's cries from far, far away.

"Very *good*, Mr. Peterson," the kidnapper said as if finally satisfied. "Well done."

Peterson sighed in relief. Soon, he would be out and would be reunited with Susan. He would have a lot of fences to mend.

His children. Tom. He would even work to make amends with his first wife, if for no other reason than to satisfy the kids.

He was going to be a good daddy again, even though his children were grown. It wasn't too late. He was going to show them. He was going to be the one they looked up to again. Somehow. Someway. This was his new goal in life. Anthony Peterson, absentee father, back again.

And then, there was the soul-searching. It was time to stop denying his history. Time to accept responsibility, if only within himself and be a better man. Nightmarish though it was, if nothing else this horrible experience had made him reevaluate his life and rethink-

"Now, there's just one more thing," that hated voice said, interrupting his reverie and fading his smile. "I'm still going to kill you and your wife."

Peterson's eyes shot open. "Wha-what?" Peterson whispered in shock. He almost dropped the phone.

"You heard me."

"But…but why? I did everything you asked. The money is all there!"

"It *is* all there. You *did* do everything I asked."

"Then why are you doing this?"

"Because you're a *bad* man, Mr. Peterson," the evil voice boomed at him. "A bad man who has done bad things! After all we've been through together over the past day, you still haven't learned that there are *penalties*?"

In the background, he could hear the scraping of a chair and the muffled sound of his beloved crying, gagged again. In that moment, he wanted nothing more than to save her.

He was at the end of his rope and resorted to bargaining.

"Please, just let her go! Let my wife go. You can do anything you want to me, but please, please, I'm begging you, just let Susan go!"

The kidnapper paused and then almost compassionately asked, "Would it hurt you more than anything else in the world to let anything happen to her?"

"*Yes!*" he said, feeling an ounce of hope again. And he meant it. Anthony Peterson loved someone more than himself.

"Well…" and the voice was silent as if contemplating the right thing to do. Peterson had hope again, and for the first time, he actually heard voices in the background. No more deception. Maybe. "Then, that's enough reason to kill her right there!" the kidnapper laughed, cruelly dashing his hopes again. "Get her in here!" he shouted.

And with that, Peterson heard a deafening sound. Something mechanical. It was… the roar of a chainsaw.

"No! No, you *can't* do this!"

"Can, do, and will, Mr. Peterson!" the kidnapper said and then gave the order to his henchman. "Make it *hurt!*"

And then, all he could hear was Susan's high-pitched scream, turned into a guttural roar as the chainsaw hit wet flesh and hard bone as it drove straight through her. He could hear the blood spattering and splashing as she drowned in her own screams.

Peterson then cried. He cried like a baby.

He had this possibility, the death of his wife, looming over his head all day, but he never knew how bad it would feel if it actually happened.

Now, he did, and he had never felt anything so painful in his life. He had never really lost anyone important to him before. Now, he had.

It was worse than the nightmares. It was worse than the fears for his own life. It was worse than tearing out his own teeth. It was worse than the loss of all of this money.

And when the noise stopped, when the chainsaw was switched off, there were no more cries from Susan.

She was dead.

There was only silence on the other end of the phone.

"Susan!" he said weakly. He dropped to his knees and wept, feeling that pain. A pain like no other.

Susan was not just a trophy wife. She never had been. Susan was the love of his life. And now Susan was dead.

He fell to the side and curled into a fetal position, helpless, wounded, and weeping.

Far in the background, he heard the sounds of dripping followed by men laughing. One of them said, "Boss, I thought you said we were going to fuck her first!"

And the kidnapper responded, "Doesn't she look fucked to you?" which evoked laughter from unseen spectators.

Peterson could not even muster anger at those words. Instead he wailed at the pain and injustice.

He had just made them rich, and they ripped out his heart. Susan.

The kidnapper spoke into the phone again. Peterson wondered why he still had it to his ear. Forced habit. "Mr. Peterson? I've got special plans for you."

And with that, the anger did return in a red rage. He could picture the blood around Susan and even imagined those skulls rising through it. This time, the skulls weren't the dead of La Aldea but were instead the faces of his own fury. Nothing mattered more than Susan. Nothing.

Every mental picture that flipped through his head now was of Susan. Susan, his soulmate. Susan, the underappreciated trophy wife he would now never have a chance to prove himself to. Susan...

Peterson cried and cursed and ground what was left of his teeth, trying to form words but managing only curses. "You fucking monsters. You fucking cock-sucking monsters."

He was a broken man.

Broken.

The hum came again, shocking his body. But what was electrocution compared to this pain he was feeling at the loss of his wife?

By now, being electrified was old hat. Peterson just jerked and let it happen.

What else could they *do* to him now that they had taken Susan away?

"You won't get the easy way out like Susan did, Mr. Peterson. You're going *to die*! You're going to die cold, scared, and alone in the dark knowing the only one you've ever loved died because of *your* actions. I'm pulling the plug on you, Mr. Peterson. Over and out!"

And with that the kidnapper hung up…and true to his words, the lights went out.

Peterson let the phone slip from his grip as he lay there, his grief and his anger vying for attention as he sobbed the name, "Susan!" over and over again.

27 Day of Reckoning

5:36 PM

"**A**nthony Peterson is a dead man!" the boss shouted, and the men and women in fatigues cheered and high-fived as if there was no dead woman ripped to shreds in a spreading pool of her own blood right there in front of them.

Calderon got it. It was the celebration of a completed job. They were getting paid, and nothing else mattered.

"My favorite part was when you said she looked fucked now," one of the hired guns chuckled.

"It just came out," the boss laughed. "Hey, open that bottle. Let's celebrate. Where's Keeler?"

A big, bald guy said, "Yeah, but I was looking forward to actually fucking her."

The boss laughed. "Every dog has his day. You get a consolation drink instead."

"Are we going to celebrate with all this blood here?" a guy with a scar running from his left ear to the corner of his mouth.

"Is there a better way to celebrate?" the boss laughed. "Anthony Peterson got what he deserved!"

The group cheered as he continued.

"And that right there?" he said, indicating the coagulating, yet spreading red puddle. "That's our reminder of that very thing." The soldiers cheered again, and the boss waved his hands to quiet them. "And as he slowly dies in his spacious coffin, my friends, he'll know damn well that these are the penalties he is facing for his choices he made. The former Mrs. Peterson over here is the bloody consequence of his path in life." He took a swig from his cup, then said, "You know? Right now...I'll bet he's searching all around the box trying to figure out a way to kill himself."

The group laughed, and a soldier named Jennifer quipped, "I wonder how long it would take a man to kill himself with a pair of pliers?" which evoked more laughter.

"Oh, man, I'd pay to see that." The boss smiled and held out his glass for another man to fill.

"It's too bad you killed the power. We could keep this party going watching him suffocate or starve to death right now," another of the troops said and took a big gulp of his strong rum.

"Ah, shit. Why the fuck didn't I think of that? Ah, well. To missed opportunities," the boss shouted and raised his glass.

"To missed opportunities," Calderon echoed as the soldiers of fortune cheered. Calderon didn't join them. He kept looking at the body, especially the calloused feet.

"Another toast!" the boss said. "This isn't a party, gang, but we've got a right to celebrate before it's all over, so let's toast! Anthony Peterson is a dead man! Here's to us!" and the group raised their glasses and cheered. "And we…" started the boss before taking a swig himself "…we are all filthy fucking rich."

Everyone but Calderon cheered again and drank.

"So, we're done, then?" Calderon asked over the bacchanalia.

"I'm sorry, Calderon, what was that?" the boss asked.

"So, it's over? We're done, then?" he asked again, this time a little too loudly, and the rest of the mercenaries immediately straightened up and silenced themselves. Calderon still managed to intimidate most any room he walked into. Even these guys.

"Yeah, yeah, Calderon, it's over," the boss said. "Your money's already been transferred. I did it from my personal account, so you wouldn't have to wait. You know, you were one of the most important parts of the entire operation and–"

"So, we're done…" Calderon cut him off. Calderon then paused and added, "…boss?" with barely masked contempt.

The boss swallowed and looked hard at him, then spoke carefully, but still happily. "Yeah. Have a drink. A job well done by all."

Calderon looked back down at the blood pool and smiled. "Well done by all," he said as he thought about Keeler's words. Calderon paused for a moment, knowing the rest of the room could not move forward with their celebration until he was finished speaking. "But you know what?" he continued. "I quit."

"You're not staying?" the boss asked, with a surprised look.

"No. I'm out of here," he said, flatly, then added, "...boss," again with sarcasm.

The boss looked to the side with a concerned expression. "We agreed to hide out here and leave a few at a time so as to not call any attention to–"

"Right. But I've got other things happening so, uh, I guess I'll be the first to leave," Calderon said. Then, almost unconsciously, he added, "I'm taking my toys and going home... boss."

The boss laughed at that, which caused the rest of the gang to laugh as well. "Well, you've earned it. We couldn't have done this without you. You are, truly, the top of your field. All of your fields."

The excited mercenaries gave their enthusiastic agreement. Calderon just looked down at the body and thought about what Keeler had said. All deaths are the same, there is no difference, so you can kill anybody. The world is random and insane like that.

Calderon had thought a lot about that, and he had decided that if all deaths were the same, that meant all deaths were the same as Justin. Or the sniped dog. Or the dead baby. Maybe in light of that, he wouldn't be killing anybody anymore. It was time to retire, after all.

He chuckled as the others continued their jubilation. He realized that in his head he sounded a lot like a Hallmark card. A Hallmark card for deeply evil people, but a Hallmark card nonetheless.

"I'll be discreet," Calderon said. "As I leave, I mean."

The boss was happy. Too happy, maybe. Didn't he realize this wasn't over yet?

The boss reached out both hands and said "Thank you again! I'll work with you anytime." He shook Calderon's hand vigorously.

Calderon turned around and packed up his monitoring equipment and carried it to the other room. Mrs. Peterson's former prison.

He opened the door and strapped on his backpack, moving around the olive-green fatigues and other clothes that were strewn messily all over the floor. He then lifted up his duffle bag with a grunt and carefully laid it over his shoulder.

"Hey, are you sure you can't stay for drinks?" the boss called after him as he left.

"Can't. Thanks," Calderon responded. "Other priorities… boss."

"Got it," the boss called again. "Hey, have you seen Keeler?"

Calderon slowed down and snickered quietly. "Earlier, yeah. She was having cigarettes with me outside. Said she wanted to see some more of me."

"Good for you both," the boss said, now standing at the mouth of the hallway, and Calderon couldn't help but notice how very different he was from the mostly emotionless madman he had been while on the phone with Peterson. One could almost forget that he was a cold-blooded killer. "Hey, on your way out, tell Keeler to come join us. She's earned this too."

"As soon as I see her, I'll tell her," Calderon said and walked to the stairs without another word.

He had already seen quite a lot of Keeler today. He had already seen enough of Keeler for a while.

He descended and exited the main door.

He did not relish the long walk he had planned down the hill with this heavy load. But then, he noticed the army green pickup truck he had been assigned to drive. It was the truck in which he had delivered Mrs. Peterson earlier. That seemed appropriate somehow, considering all.

He put down his silver case and patted his pocket. He had forgotten to give the keys back, he realized.

Convenient and appropriate.

Calderon placed the case in the bed of the truck, then opened the passenger side door. He placed his duffle bag in the seat and then fastened a belt around it to keep the cargo from shifting around. He then took off his backpack and threw that in the bed of the truck as well.

With that, Calderon slid in behind the steering wheel, started the truck, and took off for the last time.

He thought about Keeler once more, and he really had to admit as he exited the heavy gate, that he felt really, really great.

28 Alone in the Dark

6:06 PM

Anthony Peterson had not so much fallen asleep or even passed out as much as he had simply shut down. His brain had shut down as if to prevent more pain. It was Anthony Peterson's last defense.

He had lost. Susan had died.

And while it was their fault, the fault of the kidnappers, they were also right. Anthony Peterson was guilty, and all of this was because of what he had done.

Susan was now dead and gone, and soon, very soon, he was going to die and join her.

After all he had gone through, would death be that bad?

Would he really want to live after losing her and losing the game against their captors... so... very... spectacularly?

At least in death he would be with her. Unfortunately, he would also have to be with...

The phone rang again, and his eyes fluttered open in the darkness.

He looked at the phone there on the metal coffin floor and considered...why should he answer? What was left to do or even say?

Then, he realized something...something horrible, but at the same time hopeful.

This had to all be a prank.

Tom hadn't gone through all that madness. Who the hell could survive all that? He was at home with all of the other people who were in on it, and they were still playing him. They probably played all those crazy sounds on a computer. Car crashes. The crazy attack dog. And that security guard? Come on. None of that happened. The very idea was ridiculous.

And the girl? That part was rich. They had really played that one well. Overdose girl. Party monster. Hilarious touch. Hell, they even managed to get Dino and Doctor Ivy in on it.

Anthony Peterson chuckled out loud in the dark.

Susan was *fine*!

Of course she was! Susan had probably put Tom up to the whole thing, hadn't she? They wanted to teach him a lesson, and it worked.

Things were going to be different now.

Who played the kidnapper? A friend of Tom's? Maybe another employee? Or just some actor they had hired?

Oh, sure it went too far. They should never have brought up South America on a cell phone. That was dangerous. And, yes, he would need some bridges for his teeth, and he was pissed off about that. Nobody wanted dentures.

But the game had served its purpose, hadn't it? They had made him rethink his life and that must have been their goal.

It was like Ebenezer Scrooge finally learning the error of his ways and running out in the street to give long overdue gifts. That was Anthony Peterson today.

He just needed that metal cargo door to open so he could do that. Be a better man. He had so much to do. So why wasn't the door opening so he could?

He laughed again in the dark.

He bet Evan was in on it too. Even Elena might have been.

If they had presented it to them as a way to pay Dad back *and* make Dad learn a lesson, they'd bite, right? We'll play a game with your dad, scare him, but he'll come out all the better for it. He'll be apologizing soon as hell.

What a gift that would be!

Then, he would be able to make things better, and he'd never take Susan for granted or let his kids feel unloved or...

*

And, of course, that *is* exactly what happened.

Anthony Peterson was soon freed, and he was a better man for it. The first thing he did when he walked out from the container into the cheering throngs of his family and friends and newcomers was to hug Evan. He held him there, eyes closed, forehead to forehead as they had done when Evan was young. Then, he held Elena. He asked, laughingly, if he could pick her up as he hugged her, and she said it would be okay, so he swung her around just as he had when she was a little girl.

And Marie was there. He hugged Marie, his ex-wife, and apologized for all of the many things he had done wrong and told her he didn't even blame her for Sully. He would pay all her medical bills from then on and would do his best to be a better friend than he had been a husband. Marie laughed and said that sounded like a plan, and they chuckled together the way they had when they first met, all those years ago. Friends now. Not just for the kids, but for themselves. He hugged her again, and they smiled and winked at each other. They knew each other so well. They should never have parted. Even though the relationship had failed, the friendship should have stayed. That big hug proved that.

But the biggest hug he reserved for Susan. Susan was there, waiting just outside with the crowd, ever so patiently, but when it was time for her to come forward the crowd parted, just like in the movies, and Susan danced out toward him, and he hugged her tightly. It was a hug that they never wanted to disengage from. He swore he'd never take her for granted again, and she responded that she knew he wouldn't. They laughed and hugged some more, then kissed without modesty in front of the clapping crowd.

Tom made a quick speech, and everyone toasted to the new Anthony Peterson. They all laughed and joked together, especially when Peterson mock-angrily asked whose idea the tooth extraction was. Luckily, Doctor Ivy just happened to be on hand and had both painkillers and ready-made prostheses (courtesy of the craftsmanship of Dino Dennison) that Peterson was able to pop in and he felt like a new man.

Tom introduced Anthony to the guy who played kidnapper and they embraced too. He told the actor that he owed him one for helping him meet himself again for the first time. And the pair remained friends for life after that.

And that very night, he vowed to donate money to South American causes, especially to the orphans of La Aldea. It was the least he could do. He had learned his lesson after all. It was more than a pledge, it was a vow. And they did not fuck with Anthony Peterson because nobody even wanted to anymore. He was the most popular guy in town since he changed. Anthony Peterson was a new man.

Evan and Elena were even reluctantly nice to Susan, and by the end of the night, Susan and Marie had actually met and had become fast friends.

Christmases to come would have the whole family together with Evan making the occasional joke about Anthony being in one of the Christmas packages. He was, after all, cargo, wasn't he? That guy who had played the kidnapper, now one of Anthony's dearest friends, would laugh and laugh, and then offer him a toothpick while Marie and Elena would tell them how bad they were for making those jokes, and Susan just sat there laughing uncontrollably. Just like Anthony did. He was so happy he couldn't stop laughing that big, wide-eyed grin-laugh.

Why shouldn't everything work out? He had certainly had a time of it, hadn't he?

And come September, he and Susan renewed their vows in front of everyone with Tom as his best man. And this time, Evan and Elena attended, as did even Marie. At long last, everyone was on good terms. Sully even came back from the dead to officiate the ceremony. Oh, he dodged questions about whether he had actually died or not, but wherever Sully had come from, Anthony was grateful that he had made the trip. He even took Sully aside and promised that if he ever wanted to pop the question to Marie, Anthony would be glad to give his blessing and even officiate, if they'd have him.

Evan gave the speech offering his own blessing to Anthony and Susan, and Anthony just stood there on the edge of the stage that September and laughed in happiness. A drunken, sporting, full, rich laugh in front of all his friends and family. And he just laughed and laughed in happiness.

That night, he carried his wife over the threshold of their second honeymoon suite, and he made love to her like an animal on a steroids and Viagra cocktail. Afterward, he left her sleeping and satisfied with maybe a new little brother or sister for Evan and Elena to coo over growing inside of her. And instead of sleeping himself, Anthony Peterson just laid there awake and staring into the darkness laughing that satisfied, happy, goofy, glorious laugh, knowing that everything had worked out and everything was going to work out from then on out.

Anthony Peterson had won. Anthony Peterson laughed.

*

But the phone kept ringing in total darkness.

Of course it did.

Of course he wasn't in his honeymoon suite.

Of course he was still in the box.

Of course nothing had actually worked out.

Of course nothing would.

Of course Susan was dead.

Of course he had to answer that phone. He'd better do it soon before they hung up.

"Hello?" he muttered and noted the phone was broken again. Black screen. Dead.

"Anthony?"

Peterson slumped. It was Sully's voice. Sully's dead voice.

He had let himself hope this was some joke. He had allowed himself the fantasy of victory and now he was let down again.

What was real? What was real?

Was this real?

Was he in his second honeymoon suite, staring into the darkness with his perfect bride beside him, carrying his new heir?

Or was she dead, and he was now sparring with a dead man?

What was real? What was real?

"Sully," he moaned. "Let me talk to Susan."

Sully sounded patient as he said, "But Anthony, Susan is dead. I don't have her. I wasn't there. I'm dead too. We both died because of you. You don't still think I was working with the kidnappers, do you?"

"No," Anthony said flatly. "No, you couldn't be. You're dead. You weren't in on this big joke, were you? You're dead, and she's dead, so she's with you, so let me *talk to her!*"

"I'm afraid it doesn't work that way," Sully said politely.

"I knew it," Peterson mumbled. "You're not real. You never were real, were you?"

"I'm as real as you make me," Sully said without argument. "I just wanted to call and say goodbye." Sully's voice chuckled a little. "And to tell you not to worry about Evan and Elena. I'll take good care of them. Them and their mother both. If you remember, I don't make promises idly."

Peterson grunted. His subconscious was telling him exactly what he wanted to hear in that moment, all in the guise of Sully. It was nothing more than a hallucination. So, he reminded Sully again, "You're dead."

"You know?" Sully started again, completely disregarding Peterson's words. "You're right where I thought you always belonged. Oh, I don't mean in some forty-foot metal coffin, exactly. I mean that you're...alone in the dark. Dying all by your lonesome. Just like you always deserved."

"We'll see," Peterson muttered defiantly but still pained.

Sully chuckled again. "Anthony, there is no one coming to save you. You're sealed in your own perfect little tomb...forever. Peaceful, isn't it? You're halfway there, Anthony."

Softly, barely getting the words out Peterson managed to pronounce "Halfway...where?"

"You're already lying down," Sully said. "Now…just *die*."

Sully hung up, and Peterson rolled over to his back, causing the phone to fall off of the side of his face to the floor.

Peterson just lay there, looking up. No light to see the ceiling. No pregnant, perfect wife sleeping happily by his side. No honeymoon suite. Just his coffin.

Sully. Susan.

What he wouldn't give to wrap his arms around Susan's neck again.

What he wouldn't give to wrap his fingers around Sully's throat.

But no…Sully wasn't real. It was all in his own head.

Sully was dead. So was Susan. He had made sure that Sully was dead. Sully had been right about that one thing.

It was pointless to imagine revenge against Sully…the dead man talking.

Revenge.

And that was it. Sully was gone. Peterson had gotten all the revenge he would ever manage to take on Sully.

But *they* weren't gone. The kidnappers weren't gone. And he did, ultimately, have one last thing to live for.

It wasn't love.

It wasn't forgiveness.

It wasn't soul-searching and the betterment of mankind, and it sure as hell wasn't atonement.

It was vengeance!

29 Commando

7:13 PM

Anthony Peterson sat up and narrowed his eyes in angst and fury. He could see nothing, but he felt his face turning red. He hardened his heart and steeled his muscles and ground what was left of his teeth.

They had made two big mistakes, the kidnappers.

Two huge mistakes they would regret.

They had not killed him. And they had left him that phone.

Oh, sure, they knew the phone was going to lose power eventually, but they had also given him the best, shockproof battery case money could buy and it had one hell of an auxiliary battery life. Oh, sure, if he called the cops he wouldn't have a damned thing to tell them that would help. Oh, sure, calling the cops would not get him any revenge. Oh, sure.

But he did still have the phone. And Anthony Peterson did remember one other number he could call.

It was a number he did not expect to ever use again, but it was high time he used it.

He had one plan.

One last thing to live for. One more reason to keep going.

All fantasies aside, all glamors removed, all reality exposed. He had one plan and one plan only left.

He was going to pull the strings again, one last time, and he was going to love every last fucking second of it.

*

Anthony Peterson remembered that phone number like his own birthdate, though he never expected to use it again.

He brought the phone to his ear and waited, listening to every last ring.

"Speak," the voice said. It was the voice of the man Peterson called Merc. A deep, mature, masculine, military voice.

That was Merc.

"Merc," Peterson said, firmly.

The other man paused then said, "Anthony? Anthony Peterson? Sweet baby Jesus, it's been years!"

"Years," Peterson confirmed flatly, then said, "I need your help." Direct and to the point, just the way the man called Merc would appreciate.

Merc still sounded happy as he said, "Well, sure, man! Anything for my old amigo!"

Peterson coldly and deliberately recited the situation once again. "I have been kidnapped. Held for ransom. Threatened with death. They snatched my wife and threatened to kill her too."

"Wait. Are you okay?"

"No, Merc. And neither is Susan. I paid them the ten million they demanded, and they killed her anyway. Now, I've been left to die. I'm trapped inside a metal shipping cargo container. I don't know where I am, but I know the oxygen is running out, quickly."

Merc was momentarily silent, stunned at this development. "Wha–? Anthony, this is insane! Why the hell didn't you call me first?"

"Because they were fucking listening, Merc," Anthony said flatly, in spite of his emotion. "They told me that if I called the cops, or anyone not related to the ransom, Susan and I were dead." He coughed. "Looks like we are anyway."

Merc was the toughest man Anthony had ever met. Powerful and gritty. But at the moment he sounded like a concerned friend.

"Are they listening right now?"

Peterson paused. "I don't know. Maybe. I don't think so. They shut down the power. Said they were pulling the plug."

Merc said seriously "My guess is their capability to listen went with the power. That would follow, but I can't be sure. There's always that one guy who can bug anything. They had the place wired up for lights?" Merc said, clearly searching his brains for clues.

"Not just lights," Peterson said, then went on, slightly more emotionally. "Man, they *tortured* me in here. It's rigged up like one big electric torture chamber. They electrified the place over and over again. Shocked the hell out of me. I've never felt pain like that in my entire life. And they...hell, Merc, they made me pull my own teeth out, Merc."

"Jesus," Merc whispered. "And you have no idea where you are?"

Peterson shook his head in the dark. "No, none. Indoors, I'm guessing, I haven't heard any weather."

"Are they nearby? The people who put you in there?"

"I've got no fucking idea where they are, Merc. They said they could be controlling this place remotely, or that they could even be right outside," he stammered. "They threw out every possibility at me to keep me confused."

Merc persisted for clues. "Is there anything on the inside of the container you might have missed? A serial number? A shipping line? Anything?"

"Nada. I've been all over every inch of this fucker."

"Anything the kidnappers might have said to tip you off?"

"Nothing."

"Background noise. Anything?"

"I only spoke to one man. He sounded...serious. No real accent. Didn't sound foreign, so probably American. Nothing else."

"They locked you in a...a cargo container with just the cell phone? Any clues on the cell phone?"

"Not a thing. I've been through it all. It's generic. Cheap, but functional except most of the apps are blocked. It has a battery case, or else I'd have run out of power hours ago. Running low now, though."

Merc summed it up. "So, kidnapper, American or Canadian, indoors, possibly in a place that's soundproof or just deserted, and, wild guess, most likely somewhere in North America."

Peterson nodded. "Yeah, according to the people I spoke to…I wasn't missing long enough to have gone farther."

Merc tapped his finger, thinking. "So, that narrows it down to pretty much anywhere on this continent."

Peterson just sighed.

"But logically, you're probably still in the state. It only makes sense. Are you sure you didn't hear anything else at all? Think hard. It doesn't matter how trivial."

Peterson thought dutifully, then snapped his fingers. "I did hear something. Just before they killed Susan, they let me talk to her, and just for a second, way in the background, it sounded like some kind of broadcast. TV maybe. Maybe radio, but I heard talking. Maybe they had it on and forgot about it."

"What did you hear?"

"Announcer, I think saying… wait, I think he said the station identification."

"What was it?" Merc said, impatiently.

Peterson thought. This was his last chance. He tapped his free thumb against each of the four fingertips on that hand, then went back and forth across as he thought. At last, his head popped up and his eyes shot open.

"K-O-M-E!" Peterson said, almost gleefully.

"That's not a national station," Merc said, writing it down, then typing. "It must be local."

Peterson understood where this was going. "That's got to be right. Local."

Merc typed furiously. "Got it. Limited signal. The valley. Hollywood Hills, Santa Monica Mountains, maybe."

"Yes. I thought I'd seen a billboard for it around–"

"Hold on," Merc said and typed quickly again. "Checking satellite feed now." Peterson heard the sounds of an office chair rushing along a hard floor as if Merc had just kicked himself over to another workstation. More fast typing followed. "Okay, I just put out feelers to a few hundred contacts to check the word on the street for suspicious activities." Tap, tap. "And…done. Lots of cell phones going off in your area right now."

"You can text to that many phones at once?"

"Modern tech, Anthony. Gotta love it." Merc continued to type and click and then said. "Now this is interesting."

"What?"

"Hang on, let me get a satellite view. Yeah. More chatter coming in saying the same. I think I…huh…"

"What is it, Merc, what do you got?"

"Yeah, I think that's it. That would do nicely," Merc said almost admiringly. "I think we may have found your boys. They're holed up in a compound, mountainside, just like we suspected. Aw, geez, the place is a veritable fortress. Off the beaten path, easily defensible. These guys know what they're doing. They're going to be organized and well-armed."

Peterson closed his eyes tightly and asked the question he almost dreaded the answer to. "Well? What do you think?"

"Well…" Merc was brave but cautious. "I can have a team assembled in no time, but I'm not going to lie to you, these guys are not going to be easy. Our biggest advantage is that they're not going to know we're coming, but…this is no easy job. They look a hell of a lot like…"

"Like what?"

"Like *us*, Anthony. From what I can tell, they look like professional mercenaries, so it's going to be a pretty even match. I'm going to have to bring out the big guns, literally, and more men than usual, but that costs money. What do you want me to do?"

Peterson was dead serious as he said, "Payback!"

30 Exodus

Anthony Peterson was not far away, actually, for a few seconds, as Calderon drove by, although there was no way either man could have known that.

Calderon drove on, still feeling good about himself in his stolen olive-drab Toyota pickup.

There was no need to keep his cell phone off anymore, so he had activated it soon after he left the compound.

He checked his account and confirmed that he had been paid. He now had his nest egg complete. He was going to retire, just like he said he would.

What else mattered?

For the first time in forever and especially in the last several months, he felt positive. It had been a day of revelations for Calderon. It was as if everything had finally fallen into place for him, just like he had told Keeler. As his crazy mind had obsessed over Susan, Anthony, Justin, the boss, and the bizarre adventure that unfolded before his ears he started to realize the differences that he was looking for.

He started to see why.

He knew there was no way to bring Justin back. He was as dead as the men Calderon had killed over the years. And Calderon had killed a lot of men over the years. Men. Women. Even children, maybe. At the very least, Calderon was a maker of widows and orphans. And worst of all, Calderon had failed his nephew, and he was going to have to live with that for the rest of his life.

Maybe Keeler had been right in her own psychotic way.

If it didn't matter who died, maybe it didn't matter who survived.

The difference wasn't why. There was no difference. So, Calderon now had a new mission. He wanted to live the life Justin might have lived, had his uncle not failed him.

He wiped away a single tear, then coughed it away. Calderon still wasn't going to cry, goddamn it.

He thought about his epiphany as he drove the stolen truck and laughed. There was a big difference, actually. People who chose to kill were monsters, no matter the reason for that choice. Calderon was not a hero. He was as bad as Peterson or the boss or Keeler.

In Keeler's sociopathic eyes, he saw the big difference and the answer was so simple. There was no why. Because dead was dead.

Thus, he had to choose a different path and no longer be like them.

"I am become retirement," he laughed aloud.

His cell phone buzzed, and he received a message from a very familiar contact. The man known as Merc.

He was looking for… well, look at that. He was looking for the compound Calderon had just left. He laughed as he read the message.

Oh, the boss and his friends were celebrating now, but that was not going to last long.

Calderon knew Merc, and thus, he knew those assholes were never going to know what hit them.

He thought of warning them as a part of the new leaf he had turned over.

Then, he thought the words just as he said them out loud. "Nah, fuck them!"

He laughed aloud. Baby steps. He'd be a better man tomorrow and even better the next day.

Right now, he was busy. He had to drop a special package off on the way out of town, and then, he was hitting the open road to make his new life.

And as he saw the signs indicating he was nearing Bel Air, he finally felt free.

31 The Raid

9:00 PM

Anthony Peterson continued to pace, breaking only to glance at the battery life on his sole lifeline. Merc had just called him back with the team assembled as they traveled up a remote mountain road in a caravan of utility vehicles.

"We've got twenty-four men in eight vehicles," Merc shouted over the engine noise. "Nobody else is on the road, so we shouldn't have any unwelcome reporting."

"Twenty-four? Is that enough?"

"We did South America with twelve."

Those words made Peterson wince, but in reaction, he steeled himself again and grimaced. Ready to pull the strings. Ready to do to them what they did to him.

There was radio chatter Peterson could hear over the fray. The sound of professional killers preparing to do what they did best.

Merc repeated what he heard. "Snipers in place, ready to take out the guards. Multiple tangos. Shit, there's gonna be a lot of 'em. Before I let you go, it's your call. Maim or kill?"

Peterson responded coldly "Kill. Kill 'em all! Go for the headshots!"

"Kill order given," Merc repeated to the group.

"And Merc?"

"Yeah?"

"No survivors," Peterson ordered through snarling lips.

"You got it," Merc promised. "I'll report back soon."

"No!" Peterson barked. "Don't you hang up on me! They killed my wife. This is my kill. I want to hear every word. Every single scream! I want to hear them beg!"

Merc laughed. "Cold-blooded. You got it."

214

"Promise me you've got a Bluetooth," Peterson said humorlessly, thinking of Tom and his repeated fiascos.

"On it right now," Merc said as the engines roared. "Hang on, we're about to crash the front gate."

Peterson heard a loud crash. That was no chain link fence. That was a wrought-iron gate, if it was anything. And immediately he had to pull the phone back because the firefight had begun.

A loud, old-style air-raid alarm blasted through the phone. Bullet fire sounded like applause as the screams came. Bombs exploded. Men screamed. Boots stomped. People died.

Peterson paced his coffin almost to the beat of the blasts, like a caged lion, listening intently with a fierce look on his face.

Merc called out as if hiding behind a barrier. "Pinned down! We're pinned down."

A response on the radio indicated Merc's team was facing the same.

"Anthony, there is way fucking more than we anticipated. How in the name of fuck did you piss anyone off that badly?" Merc paused to fire off a few rounds, then said, "Never mind, Anthony. Don't answer that. Stupid question." Then, back into the radio, he shouted, "Stone, use the minigun! Use the minigun! Mow 'em down!"

The high-powered wail of the M134 filled Peterson's cell, and he smiled as he heard the screams. They were being shot to ribbons. He loved it. They deserved what they got.

He heard the radio buzz as one of the commandoes reported that the main door had been breached.

"Storm the main compound! Repeat, storm the main compound!" Merc yelled, and Peterson heard him rushing forward, firing a few times, before a new door was kicked in. "Freeze!" he commanded someone.

Weapons hit the floor, pleas for mercy could be heard over the shouts and the ringing in Peterson's ears.

"Anthony, we've got enemy combatants throwing down their weapons and surrendering."

Peterson's eyes went wide as he thought of Susan, his perfect bride, dead because of these bastards.

"*Waste* 'em! Make 'em bleed!" he shouted psychotically, then added "Make it *hurt!*"

Guns fired and bodies were riddled with bullets. The sounds of the men's screams indicated these were far from clean kills. Merc was going from the extremities in, grinding them to hamburger.

"Reinforcements coming from upstairs," Merc warned his men.

Peterson continued to command "*Kill 'em! Kill 'em all!*" whether Merc could hear him or not.

The battle continued loudly. Explosions, gunfire, screams, hand-to-hand combat. Peterson even recognized the sounds of some knifings. The only problem was that he couldn't tell which side was taking the most losses.

That was until Merc screamed amid a barrage of bullets.

"Commander down! Commander down!" the radio blared, and the machine guns intensified their assault.

Another voice shouted, "We need a medic. Bottom of stairwell. Stat!"

"Merc? Merc!" Peterson shouted, hopped up on adrenaline and begging for this not to be true. Not yet, at least. Merc had a job to finish.

It seemed like an eternity for Peterson, caught in this dark box with only the loud sounds of fighting as his window to the outside world. He waited and listened and tried in vain to make sense of what he heard.

Finally, he could make out coughing and gasping amid the bullets and explosions.

"I took three in the chest, but I'm okay," Merc hissed as he got up. "I'm gonna have some broken ribs, but thank God for Kevlar."

Peterson heard some of the other commandos cheer as Merc took the lead again.

"You gonna make it?" Peterson asked, concerned.

"They all hit the vest," Merc said, still straining. "I've got an extra reason for payback now." Then, loudly, he shouted, "Take the top floor. Block all exits. I'm going up!"

Peterson yelled over the ruckus, "Merc! That ringleader. I want that fucker *alive!*"

"Roger that!"

The shooting was occasional now. A pop here. A rat-ta-tat there. Another radio voice buzzed in. "This is a long hallway, Commander."

"Yeah, I'm here, I see it. Double doors at the end."

"Armored from the looks of them," the radio voice confirmed.

"Clear the rooms along the way," Merc commanded.

One by one, the doors were kicked in with reports back of "Latrine," and "Storage. Messy, but empty," and "TV and couch. Nobody there."

Merc responded, "Copy. That leaves only the armored doors at the end. Hollister! Get up here with that grenade launcher. We got a safe to crack!"

Peterson heard footfalls and another man ran to Merc saying, "Ready!"

"Nuke that mother!" Merc commanded.

Presently Hollister, Peterson guessed, shouted, "Fire in the hole!"

He heard the door blow inward and bend at the assault of the grenade launcher.

"Get that door to the side," Merc commanded. "And nobody dies beyond that door without my say so."

"Yes sir!" a number of voices said at once.

Merc pushed past the men, on his toes and ready for anything. Things settled, and Merc was heard throwing debris around looking for things.

Then, he stopped. "Oh…oh *Jesus*," Merc gasped in a shocked, disgusted voice.

Peterson didn't ask what it was. He knew from the tone.

Merc got himself together. "We…we found your wife," Merc said sullenly, "Jesus. They cut her open. Chainsaw by the look of it. Anthony, I am so, so sorry."

Peterson drooped again. Some part of him, some small, irrational part, held out hope that she was still alive. He should have learned not to hope by now.

He fell back against the wall and started to slide down.

But then, he heard another rain of gunfire, blasting through his phone's earpiece. "No!" he cried.

"Return fire! Return fire!" Merc ordered. "Pin 'em down. Give 'em hell, but leave 'em alive!"

"Where's Keeler?" someone shouted under the fray. "Tell Keeler we need her here!"

Slowly, Anthony placed the voice. It was the kidnapper with all distortions removed. He didn't sound so tough now.

"Do you copy? We need…take these guys down," the weakened voice shouted into what Peterson assumed was another radio, but there was no response.

After a time, the firing died down, and Peterson heard more weapons hit the floor. It was surrender time for his erstwhile captors.

"Don't move. Don't any of you motherfuckers move. We've got you dead to rights. Everybody on your knees." There was moaning and a collection of sighs of defeat as Peterson heard them all comply.

"Let me just take a wild-fuck guess…" Merc said tauntingly. Peterson could hear him walking back and forth, presumably in front of a kneeling audience. Merc's big boots scraped on the floor and made loud steps. After a seeming eternity Merc stopped and seemed to point. As he finished his sentence "…*you*'re the boss here."

"Please…please I can make you a deal!" that exhausted voice responded.

The voice was clear now, no longer distorted and no longer confident. But Peterson knew that was him. Peterson laughed at how beaten the once commanding kidnapper sounded now.

"Sounds like a yes. Gentlemen? Waste the rest."

Peterson heard a cacophony of booms followed by sickly splats and the unmistakable wet thumps of bodies hitting the floor.

"Anthony, I think we've found your host for the evening." He paused, and then said "Oh. Look at that. His eyes just got all wide when I said the name...Anthony. You really didn't expect this shit, did you?"

The kidnapper spoke louder, and Peterson recognized his voice. "Please, no. I can make it worth your while."

"Worth my while?" Merc said, sarcastically, "Oh, do tell."

"Double. I'll double your money. Whatever it is he's paying you. No, no! Triple!"

"What do you say, Anthony? He's trying to bribe me here."

The former kidnapper spoke louder to make sure he could be heard by Merc's Bluetooth. "Mr. Peterson. Please. I'll give you your money back. I can give you more. I can give you anything!"

Peterson smiled coldly, loving this. He had him right where he wanted him. His only regret was that he was not right there in person to watch him squirm. He now had him begging, just as Peterson had previously been begging for Susan's life. He planned to offer an equal measure of mercy.

"Merc," he said with a tone of command in his voice.

"Yes, sir," Merc responded, still sounding sarcastic.

"You and the boys soften him up...just a *little* bit!" Peterson said, almost casually. "Make him hurt. Make him *bleed!*"

"With pleasure, sir."

Peterson listened to the severe beating that was being administered and licked his lips, thinking of all the pain and torture he had gone through that day and relishing the fear his captor was surely feeling now. The fear and the pain.

"Merc!"

"Yes, sir?" Merc was laying it on thick by calling him 'sir.' It was a psychological ploy, and he knew it. He was showing the kidnapper how low he had sunk. The man torturing him now was taking orders from the man he had so recently tortured.

"Put me on speaker phone so he and I can hear each other."

Two beeps, then, "Done."

"Hey there," Peterson laughed in mock friendliness.

No response.

"Not quite the way you thought your day would end, is it?" Peterson's damaged mouth was a mile wide now.

"He's shaking his head no, Anthony."

"Good. Say, Merc? Has anybody broken his jaw yet?"

"Hmmm...looks like a no. You want me to?"

"No, no, no," Peterson laughed. "How about one of you take out ten of his teeth for me."

"Happy to do it," Merc laughed, then selected a candidate. "Skinner, dentistry at will!"

"No! No! Please!"

"Wait, Merc!" Peterson said, sounding merciful.

"Yeah?"

"Look around for a filthy pair of pliers. The kind you can actually *smell*. Don't do it with anything of quality."

Merc laughed and said "You got it, Anthony. Skinner? Store room!"

Anthony heard the commando named Skinner march away as his former malefactor continued his begging.

"Please, Peterson, you don't have to do this. I'm not the– I can tell you...I can tell you who is behind this, who put me up to it! I can help you get–"

Peterson cut off the weak pleas with laughter as he heard Skinner's boots return and Merc mutter, "That'll do it."

Peterson spoke very clearly into the phone. "Listen very closely, son," Peterson said, then cleared his throat. "I...don't... care." Then, more loudly, he commanded, "Doctor Skinner? Oral surgery time!"

The next several minutes were filled with crunches and screams, not to mention laughter from Merc's commandoes. The sounds were familiar to Peterson. They were, to his mind, the most horrible sounds he had ever heard, save his own Susan's cries for help. But he enjoyed hearing them again, considering the person it was happening to. It took longer than he realized it might. But he didn't mind the wait. It wasn't him being mutilated on the floor this time.

"How's he looking now, Merc?"

Merc laughed. "A lot like raw sausage, actually."

"How's he sound?"

Peterson heard Merc hold the phone close to the man's face, and all he could hear was the sickly gurgling of a man who had been beaten within somewhere around a millimeter of his life.

Peterson just laughed and laughed.

He thought about the kidnapper's last pathetic offer, about the real ringleader as it were and he chuckled to himself.

Had this happened twelve hours ago, he would have asked Merc to find out who the man was. Go through everything and figure out his name and what the connection was.

But now?

Peterson wasn't the same man he had been. Now it just didn't matter anymore. Anthony Peterson had changed. He was a man with nothing left to lose, and who this kidnapper was in life didn't really matter at all to him. Who the mastermind was, if they weren't one and the same, truly didn't matter either.

All that mattered now was his death and making damn sure it was as painful as possible.

"Merc?"

"Yes, sir?"

"Did you happen to bring with you...the axe?"

"Oh, you know it, Anthony," Merc laughed. "Don't leave home without it."

There was a metallic ringing sound, almost like a sword being unsheathed as Merc grunted through the pain of his broken ribs and held the axe up high.

"No! No, please! Don't. You'll be a millionaire if–"

Another commando silenced him with a punch.

Peterson could hear him, still gurgling, still whimpering, still alive.

Peterson whispered into the phone, just loud enough to be heard, but sounding immensely serious. "Hey. You. You on your knees there, bleeding and begging and crying. You. The one who had me kidnapped, tortured, killed my wife. Yeah, you. I suggest you listen closely, little man, because these are the last words you are ever going to hear."

Peterson then paused as the kidnapper often had on their calls, letting the words sink in, letting the terror sink in, before he continued.

"You know something?" Peterson said sinisterly. "You *were* right the first time. I *was* setting an example. But you...you had to learn it the hard way. And it's the last lesson you'll ever learn." He clenched his bloody teeth and snarled, "*Don't...fuck...with... Anthony...Peterson!*"

Peterson waited for the kidnapper to cry out in fear, then said "*Merc*, give him the *Red Queen Special*."

Pleas and high-pitched screams rang out. They would be horrible and bloodcurdling in any other situation, but Peterson loved every bit of it.

After a few swings, Peterson heard what he was waiting for. His erstwhile captor's head fell to the floor, bounced once, and rolled to the wall, just past the phone.

"Merc?"

Merc was out of breath but responded, "Yeah?"

"Before you clear out of there, take his head outside, and stick it on a pike."

Merc laughed a far-too-friendly laugh for the situation and said, "Just like South America?"

Peterson felt the rage dying again, and he shivered at the words. Hoarsely he responded "Yeah. Just like South America. Just like in La Aldea."

"Ha-Ha! Now you are a vicious bastard, aren't you?"

But Peterson didn't feel vicious all of the sudden.

It was a strange sensation, this shifting of mood. The closest thing he had to compare it to was a kid anticipating Christmas all year and then feeling let down once the presents were all opened. There was nothing left to look forward to.

And in Peterson's case, that was true. He had wanted this revenge moment so badly and he got exactly that. Now there was nothing more to anticipate and he felt himself settling into the darkness again.

The head on the pike, the reminder of La Aldea brought back the visions that had been torturing him all day. The blood and the skulls of La Aldea. Even more than the sadistic kidnapper and his electrified box, those visions tortured him.

And worst of all, there was Susan. Susan was gone. And now, he could see the shape of her face in each of those skulls.

Susan.

And every time the skulls floated up and the jaws opened, he heard Susan's scream again and again and again.

Peterson shook his head and grunted. "Go through his stuff. See if you can hack into his computer and–"

"We know what to do, Anthony!"

"Keep me posted," he said and hung up without another word.

32 The Remains of the Day

10:40 PM

Anthony Peterson's day was almost over, and Merc knew that meant his time was running out.

His old friend Anthony was told he had twenty-four hours of oxygen. So, when was that time up? That was not an easy thing to pinpoint. Too many variables and this idiot on the floor didn't quite seem to have been a physicist any more than he was a physician.

"This was one of our biggest jobs in a while," Anderson said as they rummaged through the room.

"Yeah, big enough to be heard, so we need to get done and get gone," Merc responded.

Shanks was busy on the laptop, hacking in, and hopefully pulling all of the information he could before the time was up. Meanwhile, Tapping and the man they called Judge were going through all of the paperwork they could find while Skinner and Hollister searched the rest of the building for anything they could find.

Medic walked in, and Merc turned around to greet him. "Hell of a job. Casualties?"

"A lot of injuries. Yourself included. These guys were tougher than expected."

"And?"

"And two deaths."

"Damn. Not bad considering all. Who did we lose?"

"Grant and Goldsher."

"Damn. Let's get them loaded up. Can't have them found." Merc sighed. His chosen line of work was exhausting to say the least. "What about these guys? Any of them ours?"

That was always a possibility with soldiers of fortune. You could be shoulder-to-shoulder with a guy one month and then have his blood all over you the next.

Judge looked up from the papers he was rummaging through and said "Looks like a no. They hired a few outside guys, but most of them were here in the compound training for some time."

"What are they, like a doomsday cult?" Merc asked.

"Survivalists, maybe? Clearly not very *good* survivalists," Tapping joked. "I don't know. There's nothing here about an ideology or mantra. They seem to be another group of mercenaries on contract. It's all about Peterson."

"All right," Merc said. "But this is a hell of a lot for one man… one job. Keep looking and make it fast. We need to clear out soon. Holloway?" he said into his radio.

"Holloway here."

"Anything?"

"Nothing living. Somebody has even taken to gutting wild squirrels around here. Must be a real sociopath."

"Disgusting. Must have been a really bored sociopath. Anything else?"

"Yeah, I found a good bit of munitions, actually."

"Anything we can carry?"

"A few crates. At least enough to reload us for the night without having to head home."

Merc smiled. "Convenient. I'm ready to hit the rack, though, goddam it. Hell of a night."

"I second that," Medic responded.

"Shanks?"

"Almost in."

"Good," Merc said and decided to be patient.

He looked at the bodies all around and was happy that he didn't have to clean all this shit up.

And then, there was the wife. Poor lady. Merc had never met her. Not the previous wife either. Merc was not the kind of associate you brought home to meet the family. Still, Anthony had become a friend, and he felt bad for the lady.

He hunkered down and looked at her destroyed form. Fit body, he could still tell. He reached down and removed the burlap bag covering her head and saw her lifeless face with the gag stuffed in her mouth.

Pretty lady. Shortish brown hair. Maybe dark, but it was hard to tell with the blood. Brown eyes. Nice enough face. Cute. Playful. Not exactly the type he expected Anthony Peterson to be with, but not a bad catch nonetheless…at least from what he could tell in her present form.

"Hey, look around…" Merc pushed the button on the radio to relay this message to everyone. "…look around for any women's jewelry here. Mrs. Peterson is not wearing any. Must have…taken it off of her," he said, with a yawn. "I'm sure Peterson would like to have her wedding ring back."

Merc listened to the responses of "right" and "copy" and "you got it" before moving on.

Next up was the body of that kidnapper.

"I'm in!" Shanks called over his shoulder, getting Merc's attention away from the other body.

"Excellent. Location first! Identities and money later. My friend might be dying in there."

"On it," Shanks confirmed.

Merc walked over to the wall and picked up the severed head and spun it up to look into its dead eyes.

"Do I know you?" Merc asked thoughtfully. He studied the features and thought about it. The face, or what was left of it, looked like any old grunt out there. Like one of a hundred thousand mercenaries out there. Dark hair, short, but not regulation crew cut. Tan skin, brown eyes. He flipped the head around. No facial hair. No tattoos above the neck. Why bother?

"Hey, Busby?"

"Yeah?" the other mercenary called back from the hallway.

"You're on pike duty."

Busby laughed and entered the room just in time to catch the head Merc threw like a basketball.

Then, he returned to the body.

He realized he was just bored. Occupying his time until Shanks, Judge, and Tapping were finished. But...

But who would do this? Who would spend this much money and come up with such a sadistic plan to do all of this?

Sure, Anthony Peterson pissed off a lot of people, but this seemed needlessly elaborate. Hell, he could have just kidnapped the wife, extorted the money, then popped Peterson on the street the next week.

No dog tags on the body. He searched the pockets. Not much to go on. Picture of an exotic girl. Might've been a sweetheart. Well-worn. No wallet. Cell phone...smashed by the beating. He might be able to get something off of it later with his equipment at home, but...not much else.

Wrist watch. Expensive, but not luxurious. Durable, like a warrior would wear.

He pushed the sleeve of the headless man up the dead arm. Interlocking tattoos. Tribal. Typical. After Mike Tyson got that idiotic tattoo on his face, every tough guy and his brother wanted a full sleeve of tribal tats in all black.

Tapping spoke up "Merc, I've got a delivery location for the container on this paper. Looks like it's at the pier. Warehouse. No activity. Might have been all bought up?"

"Read me what you got, let me look here."

Tapping read it to him, but Merc wasn't concentrating on their conversation.

Out of an equal mixture of comedy and boredom, Merc ripped down the dead kidnapper's sleeve and looked at the full arm. The tribal tattoo seemed to snake up into a mesh toward the top, all surrounding another emblem...a disk-like imprint.

Merc ran his fingers over it. It was a scar tattoo. No ink. This man had been branded. He grabbed his cell phone and shined the light over it.

"No," he said aloud.

One thing Merc knew very well from his line of work was scarring. This scar tattoo was over a decade old, and the man was clearly proud of it to frame it like this.

And Merc had seen it before.

Outside was a circle. Inside was what appeared to be an inverted wave with the edge tapering into the form of a blade.

No. He remembered it now. It wasn't a wave. It was a shark's tooth.

He grabbed his radio. "Hey, anybody see tattoos on the bodies all around here?"

Folmer radioed back "Yeah, they all have tats it looks like. They're mercenaries. Well, they were."

Merc scoffed. "I'm looking for this, specifically. I'm sending you all images. Check for it."

He snapped the photos with his phone and send them to the group he had created for these mercenaries at the beginning of this mission.

"Checking," came several responses.

"Shanks, how we doing?"

"I got it!" he said. "Tapping's right. Abandoned warehouse. I've got the address ready for you. Pier and building number."

"Right, let's finish this up," Merc said and turned his attention back to the headless body. "Any word on those tattoos?"

The responses of several team members came back in the negative.

"So, you're the only one," Merc said aloud.

"Sir?" Tapping asked.

"Nothing." He pushed the radio button again and gave instructions. "All right, guys and dolls, the plan has changed. Let's get everything useful we can carry and bring our dead inside with the rest. We're going to detonate the remaining munitions as we leave. I don't want any more of…" he paused "…this getting out. Let's get moving, children, we gotta go get my friend out of his hell hole."

Everyone responded in the affirmative and began moving double time.

He leaned down again and took another last look, ignoring Shanks.

Impossible, he thought. *You should all be dead.*

He knew the emblem that tattoo represented. It was the sigil of the people Peterson's company had been dealing with a decade before.

La Fraternidad del Tiburon. They were the ones who double-crossed Anthony. And that double-cross had been the reason Anthony had rained hell on La Aldea that day ten years back.

"La Fraternidad del Tiburon," he said. "You were *there.*"

The sooner he could get to Anthony and detonate this place the better. He suddenly had a very cold feeling as if his blood was chilled, then pumped back inside him.

"Merc. I'm into the account now," Shanks said. "I've got the money here. And there's more."

"More? What?"

"I think we see now what Brom Bones over there was trying to tell us."

"The real guy behind this?"

Shanks brought up the document he had been looking at and focused heavily on the name at the very end of it.

"Harrison S."

Merc narrowed his eyes, then looked back at the body. He almost laughed. "No. Really?" He then looked up at the far too recent date on the document and said, "No. Not possible."

"What is it?" Shanks asked.

"It's time to go is what it is," he said. "Everybody, let's double time it. I'm calling the man right now. I want that fuse ready to light and everything worth taking in the trucks. Let's GO, people!"

He retrieved his phone again and dialed Anthony's very temporary number.

"Oh, Anthony, buddy, you are going to love this," he said aloud as he listened to the rings.

33 La Aldea

11:11 PM

Anthony Peterson had moved back to his sitting position, right in that same spot he had cultivated over the past day. Even in the dark he had somehow sensed where it was and banged the back of his head a few times in that familiar way as he waited, just to get the feeling.

And to keep his head clear. He had been doing quite a bit of thinking since he hung up with Merc.

Plans changed. And this one had evolved.

He had won the final battle, but it was so pyrrhic that he knew he had lost the war.

Susan...

He had lost...Susan.

The one innocent in all of this was Susan.

The kidnappers were conniving bastard murderers. Tom was an underhanded, money-grubbing snake. Merc and his mercenaries were soulless killers. Sully, in life or death, was far from a prince and had been sleeping with Anthony's wife for God knew how long. Even Evan and Elena were greedy, entitled kids who never worked a day in their lives.

But that was his fault, wasn't it?

Wasn't all of it his fault?

And all of it...one way or another...went right back to one man. To Anthony Peterson.

Anthony Peterson was the greatest monster of them all, wasn't he?

And maybe he did deserve all of this. The rage that drove him had reared its head again today as he relished the sounds of those men dying. There was no more denying what kind of man he was. Maybe he did deserve what he got.

But Susan…she was the sweetest person he had ever met. She didn't deserve any of this. She hadn't even deserved the things Evan and Tom had said about her. But to die like that? She was the only innocent in all of this. She didn't deserve to die at all.

But she was gone now.

He had avenged her, but she was still gone.

But still, had he not won in the end, just as he knew he would?

He could scarcely help but think that if Anthony Peterson really had won this final battle…that meant that the bad guy won.

Anthony Peterson was the bad guy. That was the only thing that he and his kidnapper could possibly have agreed on. This all went back to Anthony Peterson, and he saw that clearly now.

Same old story, same old song and dance. Anthony Peterson was as soulless a killer as Merc, as the kidnapper, as anyone. But Anthony Peterson was also an effortless killer. Same as it ever was. He waved a hand and ordered the killings. He never even had to get his hands dirty.

Anthony Peterson understood it all too well now. He really was a bad man.

The phone lit up once more, and after a couple of rings, Peterson picked it up.

"Merc," he said without checking.

"Anthony! We're done, and man, we've got a lot to tell you. First things first, though. We got your locale."

Anthony lolled his head in the dark and asked, "Where am I?"

Merc responded "Abandoned warehouse out in Los Angeles Harbor. All he buildings around it are empty. They must've bought the whole pier. Pier X it says. Building number…oh, you're going to *love* this one. Building number six hundred sixty-six," Merc chuckled. "We'll be there ASAP and fill you in on the rest while you get patched up."

Peterson listened reservedly and took mental notes but didn't release the line. "Got it."

"Anthony, there's more."

"I know."

"No, I mean more that I should maybe tell you now. Anthony, the guy, the kidnapper, he's–"

"It doesn't matter, Merc."

"But he wasn't alone. And he was there!"

"Of course he was."

"Anthony, he was there, at La Aldea."

"It doesn't matter anymore, Merc. I don't care."

Merc paused, attempting to read him. "You're in shock, Anthony. After what you've been through, you're in shock and exhausted. I get that. We'll get you out fast and–"

"The money?" Peterson asked, cutting Merc off.

Merc seemed to smile as he said "Every penny back, my friend. You are covered."

"You did a hell of a job today, Merc," Peterson said quietly. "Take your fee, plus a million on top of that."

"Well, well, Mr. Generosity," Merc laughed.

"Pay your men…and the rest…give to my children. Clear out the account, give it to them."

"Will, do my friend! I'll get it done just as soon as–"

Peterson abruptly, yet still flatly responded "Can you do it now?"

"Now?" Merc was surprised. "Anthony, you're running out of–"

"I need you to do it now, Merc. I have the account and routing numbers memorized."

"Well…okay," Merc said, sounding suspicious. What could Peterson be up to? Why wasn't he doing it himself after all of this?

"Thank you," Peterson said and listened to Merc's typing and clicking.

"Done," Merc said. "I got mine, plus a million. Men have been paid their fees, plus the bonuses for the families of the casualties."

"I'm sorry to hear about that."

"It's business, Anthony. Me too, but it is our business," Merc said, "And your kids are now millionaires again. The account is empty."

"Thank you, old friend."

"Happy to help. But, uh…Anthony? That clears out the entire account…won't you–" Merc seemed to sense something was deeply wrong, so he quickly said, "Listen, we'll have you out of there in no time at all, so you just relax. Kick back and relax."

"Listen Merc," Peterson breathed and nodded to himself as if finally resigned. "No. I don't want you coming here. I need you to make yourself scarce."

"Scarce?" Merc's seriousness shifted into the grave concern. "Why? What's going on?"

Peterson took a deep breath and continued, "I'm gonna be calling the police as soon as I hang up here. I'm going to confess everything."

"You're what? Are you out of your fucking mind?"

"And I'm going to be turning state's evidence on everyone… including you."

"You *what*?" Merc cried, sounding betrayed and furious. He had every right to be. Soon, Merc calmed himself and responded, "Anthony, just…just calm down, okay? You've been through an ordeal. You're in shock, and you're not thinking straight."

Peterson felt around his missing teeth with his tongue. "No, Merc. For the first time I actually am thinking straight. This is the way…and I've made up my mind. This is the only way. And once they investigate me, they're going to find out about you."

Merc was indignant. "So, you set me up. I did all this, and you set me up, you son of a bitch! Well, then why the fuck are you even telling me this?"

"Because you're my *friend*, Merc," Anthony said, with uncharacteristic sincerity. He remembered Tom's words about the meaninglessness of friendship and shook his head. "I have to do this, but I want you to get a clean head start."

"To what?" Merc scoffed. "Get lost? Get out of the country? Anthony! Why the fuck are you doing this?"

Peterson sucked in air through his damaged teeth and patiently answered, "I'm a…bad…guy, Merc. I know that now.

Maybe I've always known that, but…now, I don't have anything else out there."

"Anthony," Merc said, trying to contain himself and reason with his former friend. "You know what I'm gonna have to do if you do this."

"Goodbye, Merc, and thanks. I gotta go make a call," Peterson said, then paused and thought of Sully. "See you around."

As Peterson reached for the hang up button, he heard Merc's bloodthirsty cries of "Yeah? Well, not if I get there first, asshole."

34 Disclosure in Blue

11:22 PM

Anthony Peterson was still the subject of the day and with all of the chaos surrounding his disappearance, rightly so. Desk Sergeant Burns had never seen anything quite like it and was unlikely ever to again. It was a wonder they managed to keep this out of the press so long. Maybe the unconnected nature of these separate incidents wasn't quite hitting the reporters, especially as Peterson was not yet confirmed missing. Hell of a tale he would have to tell one day.

Luckily for all involved, overtime was approved. The day had turned to night, and the case was nowhere near resolved.

Detective Gilley ran through the main lobby again, dodging other cops and hopping over the half door. Burns took another good look at the Detective who – Burns could never not see it – looked a bit unstuck in time. With the bushy hair, mustache, western wear, and sideburns, Gilley could've been the lead on a cop show, albeit decades earlier.

Things had gone from strange to outright insane once Officer Nash had called in. The big guy had woken up butt-ass naked in the middle of an alleyway in a very bad area of town. Turns out when The Hulk had woken up, a couple of friendly hookers guided him, still naked as the day he was born, to a pay phone and gave him a quarter to call in. They had offered to let him borrow some of what they were wearing, but he flatly refused and stayed flapping in the wind until picked up.

Once Nash was confirmed okay, the story elicited no small amount of laughter from the precinct. It might even have continued if Nash hadn't been such a giant. Nobody wanted to piss off Nash.

Oh, but somebody sure as hell had. Whomever it was that kidnapped Pocase and the Petersons and stole Pocase's (and then Nash's) car had really pissed Nash off, and he was champing at the bit to get into his clothes and go find the guy. Unfortunately, Nash's rage-filled report didn't include much that the task force didn't already know, aside from the fact that Nash wasn't as shy as the kidnapper had hoped or the rest of the precinct had believed.

Luckily, the GPS locator fiasco had been worked out, reportedly with a service revolver to the IT analyst's head. From the look on Gilley's exasperated face, however, the news was not quite the best that it could be.

Gilley walked back into the main room with Lieutenant James and Burns walked over to listen in.

"All right, Gilley, what's the latest and the greatest?" James asked.

Gilley scoffed and looked over to Burns in annoyance with James' question and reported.

"All right, the great latest then," Gilley sighed. "So, we traced Nash's squad car to a fence just outside of town."

Lieutenant James gaped. "They *fenced* a cop car?"

Gilley chuckled. "Yeah, I couldn't believe it either. Thing is, GPS worked. Nopke and I headed out there with a couple of squad cars to back us up."

"You brought Nopke?" Burns asked.

"Yeah, the rookie seems obsessed with finding Peterson for some reason. Anyway, we get there and it's this pawnshop-army surplus store called Dino's run by some old hippie biker-type guy name of Daniel 'Dino' Dennison. He doesn't answer the door, we pull around back and knock on his back gate of some... fenced-in area he's got back there. He says they're closed. I say I don't care, we've got reason to believe he's in possession of stolen goods."

"Which I assume he was," James said.

"That's putting it mildly," Gilley laughed. "So Nopke and I kick open the door – probable cause and all – and we find this guy Dennison literally working on removing and disabling the GPS right there in front of us. Red-handed, baby!"

Burns laughed.

"So, this guy, he knows he's screwed, right? So, he doesn't even bother with the old lame excuse. I was expecting something like 'I just found it' or 'how was I supposed to know the cop car was hot?' or some such stupid shit but no! He just puts up his hands and says we got him and that's it. But he won't say anything about the guy who sold him the car."

"Of course not," said James.

"Right. But the court order came through, see, the one about Pocase's phone?"

"Peterson's assistant?" Burns asked.

"Exactly, so Burns here has the boys send me over the PDF of Pocase's calls, as an SMS attachment, you know? And hoo-boy, he's been on the phone all day with one number in particular. Dennison says he's got no idea whose number that is, right? I mean what else is he gonna say?"

"Well, what I'm gonna say is cut to the chase, Gilley." Lieutenant James said. "I'm a busy man here."

"Sure, so while we're questioning this guy, Nopke over there starts casually fiddling with the guy's phone. Landline. Cordless job with the LCD readout? He calls over to me to read the number back and bam, there it is right there on the caller ID. It's the number Pocase has been on the line with all night and day. So, we say, hey, we know that number belongs to either Peterson or the people who've got him and he admits it, right there, but won't give us any information. Figures he's protecting an old buddy, I guess, I don't know."

Lieutenant James nodded. "So, you called the number?"

"I put another uniform on that. Officer Leahy. He kept dialing, but nobody's picking up. If it's the kidnappers, they're not answering. If it's Peterson, he's not taking the call."

"Or worse," Burns added.

"Well, yes, and Leahy's still calling, trying to get through but that's when Hall comes out of the back with a big tray Dennison had been lookin' at and maybe appraisin'? A couple million in jewelry right there."

"You're shittin' me!" Burns said.

"And they matched what was taken from the Fairfax store. Some of them still had the goddam price tags on them."

James laughed. "Guess they didn't expect us to move so fast, did they?"

"Guess not. But the thing is, why does a pawnshop owner and part-time fence have a couple million lying around to buy all this crap? Nopke says two words to him, 'mob money,' and Dennison starts singing like a canary."

"So, where's Peterson?" Lieutenant James asked.

Gilley's smile faded. "That's the problem. We don't know, still. Dennison claims he didn't even know Peterson was in that kind of trouble. Says he 'don't ask no questions,'" Gilley said, affecting a dumb street thug-sounding voice. "But he does say he talked to the guy, so we know he's alive. Then, Dennison describes the guy who sold him all the goods, and it just matched a bit too well."

"Pocase?"

"Pocase. We showed him a digital pic the wife sent us, and, yep, Dennison confirmed that was the guy. Says he loaned Pocase a junker and sent him on his way. Claims the guy was heading to the bank, then home."

Lieutenant James coughed again, then said in his dull voice, "And you believe him?"

Gilley scoffed again. "Lieutenant, this guy was so scared after the jewels got found, he's willing to tell us if he likes wearing pink silky garter belts. Yeah, I believe him! Pocase is our man. That doesn't mean he's the kidnapper. Hell, maybe he's helping Peterson, but we do have him for moving violations, selling stolen property, suspicion of two B&Es, and, let's not forget, suspicion of murder."

"We gotta pick him up, then!" Burns said excitedly.

James cleared his throat. "Let me guess, that's what Nopke is doing right now."

Gilley chuckled and nodded "Nopke insisted on it. So, Hall is booking Dennison right now for possession of stolen property just to start with."

"Aren't you going to interrogate him?" Lieutenant James asked.

"I'm hoping I won't have to. I'm waiting for the next shoe to drop with Peterson."

Lieutenant James raised his voice in annoyance. "Look, Gilley, I don't care what your gut tells you. Dennison in there might *be* the next shoe."

"I think it's Pocase." Gilley asserted.

"Pocase isn't here yet. Officer Nopke is getting him. I want you focused on Dennison."

"The guy is a dead end. He's telling us all he kno–"

"Look, Gilley, we've got SWAT on standby. I need every lead chased as soon as possible. This is not something you can just throw on the back burner 'cause you've got a feeling!"

Burns was riveted by both the revelations and the exchange, but had to break away because his phone was ringing. "Goddamn it. I'll be back, guys," he said and jogged through the desks back to his own as the other two men continued to argue.

Putting aside his excitement, Burns answered with a very professional "LAPD."

On the other end of the line, the caller took a deep breath and spoke slowly as if trying to make this call as clear as he could.

"My name is Anthony Peterson," the voice said.

"What's the emergency?" Burns asked absently before the name registered. Then, his jaw dropped open.

"I've been kidnapped and held for ransom. My wife Susan was murdered by our abductors this evening. I then sent a group of hired mercenaries to eliminate those same abductors. They're all dead now. All of my captors are now dead, thanks to these mercenaries. You will find the bodies in a compound in the mountains outside the city along with the body of my late wife."

"Wait. Anthony *Peterson*? We've been looking for you, let me—"

But Peterson continued, oblivious to Burns' words in a drone that Lieutenant James would have envied.

"I employed these same mercenaries for the murders of several people in South America ten years ago when a business deal went wrong. You would have seen this in the news. La Aldea Massacre. The culprits were never found, and my connection was never even suspected. You will find all of the details recorded in my personal files in my private office at my company's headquarters."

"Whoa, whoa, whoa, slow down now, Mr. Peterson. We've been looking for you, let me get you over to—"

"Don't transfer me. There isn't time," the voice said, and that was the first time Burns could be sure this wasn't a recording. "Write this down and come quickly. I am trapped in a locked cargo container in an abandoned warehouse, building number six hundred and sixty-six in Los Angeles Harbor. Pier X. You should send a team to arrest me immediately."

"Whoa, now, what? Who—?"

"Officer. I assure you this is not a joke and that time is of the essence. Pier X. Building six…six…six. Thank you."

And with that, the phone went dead.

"Detective Gilley! Lieutenant James!" Burns called across the large room.

"Just a minute, now, Burns!" Lieutenant James barked and turned to continue his admonishment of Gilley.

"Oh, no, no, sir. You're going to want to hear this one right away." Burns said, holding up his note paper.

Nopke was going to hate that he missed this.

35 Dead Men Talking

Anthony Peterson coolly hung up the phone and breathed deeply. The cop got the message. Police calls were recorded, and this was to be his confession and testimonial.

And now, all there was left to do was wait.

He stood up, painfully on shaking legs and started to pace, one last time, perhaps only out of habit.

He would be dead soon anyway. What else was there to do but pass the time?

He had to ask.

The phone rang one last time. Was it the police calling back?

He brought the phone to his ear but did not answer.

"Anthony," the voice said proudly.

"Sully," Peterson responded emotionlessly.

"Tell me…how long have you known?"

Anthony shook his head in exhaustion. "Known what, Sully?"

"Well, who was behind all this, of course."

Peterson grunted angrily. "I don't know," he said to the dead man. "Don't you get it? I'm never going to know, Sully. I don't want to know anymore because it doesn't fucking matter. I'm gonna…" Peterson paused and leaned against the wall and forced out the words. "… I'm gonna die not knowing because it doesn't matter."

"Doesn't it?" Sully asked in that same, annoyingly pleasant tone.

"It really doesn't. All that matters is what's next. Payback."

Sully chuckled. "Payback? But the kidnappers are all dead, aren't they? You took care of things like you always do. They're dead now."

"That's not what I meant, Sully," Peterson sighed and then added, "It's time for my payback."

"Oh." Sully said, far too pleasantly for the situation (for any of the situations) and took his sweet time thinking about that. Finally, he said, "Well, Anthony…looks like you're gonna win after all."

"In a matter of speaking," Peterson mumbled, dejected.

Sully paused again for a few moments, and Anthony could tell, somehow, that Sully was smiling on the other end of the line.

"Atta boy!" Sully said.

Peterson violently threw the cell phone at the floor and heard it pop out of its sturdy case, then shatter against the metal wall.

"*I'm not your boy!*" he shouted.

And the rest was silence.

36 Gunmetal Grey

12:00 AM

Anthony Peterson sat calmly in the dark with his back against the container wall.

His prison cell.

His forty-foot coffin.

He knew now that he was a bad guy. He knew now that a man could lose everything and still have more to lose.

He knew now that the nightmare of the previous day had never really ended.

And he knew he was ready to face his fate.

For the first time in what seemed like forever, he heard some sounds from beyond the container that did not come from his phone.

Cars, several of them, rushing to surround the building.

Eight cars? More? He couldn't be sure. He heard many men getting out and shouting orders at each other. A heavy warehouse door was slid open with a loud, rusty screech.

Door number six-six-six.

More orders were shouted, and guns were cocked.

Peterson stood slowly and painfully in the thin air. Every joint he had popped, and although everything hurt, he didn't change the stoicism in his face.

Anthony Peterson was resigned to his fate.

He walked to the middle of the container and stood there, staring at the double metal doors and waited.

He was ready.

More guns cocked, more shouts echoed, and finally he could hear the distinctive sounds of locks being cut and chains being thrown aside.

He took a step forward as both doors creaked open in unison, letting in a hiss of fresh, full air and a blinding burst of white light.

He had been in total darkness for…how long? Hours, he guessed. His phone, his erstwhile lifeline, was now smashed and even had it not been, the battery was surely long dead. Regardless of how long he had been in the darkness, this new light was like the very sun. Any light would have blinded him, but this was like staring into the core of a star.

He squinted at the onslaught of light and waited until his eyes adjusted. Everything had gone completely quiet. Peterson guessed that meant the time was finally up.

Slowly, his vision went from a painful bright blur to some form of clarity. The light was still bright, but now he could see the heavy dust in the air.

And then, he saw red.

He looked down and saw a red dot on his chest and followed the beam through the dusty air into the amorphous glow before him.

It was the laser sighting of a gun. Soon, it was joined by another red dot. And then another and another and another.

He looked down again and noticed there were over a dozen of them on him. Ready.

Every one of them was redder than the blood he kept seeing. The light before him was a violent white, like the glow from a polished skull.

Death had come for Anthony Peterson and had brought friends.

Whoever was out there, they just stood where they were as if to taunt him by making him wait. Was it the commandos? The police?

It didn't matter. There was nothing more that could be taken from him. The raggedy man had been pulled to shreds.

Anthony Peterson was not even a man anymore.

He was *cargo*.

He looked out into the deadly light, beaten, bloody, and weary as he stood before the invaders to accept his fate.

And Anthony Peterson remained unafraid, even when a new, yet somehow familiar, laser sight appeared right on the dead center of his forehead.

Acknowledgements

[*C*]*argo* would literally not have been possible without my good friend and collaborator James Dylan. We began discussing the film version of [*Cargo*] back in 2012 and over the years we developed the concepts that lead to James' original screenplay. Special thanks to James for directing this film we produced together, for writing this intense screenplay and for trusting me to expand his concepts "outside the box" into a full-length novel. There is much, much more to come!

I would be remiss if I did not acknowledge the contributions of the cast and crew of [*Cargo*] who influenced the voice of the novel. Thank you to actors Jose Rosete, Eliot, Danika Fields, Mark Wood, Corbin Timbrook, Ivy Burns, Matthew Rosvally and especially our star, Ron Thompson. A bit of each of you is in this book. Thank you also to Thorsten Quaeschning of Picture Palace music and Tangerine Dream who composed our compelling score.

Thank you to everyone in "The Bloodhound (Books) Gang" and especially Publishing Director Betsy Reavley. You encouraged me to expand the novel to its full length and gave the complete version another look. [*Cargo*] would not be the book that it is without you.

Special thanks to my supportive family including both my parents who remain two of my biggest cheerleaders even from their separate homes far across the country from me. I especially wish to extend both acknowledgement and thanks to my daughters Lexi and Nixie and my wonderful wife and muse Christine. Your encouragement, love and patience truly made all of this possible. Thank you! I love you!

Made in the USA
Middletown, DE
21 January 2018